Star Gazer

Jeanne McCafferty

First published in Great Britain in 1995 by
HEADLINE BOOK PUBLISHING

First published in paperback in 1995 by
HEADLINE BOOK PUBLISHING

A HEADLINE FEATURE paperback

10 9 8 7 6 5 4 3 2 1

ISBN 0 7472 5086 3

Typeset by Avon Dataset Ltd, Bidford-on-Avon, B50 4JH

Printed and bound in Great Britain by
Cox & Wyman Ltd, Reading, Berks

HEADLINE BOOK PUBLISHING
A division of Hodder Headline PLC
338 Euston Road
London NW1 3BH

To the one who believed
first and most,
this one's for my mother.
And
in remembrance of my brothers
Patrick J. McCafferty and William F. X. McCafferty;
they would have been proud.

ACKNOWLEDGMENTS

With thanks for their assistance:

To my family, the whole extended lot of them; with special thanks to my sister Maureen for the never-ending supply of laughter and talk; to my nephew Brian, whose sharp eye and fast pencil cleaned up the first draft, and to my nephew Dan, whose steadfastness in pursuit of his own dream has been an inspiration.

To Julia McLaughlin, a true friend, for her early reading and important encouragement.

To Patricia Shannahan, friend and music professional *extraordinaire*, for having information at her fingertips when I needed it.

To my friend Annamaria Lepore, PhD, for her enthusiastic and insightful comments, and for the use of her apartment (in more ways than one).

To my friend and former colleague Bobbie Geary, whose precise critique and warm praise meant more than I can say.

To Laura Myre, MD, for heading me in the right direction.

To librarians everywhere, but especially those in Old Lyme, Connecticut, and Albuquerque, New Mexico; they are the saints of our secular world, devoted to helping others, and I honor them for that.

To Wendy Schmalz, professional colleague of recent vintage, whose patience is appreciated, and to Leonard J. Charney, Esq., friend and colleague of my professional lifetime, whose guidance and advice have been invaluable.

And to Reverend Kay Davis, for helping me to find that encouragement within.

My gratitude.

Tragedy? This was no tragedy! This was freedom!

Nine at last. The funeral director – God forbid anyone call them undertakers anymore – was reciting to her again the schedule of events for the next morning. She nodded her agreement to everything he said, struggling to put on her winter coat and to pick up the pace as they walked down the hall to the exit. Yes, yes, anything – just let me out of here.

Home. Quiet. No sweet aroma of flowers here, just the lingering scent in the air to let you know there was a sickroom in this house. She walked quickly down the hall to the den at the back of the house, stripping off the jacket of the black funeral suit she'd worn all day. Maybe she would fix herself something to drink – but not until after she saw him first.

The screen glowed, with a little trace of sound coming out of the set before the videotape caught and she heard his voice. The light from the television played over her face, a pastel glow in the dark room. There he was – all hers. The image she had become so familiar with drove home, straight to her gut, as it did every time. The sculpted face, beautiful but unmistakably masculine, the long flowing hair, hazel eyes that were kind, and the expressive mouth. A wide mouth, with full, sensuous lips. Lips that she knew were soft. She sank into the armchair and sighed deeply. He was hers for almost an hour.

The video cut to a long shot. He was dressed almost completely in black, a loose jacket with sleeves pushed up revealing strong forearms, a white silk shirt highlighting the golden glow of his skin, elegantly cut trousers showing the powerful thighs as he swayed to the music.

It had taken her a while to compile the tape, because she'd done it herself. It had taken concentration and readiness in every spare moment, but she had recorded his videos three or four times each on one tape. Of course, there were other ways she could have gotten them, but this way she didn't have to rewind so often or change tapes. She could watch and relax and enjoy. Sometimes the beginnings were a little ragged and the sound was dissonant while the picture swam into place; those were the times she'd had to leap for the remote to start recording. It wasn't perfection she was after, anyway. It was him. Besides, there was no one to notice little flaws like that. No one but her.

Now she had him for an hour. She could breathe again. No more murmurs, no more flowers, no more smiling.

Maybe she would get that drink. She pressed the Pause button and his image flickered, then froze on the screen.

ONE

May 24

They found the body just about quarter to nine in the morning. Actually, 'they' didn't find the body. Charley Fleischer did. Once more, Charley's enthusiasm got him into hot water.

Charley was one of those lucky people who loved what he did for a living. He was director of operations for Metropolitan Productions, and he thought it was the greatest job in the world. Charley had been in and around the electronics/communications/media/entertainment business since he started selling televisions in 1951; he, of course, had thought *that* was the greatest job in the world.

The only thing that marred his mornings was getting stuck in traffic on the way in from New Jersey. So he avoided the delays by leaving home at 5:45 and getting through the tunnel before the backups started. By the time he had parked his car and stopped to pick up the paper and two cups of coffee, he usually walked into the building by seven.

This morning was no exception. He was at his

desk by 7:08 and by 8:45 he'd not only gotten through his two cups of coffee and the first section of the *Times*, he'd also made it through at least half of his In basket. It was time for his morning patrol. Charley loved walking around the building as the employees arrived. He thought it gave them a sense of leadership, a feeling that somebody was in charge. Besides, he liked seeing who was on time, who was smiling, who looked hung over. You could get a sense of what the day was going to be like. Charley loved being on top of things.

Besides being enthusiastic, Charley was also quite good at his job. At any given moment, he could tell you the video production facility's schedule for the next week, in detail, the tentative bookings for the next month, and the percentage-of-use for the small Stages A and B versus the medium-sized C and the largest Stage D. So Charley knew something was wrong as soon as he got off the elevator on the fifth floor. The monitor on the wall showed that the lights were on on Stage C, and Charley knew that there was no booking for Stage C for another four days, not until Tuesday morning at eleven.

Charley abhorred waste and as soon as he found out who was responsible for leaving on those lights, they'd get a piece of his mind. Those stage lights ate up the juice like there was no tomorrow, he thought as he hustled down the hall and into the stage entrance, and not even a client to bill it to . . .

That was when Charley saw him, caught in the

full glow of one of the spotlights. Marty, that nice young editor who'd been with them for about a year and a half. Stretched out on the floor like he was taking a nap. But one hand lay across his stomach in an odd position; as Charley got closer, he saw that the hand held a flower – a rose.

When Charley hunkered down and touched his other hand, preparing to shake him, some animal awareness screamed in his brain that the flesh was just a tad too cool. Shaking wasn't going to wake up this guy.

Nice fella he was. From Chestnut Hill, Pennsylvania. Charley had met his parents when they came to New York last Christmas to see how their boy was doing. Good people. He hoped he wouldn't have to be the one to tell them their son was dead.

TWO

Lt Mario Buratti glanced around the corner, hoping that she wouldn't be there just yet. He was babying the last inch and a quarter of his cigarette, trying to make it last. Hard to believe he was consigned to smoking on the street corner again, just like when he was a kid.

Pretty soon the nonsmokers of the world were going to start shooting smokers, he groused to himself. At least he had a nice day to stand on the sidewalk and smoke. Nice, hell, it was gorgeous, the kind of perfect day that New York gets only in May and October. A light breeze was blowing, the air smelled fresh, the sky was blue, and it seemed like you could almost see Pennsylvania.

But still, who woulda believed cops – his fellow officers – would be chasing him outdoors to smoke. And how long until they start banning smoking even outdoors? What the hell was the world coming to?

At least he had the excuse of waiting for Mac. He peeked around the corner again and spotted her, just about a hundred feet away. Perfect timing, he thought, as he dropped the butt onto the sidewalk and crushed it with his foot.

He stepped around the corner this time, and watched as she approached him. Mackenzie Griffin, PhD, looked just about the same as the fresh-faced twenty-five-year-old he had first met six years ago. He could still see her then, a newly minted doctor of psychology, preparing to lead a seminar filled with police veterans who were more than ready to make life miserable for the novice teacher. Mac had stood her ground and won them over. She had more guts than a cat burglar.

She was still a little preppy and she looked more like a coed at a small New England college than a member of the psychology faculty at CUNY's John Jay College of Criminal Justice. Her straight golden blond hair was down, with a soft wave just kissing her neck. A scarf was draped over her shoulder, topping a simple skirt and a knit top that hugged her figure attractively; everything she wore was in different shades of purple and lilac. She had a classic look to her, that's for sure. For a WASPy type, she was definitely a looker, Buratti thought. Any Italian mother would say she was entirely too thin, but on the whole, not bad at all.

'Hey, Mario,' she started from several feet away. 'Still smoking, I see.' She came to a full stop in front of him.

'Whaddya seeing around corners now?'

'No. I saw you peeking around the corner before. So how's Gloria? And Angela? And Tony? And Michael?' Anyone who'd known Mario Buratti for more than a day knew about his family. Dr Griffin had spoken to Gloria Buratti only once and had seen only pictures of the kids, but she felt as if she knew the whole family.

'Gloria's fine. Tony made the dean's list, if you can believe it. Michael has just discovered girls, God help us all. And Angela – well, Angela's senior prom was last night, and we're still having a discussion about how the senior prom is different from the graduation dance which is next week I think and how she needs a different dress for both a them.'

'Absolutely.'

'Absolutely what?'

'She needs a different dress for the prom and the graduation dance. Wearing the same dress to two dances simply isn't done.'

'Do me a favor, will ya? Let's keep that between us. I almost got her convinced.'

'So what are we doing here, Mario? Much as I like standing on the corner with you . . .'

'Let's head this way.' Buratti guided her arm until they were both heading westward, and started walking at a slow pace. Mac noticed the police cars and other official vehicles parked just ahead. 'I'm not really sure how you can help. But I got a hunch.'

'It's intuition, Mario. You're listening to your inner female.'

11

'You know you make me crazy when you say things like that. It's a good, old-fashioned cop's hunch.' He came to a stop in front of an impressive double doorway. A tasteful plaque to the left of the door read 'Metropolitan Productions.'

'Whatever you say, Lieutenant.' Mac loved it when she could rile Mario. It was so easy.

Buratti held open the door for her and they stepped into the lobby. To the rear was a reception desk, now manned by a uniformed guard. In front of the desk was a lectern that held a sign-in book and a pen attached to the lectern with a chain and black electrician's tape. Buratti waved to the guard and turned to the left toward the elevators.

'We got a few minutes waiting for this one. These elevators are almost as slow as the ones we got.' Buratti sighed a deep one; it sure seemed a lot later than ten-fifteen. 'Here's what we've got so far. A white male, age twenty-eight, found early this morning on a stage C up on the fifth floor.'

'Stage? What is this place?' Mac asked in a low voice, with a glance toward the guard.

'Video production facility. The victim, Martin Jury, was an employee – a video editor. Time of death estimated between one and three a.m. The body was found about eight forty-five when one of the honchos was strolling around.'

'A basic question, Mario. Why are you telling me all this? Why am I here?'

'You'll see when we get upstairs.' The elevator

slid to a stop and the doors opened slowly. They got in and Buratti pressed the button for the fifth floor. The elevator doors closed just as slowly and started up.

'Cause of death?' Mac leaned against the back wall.

'We don't know yet.'

'Hmmm?' She stared at the numbers; this elevator took one hell of a long time between floors.

'Like they say, the immediate cause of death was that his heart stopped beating. What the bright lights at the ME's office have to figure out is *why* his heart stopped beating.'

'How about the obvious – drug overdose?'

'Nope. No history. No evidence. No nothing. They're growing a strange breed in rock 'n' roll these days. A bunch of them seem to be health nuts.' The ones he ran into this morning sure as hell wouldn't let him smoke in the same room.

'Rock and roll?'

'Yeah. Well, the music business anyway. Jury's main job was editing music videos. Metropolitan has contracts with a few of the big record companies to' – he checked the notebook he pulled from his side pocket – 'provide post-production services on music videos. And some of the videos are shot here as well. They've got four soundstages on the premises. It's one of them where the unlucky Mr Jury was found.'

'What else have you got?' The elevator jerked a bit as it stopped at the fifth floor. Buratti motioned for Mac to leave the car first, then guided her down the hallway to the left.

'Not much. The victim worked until about seven last night. He was a reliable guy, never a problem, no bad habits or known enemies. He just showed up at work this morning very early and very dead.'

'Another basic question. Are you sure it's murder?'

'Always a chance that the ME will come up with something weird, but we're ninety-nine and forty-four hundredths percent sure.' Buratti checked his notebook again. 'Jury did come back to the studio last night after midnight and he had somebody with him. The guard saw him at the front door, just as he – the guard – was about to take his usual potty break. Jury worked a lot at night apparently, and the guard knew him, knew he had keys, so he waved at him and took his break. The guard says Jury was holding the door for somebody, but couldn't say who. Couldn't even say man or woman, black or white, short or tall. Anyway, they have a sign-in system, and Jury signed in at twelve-twenty with "plus one" in the guest column. Guard was on duty till seven, didn't see anybody leave. 'Course, he didn't let us know how many other potty breaks he took either, and the door is locked against people coming in, not going out. So we got somebody who came in with Jury but didn't sign out, and a cold one on the soundstage. Yeah, I'm sure it's murder. And you will be, too, soon as you see this.'

They passed several closed doorways; finally

Buratti opened an enormous one to the right, and they entered a dark backstage area. 'Wait here,' Buratti said. 'I want to make sure you see this the way I did.'

Mac glanced up and around to assess the large space – it really was too large to be called a room – and tried to estimate the size. The doorway they had entered through was probably fifteen feet high and the upper reaches of the walls seemed to disappear into darkness at about twenty feet, although she was sure there was a ceiling up there someplace. The area of the stage that was lighted was at least twenty by thirty, and that appeared to be only the center of the stage. Mac lifted her shoulders as a slight chill raced through her. Standing in the dark at the periphery of the 'room,' Mac realized that the air was much cooler than it had been in the corridor.

Buratti had walked through the darkness into the lighted stage area and spoke to the head of the crime scene unit. The man nodded and said a few words to the other members of the crew. Within a few moments they had stepped back away from the victim, and Buratti called to someone in the control booth to reset the lights. He returned to where he'd left Mac and said, 'Okay, it's pretty much the way we first saw it. Come on in.'

Mac slowly approached the prone body, trying to absorb as much of the setting as she could. The body of Martin Jury lay on its back, legs fully extended, the left arm angled in slightly so the hand rested atop the left thigh, the right arm bent so that the hand rested high on the stomach, the right hand holding a rose. The head was not centered, but turned to the right. Some lights had been on when Mac had first entered the stage, but the addition of the lights that Buratti had called for created a stunning effect. The blue, red, and pink gels on the spotlights shaded and sculpted the scene so that it looked like a meticulously staged photograph.

'Well, whoever is responsible for this death has a real sense of theater,' Mac said quietly. Only Buratti was close enough to hear.

She hunkered down slightly to get a better look at the body. Martin Jury was – or had been – an average-looking man. Clear skin, even features, nothing really distinguishing about his facial appearance except his hair. He had long, curly hair that must have reached past his shoulders when he was standing. But his hair was now fanned up from his head like a halo.

The hair was above his head for the same reason his shirt was taut across his chest: The body had apparently been dragged into its present position. It hadn't been dragged far, judging from the position his shirt and loose jacket were in, just above his waist in back.

'The body was dragged? Not your guys, I presume.'

'Right,' said Buratti. 'He's right where we found him. We figure he was dragged maybe a foot or so.'

So much for suicide or accident. Dead men, even

16

unconscious men, don't drag themselves into a better light position. And that's exactly what Mac sensed – this body had been posed and placed in the best possible light.

'So whaddya think?' asked Buratti.

Mac straightened up and spoke to Mario while still looking at the body. 'An empty stage, a dead body, the spotlights right on him. The rose is a nice touch. Shows a flair for the dramatic.'

'And . . . ?'

She finally turned to him. 'Okay, assuming it's murder, and I think you're right on that, there is a lot of power in this scene.'

'How do you mean?'

'This scene took a lot to accomplish. It's very dramatic. The lights, the flower, the whole feel of this place. That took a lot of thought. And it was apparently very important to whomever – the murderer – because it would take a lot of effort, too.' She looked at Buratti as he jotted notes. 'What I'm saying is this is *not* your garden-variety homicide, Mario. It's not random, it's not impetuous, it's not particularly violent.' She looked back down to the body. 'What it is, is very chilling. Murder scenes aren't supposed to look this good.'

'Mac,' Buratti said quietly so she would be the only one to hear, 'the little voice inside me says this ain't the whole picture. You know Peter Rossellini?'

'The singer? Sure, I know *of* him. He's going to be playing at Radio City pretty soon? I remember

17

something in the papers about how they sold out all the performances in just a few hours and they had to add a bunch more. And he's had that big hit recently, what was it? God, it was a great song . . .'

' "One Heart." '

'That's it. Every time you turned on the radio – no matter what station – that was playing. I love it when that happens – if I like the song, I mean.'

'You seem pretty up on this stuff, Mac.'

'I never stopped listening to pop radio once I started in high school. Much to the horror of friends and family, I might add. Peter Rossellini is *the* big star of the last year or so.'

'Rossellini's had a good year, all right. This guy here told me his album went triple platinum, like they say, a couple months ago and it's still selling. And according to this same guy, Rossellini's starting a tour next month that's gonna bring in some serious bucks.'

'And . . . ?'

'Jury edited Rossellini's last video. March, April, whenever. But that's not the only connection.'

'The connection . . . ?' Mac was getting impatient.

'Let me get somebody over here.' Buratti stepped into the darkness again, toward the control room, and motioned his hand for someone to come out. Mac was left standing near the body, the full glare of the lights on her. She became aware of the sensation of heat on her skin. The temperature was amazingly different from where she had stood just a few feet away. No wonder she'd heard the reference to working under the hot lights.

A studious-looking, lanky young man dressed plainly in jeans and a white shirt walked up to Buratti, and the two of them moved back into the light toward Mac.

'Mackenzie Griffin, this is Joe Kahn.' Mac and the young man both caught one another's eye and nodded fractionally. Buratti continued: 'Joe is a video editor here as well, and he's been giving us a hand. Tell her what you told me before.'

Mr Kahn was nervous, Mac could tell just looking at him. His eyes kept darting to the body. Professionals like cops and medical personnel keep forgetting how unaccustomed most people are to dealing with death, Mac thought. 'Would you like to step over here?' she said to Kahn quietly, taking his arm and turning him toward the rim of darkness that circled the stage. He eagerly accepted her suggestion. Buratti was a step behind them.

'I don't know if it's any big deal, like I told the detective.' Kahn spoke quickly, as if he could get this over with very soon if he got out all his words in record time. 'It's just that this was the studio where it was shot, and that was sort of how it ended.'

'How what ended?' Mac asked softly.

'Rossellini's first video – "How Can I Show You." It was all a studio shoot, pretty low budget, just the band and Rossellini. But at the end he picks up a rose off the music stand, and holds it like this' – he held his lightly fisted hand in front of his sternum – 'and the camera closes to an ECU – extreme close up – on the flower and then goes into a paintbox effect.'

Kahn glanced back at the body, still in the glare of the spotlight. 'And it was a rose just like that. And Marty is sorta dressed like Rossellini was, too.' He stopped and looked at Buratti. 'That's all I got to say, really. Can I go back to the booth now?'

'Yeah,' Buratti said. 'And thanks.' He turned to Mac when Kahn had left the immediate area. 'So whaddya think?'

'Not looking good.'

'Nope. And that's not all. There's something else.'

'What?' Mac asked. She opened her purse and withdrew a slim notebook. This situation definitely called for notes.

'Jury looks like Rossellini. Or looked like him. Vaguely. Same build, same coloring, same hair. Little younger.' Buratti paused for a second. 'Mac, I hate to say this, but . . . I think there's a possibility we've got some weird kind of stalker on our hands.'

She'd known that's where they were heading. Star stalker. An unfortunate by-product of the media age.

You didn't hear about it as much in New York as in Los Angeles. New York was relatively safe for celebrities – there were so many of them, and the legendarily blasé attitude of New Yorkers did have some basis in fact. But nobody could forget John Lennon . . .

Events over the last few years, especially in LA, indicated that celebrity obsession was not an isolated, freak incident. Several actors and actresses, musicians, newscasters, and celebrities of all ilk had been stalked. They had received threatening calls and mail; a few were hurt in attacks. At least two had been killed.

Los Angeles had finally set up a Threat Management Unit to deal with stalker cases. NYPD had been developing a similar special unit last year and Mac had consulted with the LAPD psychologists to help in setting up the team. That was before the latest fiscal crisis hit the City of New York and killed any new special projects.

Mac had kept Mario informed when it looked like they'd get a team organized, and he had shared her disappointment when all that work had gone down the drain. This morning, as soon as he had a glimmer that this case was a possible stalker, Buratti had called Mac at her office a few blocks away. Maybe all that work wouldn't be for naught. And even if she wasn't official with the department, she was still the closest thing he had to an expert on the psychological profile of stalkers.

'Mario, you realize' – Mac looked at the scene and then back at Buratti – 'you're going on very little information here.'

'I know that. That's why I called it a hunch. I've got to hedge on this. Somebody might be out for Rossellini. And that's why I called you in.'

'What do you want me to do? And am I official on this, or is it another freebie?'

'Freebie for now, until I get something more. You know Captain Lenox – somebody would have to take a shot at Rossellini in his own john before Lenox would think he was in danger. No, I'm sure I'll be doing a whole by-the-book investigation on Jury. This is on the side for now.'

'Okay, what can I do?'

'Go over the whole profile with me. Brush up on Rossellini and try to figure out who might be after him.'

'And after I take care of that, would you like me to solve the traffic problem in the city?' Mac answered in an innocent voice that belied her sarcasm.

'Look, I know it's a lot, Mac. And I'm going to be running down everything on Jury anyway, so I won't need this till maybe Monday.'

'It's Friday, Lieutenant Buratti. Friday of Memorial Day weekend in case you hadn't noticed the city emptying out already. I'm going to see my parents this weekend.'

'Okay, then Tuesday. C'mon, Dr Griffin, you know you can't resist this one.'

Mac sighed. He was absolutely right.

INTERLUDE ONE

She got home late. She closed the door and slumped back against it, inhaling deeply. Home. Home at last. Now she could let herself remember.

It had been hard to make it through the day. It was almost like she had to hide all day. She hadn't been able to let herself think about it, but now she could. A laugh bubbled out of her chest.

This one had been so good. So much better than the first one. More real. More romantic. Gentler. And Martin had been much more cooperative. A real gentleman. He'd looked so handsome there on the floor. Just like Peter.

She stepped out of her dress, pulled off her slip and pantyhose, and stretched out on the bed. She grabbed the pillow and hugged it to her, rocking back and forth, back and forth. The friction of the spread's ribbed fabric felt good against her skin.

She had loved being in that place, that stage where he'd worked. She had felt the lights on her face, the heat warming her skin just as it had warmed his.

She had stood where he stood, where he sang that song just for her. Only for her.

Yes, it had been good, so good. She shivered at the memory, holding the pillow tighter and tighter. She was ready for Peter now. No need to practice anymore. It would be soon. Very soon.

She took a deep breath. Funny. She had no desire to watch the video now. She didn't need to watch it; she'd lived it. Now she could just remember.

THREE

May 26

Mac climbed a few feet to the top of the dune until she could spot the swans. There were dozens of them gliding around the inlet, and she watched, entranced, for several minutes. This particular stretch of Long Island Sound, just at the mouth of the Connecticut River, was home to hundreds of swans. And they were gorgeous, even if they were the meanest birds in creation.

She quietly turned and stepped down the dune carefully, trying to avoid getting sand in her shoes. Once back on the level beach, she picked up her pace and headed back to the house.

This was her favorite time at the beach: early morning low tide. The receding tide made more of the beach walkable, so from the house to the point and back again, she could walk over a mile and a half. This was her favorite time of year as well; the beach was almost empty in spring. Over the next few weeks, the tourists and the summer people would be arriving, and the beach wouldn't be hers again until the fall.

She came around a curve in the beach and spotted the house. It was quiet now. Her parents were off to church services and the housekeeper wouldn't be back until close to noon.

Mac was glad she'd made it up this weekend. It had been several weeks since she'd seen her parents, and with the coming of the summer crowds, it would probably be several more before she was back. As much as she loved her parents, life was easier and a little less complicated if she kept the visits to a minimum.

Mac was about twelve when she began to realize that her parents were genuinely odd. Well, different, anyway. The parents of the other kids in seventh grade seemed to know what a Sadie Hawkins Day Dance was; hers didn't.

As she got older, she began to understand. To begin with, their entire life could be described in an oxymoron – they were wealthy academics. They didn't consider themselves wealthy, of course, having come from old Yankee stock, among whom financial security was something assumed and never talked about.

Both her mother and father had come into a few trusts at various ages. The income from the trusts was simply reinvested, supervised by a trust manager at one of the local banks, who transferred an agreed-upon amount into their checking accounts each month. Their allowance, her mother called it.

Their material needs were actually very few. The home they lived in and had lived in since a few months before Mac was born was inherited from her father's maternal grandparents. They each bought a very good car every five years. They traveled when time allowed.

Mac knew that her parents didn't consider themselves wealthy, but by the time she got to college and looked around at her classmates and their families, she realized that her parents had never had to do anything they didn't want to do just for the sake of money, which in its own way was an incredible wealth.

Their financial status wasn't what made them odd, though. Mac knew plenty of people who were well off. And it wasn't that her parents worked for a living. Some – not many, but some – of her parents' friends did, too.

What made them stand out was that they had little genuine contact with the real world of the twentieth century. Her mother was a professor of classics and her father was a professor of American history specializing in the Settlement and Colonial Period. They both taught at Riverside University, some twenty-five miles north. Their studies were extraordinarily real to them. They talked of Aristophanes and Ovid, Roger Williams and Thomas Jefferson as friends of long standing who'd been to dinner last Tuesday. Their academic lives totally captured their imaginations.

What rarely occurred to them and what they rarely had to pay attention to were the details of everyday living: Their food was prepared for them, their clothes were bought for them, the nuts and bolts of their lives were taken care of by other people. Except for their children, the twentieth century almost never intruded on their consciousness.

Her parents' marriage was living proof, Mac thought, that there are gods of romance. After all, these two had found one another.

By the time Mac was thirteen, Stella the housekeeper was consulting her on the household decisions. 'You're gonna have to learrrn earrrly, my girrrl. Those two dinna have the sense to come in outta the rrrain.' Stella had come from Scotland the year before Mac was born; even now, thirty-two years later, her burr was undiminished. 'Sometimes I wonderrr how they got the thrrree of you. Not that there's anything peculiarrr, mind you. It's just a wonderrr that they got theirrr noses out of theirrr books long enough.' So it fell to Mac and Stella to decide which roofer to contact, if the driveway should be graded again, and when the house should be painted.

Through her adolescence, it was Mac who made sure that her father's car was inspected, Mac who got her siblings ready for camp, Mac who scheduled the family physicals and dentist appointments.

By her second year of college, Mac had decided that not only was she going to major in psychology, she was going to specialize in criminal psychology. She told her parents with some trepidation, anticipating the knee-jerk reaction that would have come from ninety-nine percent of the starched New Englanders she knew, to the possibility that their daughter would be associating, even academically, with a criminal element. But her mother's response had been, 'One of the social sciences, my dear? Are you absolutely certain?' Her father had muttered his agreement to the question. When she said 'Yes,' that was that, and her decision was never discussed again.

They were absolutely daft and she loved them.

She turned up from the beach and onto the wooden walk that led to the side kitchen door. The house was an immense turn-of-the-century charmer that her great-grandparents had built as a 'cottage' to escape the Hartford summers. The land it sat on rose gently, and the house was angled slightly so that it had a view both of the Connecticut River and Long Island Sound. Mac's favorite vantage point was from the small porch next to the side door; you could look over the marsh grasses down to the beach and out over the Sound without seeing a trace of civilization.

The aroma of coffee welcomed her as she entered the kitchen. The automatic pot had almost dripped through. While waiting, she sorted through the Sunday papers sitting on the counter. Given the choice between *The New York Times* and the *New*

Haven Register, she immediately reached for the *Register*. As wonderful as *The New York Times* was, it still had one major flaw. No comics.

A headline on the front page of the local news section caught her eye. 'DEATH AT LOCAL BEACH CLUB REMAINS A MYSTERY.' She stopped riffling through the paper and read the brief article. Her eyes widened and the little hairs on her arms prickled as she read; when she was finished, she exhaled on a long, slow whistle.

Her parents walked in just as she returned to the kitchen with her briefcase in hand. 'Hi,' she said hurriedly. 'Coffee's done. I just have to make a quick call, then I'll start breakfast.'

'Thank you, darling.' Her mother shrugged off her linen jacket into her husband's waiting hands. 'It's wonderful to walk in and smell the coffee, isn't it, Walker?'

'Yes. Wonderful, dear, wonderful.'

Mac held the phone book in her left hand and tapped the numbers with her right, holding the receiver between her ear and her shoulder.

'Buratti.' The voice sounded clipped. 'I mean ... hello.'

'Forgetting that you're at home, eh, Mario?'

'Mac, is that you?'

'Yep. Got something for you. Real interesting.'

'What is this? I thought you were spending the weekend up in Connecti-cute.' Buratti was one of those New Yorkers who could not fathom why some people willingly – God forbid eagerly – left the city on weekends.

'I am.' She stretched over to the counter and picked up the paper. 'Let me read you something. Page One. Section B. Local News. The *New Haven Register*. Headline – death at local beach club remains a mystery. Text – Branford police have no new information to report on the death of Randy Vos comma twenty-eight comma the Branford resident found dead early last Sunday at the Colony Beach Club. New paragraph – Vos's body was discovered on the beach in front of the Colony Beach clubhouse at five-thirty a.m. by Mr and Mrs Paul Salazar. The New Haven County Medical Examiner's Office has been unable to classify the death as a homicide or as an accident. Quote they found alcohol in his blood said Sergeant Richard Swett of the Branford Police Department but nowhere near enough to kill him unquote. Swett said that until they hear otherwise from the examiner's office comma they are treating Vos's death as a possible homicide due to the quote unusual circumstances unquote in which the body was found. Sergeant Swett declined any further comment. Didja get all that, Mario?'

'Yeah.' His voice was both questioning and hesitant.

'The article continues. Colony Beach Club is a favorite among the locals and the summer tourist population and is preparing for its busiest season yet said manager David Fremont. It attracted much local attention earlier this year when it was the scene for the filming of a music video by popular singer Peter Rossellini.'

'Ah, shit. You mean there's two a them now? Shit,' he repeated. There was silence on the phone for a second or two. 'Mac, you still there?'

'I'm here, Mario. Just thinking.' She shifted the weight on her feet and the difference in her body reflected in her voice. 'I wasn't really certain Friday, but I'm certain now. You've got a real problem on your hands.'

'Tell me about it. Some star stalker video freak who kills.' Mario's voice held a tired resignation.

'More than that. This is a twist on the usual profile. I've never heard of one like this, so indirect, where they go after someone who resembles a celebrity, or maybe someone who just happens to be in the same place this Rossellini guy once was. And now more than one victim? Really unusual.'

'Great. Just what I wanted to be doing,' said Buratti. 'Breaking new ground for the psychologists.' He paused. 'Mac, what do you think the chances are of these two being coincidental?'

'You mean these two bodies show up at places that just happen to be the site of Peter Rossellini's videos, but the two deaths have nothing else in common? Is that what you're asking?'

'Yeah,' he said reluctantly.

'You've got to check it out, of course, see if maybe

Vos had a jealous husband after him or something. But basically, I think the odds are about a kajillion to one.'

'That's what I figured.'

'Well, Mario. Glad I could perk up your Sunday morning. Talk to you—'

'Wait, Mac. I got a favor to ask of you.'

'Another one?'

'I'm talking to Rossellini's manager first thing Tuesday morning, at her office. Gonna ask about Jury, any connection to Rossellini, any threats to him. Not questioning, really. But I want to kind of alert them, without scaring anybody. You know these fan nutcases better than anyone around, Mac. Will you come with me?'

'That's it? You just need me to give a rundown on the stalker profile?'

'Yeah. Remember, I don't want to alarm them. I just couldn't sleep at night if anything happened to Rossellini and I had this hunch—'

'Intuition.'

'Right, intuition, and didn't do anything about it.'

Buratti listened carefully to the silence on the other end of the line. Finally there came a thoughtful sigh. 'Okay,' Mac said. 'Where and what time?'

FOUR

May 28

Buratti knew from previous experience that Dr Griffin was one of those people with a gift for punctuality. She swung through the revolving doors at precisely nine fifty-five a.m.

'You clean up good, Mac.'

Mac smiled and dropped her head in a mock bow. She knew she looked pulled together – her hair tight to her head in a French braid, a linen suit in a golden beige not that different from her hair color, the leather briefcase. All the image of the cool, controlled shrink.

They started for the rear elevator bank, the one that served the higher floors, and Buratti pressed the signaling button. 'Before we go up . . .' 'How do you want to handle this . . .' Their words tumbled over one another. Mac had to smile.

'Great minds et cetera, isn't it? Go ahead, how do you want to handle this?'

'Leave all the facts about Jury's murder to me. And the guy up in Connecticut, too. As soon as I

35

mention the possibility of a stalker, I'm sure all hell is gonna break loose. That's where you come in.'

'I think you brought me along for protection, Buratti.'

'You got it, kid.'

Mac glanced over to the lighted panel that showed the whereabouts of the elevators, and then looked back at Buratti. 'Were you able to talk to anybody up in Branford yet?'

'Nah. Made a few phone calls Sunday and yesterday, but none of the people who worked on the case were around. Seems they take their holiday weekends pretty seriously up in Connecticut.' He reached over and pressed the signaling button again, hard, just as the door opened. 'I'm supposed to talk to the lead investigator later this morning.'

Buratti stepped to the rear of the empty car and spread his arms along the handrail, sighing deeply. 'Hard to believe it's only ten o'clock.'

'What have you got on Jury so far?' Mac asked.

'A little less than not much. Saw his landlady. He was a model tenant, no loud parties, no trouble, no nothing. His apartment was pretty neat for a guy livin' alone. Seems like all he did was work and go home. Not much of a social life. Talked to a few friends, but they couldn't tell us much. Nobody knew what he was doing back there at midnight, or who he was with.'

'How about the crime scene? Anything from there?'

'Nothin'. Not a hint that another person was there. No fingerprints that mean anything. Of course, we figured the only surfaces they would've *had* to touch were the doors and the elevator buttons, and there's maybe only five hundred prints a day going on both of those.'

The elevator doors opened with a *ping!* onto a glass-enclosed foyer. The carpeting, very plush, very expensive, very taupe, let you know you were in the vicinity of some real money. The glass doors at the left led to the office of a public relations firm. To the right, the doors were almost entirely covered with a highly stylized double *B*, the logo of Berman and Bennet Management.

The receptionist, an eager-to-please young woman in her early twenties, was conservatively attired in a linen dress with contrasting jacket; Linda Campbell, according to her engraved nameplate, would have looked equally at home in a bank or brokerage house. She had obviously been alerted to their arrival and immediately buzzed into the inner offices. 'Michelle will be right with you,' she said.

If Ms Campbell would have looked at home in any Fortune 500 company, Michelle could have been the gatekeeper at a cloistered convent. She wore a dress in taupe, almost the color of the carpet. It was a color that had been trumpeted in all the fashion magazines as a classic neutral; on her, though, it simply came across as no color. Adding to the nunlike appearance, she wore little or no makeup, and her hair was pulled to the base of her neck in a plain ponytail.

'Mr Buratti?' she said in an unpleasantly nasal voice as she neared them. 'Oh, you brought someone with you.' She was not pleased. 'This way.'

She led them toward Rachel Bennet's office. Michelle Wenzel, or so said the nameplate on the desk that they passed, was one of those people whose age was hard to guess, but Mac took a chance at around thirty. She was a little taller than Mac, five seven or thereabouts, and probably would have had a good figure, but her slumped-shouldered posture ruined any grace of line.

She would look so much better if she simply stood up straight, thought Mac. Then her eyes widened at what had just passed through her mind. Many of her friends had confessed recently that they'd found themselves sounding exactly like their mothers. Mac could avoid that with no difficulty; her problem was that, lately, thoughts that danced across her mind and occasionally right out her mouth sounded so much like Stella, it was a wonder she didn't speak with a burr. She could almost hear it now. 'Strrraight, girrrl! Stand yourrrself up strrraight!'

'Have a seat,' Michelle Wenzel ordered when they reached the office. 'Do either of you want coffee?'

'Not for me, thanks,' Buratti said.

Mac smiled apologetically as she declined with a 'No, thank you,' acting as though Ms Wenzel might have overheard her earlier mental criticisms. The chilly expression on Michelle's face faded to mere confusion, then she left them alone with a curt, 'Ms Bennet will be right with you.' She closed the door behind her.

'Another one who loves her job,' said Buratti as he turned to assess the office appreciatively. You could drop three or four of the cubicles he called an office into this baby and have room to spare. The office had windows on two sides, along the back behind the desk and along the left side. The whole room was done in variations of gray – carpet, draperies, leather. Not boring gray – expensive gray. The furnishings were medium-toned oak – real oak – a large desk, comfortable-looking executive chair, an eight-foot-wide credenza in back of the desk holding a complete array of every type of sound equipment one could imagine – cassette player, compact disc player, turntable, amplifier, receiver, speakers – plus a fifteen-inch television and two kinds of videotape players. In front of the desk sat two guest chairs in a tone slightly lighter than the desk chair, a tone to match the U-shaped couch that must have totaled fifteen feet in length if it were straightened out. Inside the U of the couch, a coffee table in the same oak finish. This coffee table was so big, Buratti thought, if you wanted to play cards on it, you'd have to have arms like a baboon. He strolled toward the windows while Mac placed her briefcase at one end of the couch.

'Would you get a load of this view, Mac? Practically river to river *and* the park.'

Mac joined him at the windows. 'Working in the private sector does have its rewards, that's for sure.' She stood staring past the smaller buildings on Fifty-eighth and Fifty-ninth Streets toward the late-spring canopy of Central Park. She glanced toward Buratti. Like any New Yorker, he was transfixed by the sight of greenery en masse.

The door whooshed open and Rachel Bennet glided into the room. 'Sorry to keep you waiting.' Here was show business at last. Bennet was an attractive fortyish woman, very well maintained. The haircut was perfect, the body trim, the skin glowing, the nails done in an elegant French manicure. Mac knew that the monthly cost in Manhattan for maintaining this kind of natural, please-God-let-it-appear-effortless look could pay for a decent apartment elsewhere in the country. The khaki-colored linen jumpsuit and the low-heeled kid shoes would easily be another month's rent.

Bennet stopped midroom and let the two visitors approach her to accept her outstretched hand. 'Lieutenant Buratti, I presume, and ... ?' Buratti jumped in, 'This is Dr Griffin, Ms Bennet. She'll be consulting on this case.' Not if Captain Lenox has anything to say about it, Mac thought, but she placidly played along with Buratti's introduction.

'Please, have a seat' – Ms Bennet gestured toward the two chairs in front of the desk as she circled it to take her own seat – 'and perhaps you can fill me in. As I said to you on the phone, Lieutenant, we're more than happy to cooperate with the police. But I really don't see how we can be of much help. And if there's going to be a lot of . . . ah, adverse publicity, I'll want to keep my client's . . . cooperation with you as confidential as possible.'

'We're lookin' to keep a low profile on this one, too, Ms Bennet. And so far, so good. But you know I can't promise anything. Freedom of the press, and all that. As for filling you in, I think we should wait for Mr Rossellini and lay the whole thing out once.'

'Okay, Lieutenant.' It was not okay, and the change in Bennet's body language and voice indicated that her promised cooperation had just decreased by a few percentage points. 'Peter should be here shortly. His lawyer will be joining us as well. Irwin thought it best.'

'Sure, sure, that's fine,' Buratti said. He was lying. Among the many things he didn't need right now was a silk-suited entertainment lawyer who was more accustomed to licensing T-shirts than dealing with a homicide investigation.

'In fact, I think that's Irwin now,' Bennet said, looking toward the door. Irwin Steinfeld, Esq., was almost always heard before he was seen. The muffle of noise accumulated and finally burst through the door, as the pudgy, midforties Steinfeld appeared. Following him, still engaged in a teasing conversation with the noticeably less stern Michelle Wenzel, was Peter Rossellini.

As Rachel Bennet made the introductions all around, Mac was experiencing the peculiar sensation that 'civilians' encounter when meeting a celebrity. The face is familiar, the voice even more so in Rossellini's case. The brain gets mixed signals. While the hand is offered in greeting and the mouth is murmuring 'How do you do,' the eyes and the ears are whispering to the brain, 'But I already know this person!'

Peter Rossellini was handsome in his photographs; in person he was stunning. Tall, about six foot three, in his midthirties, and well built: broad shoulders and chest tapering to a trim waist and long legs. His outfit complimented his physique but didn't particularly draw attention to it: a white cotton shirt with a large collar, an oversized natural-colored linen jacket with the sleeves pushed up his forearm, khaki-colored trousers. The neutral tones blended perfectly with his medium-brown hair, curly and shoulder-length, his lightly tanned face, and his hazel eyes. Mac's first thought was that this was one very attractive man; her second thought was that Martin Jury did bear a passing resemblance.

Rachel got everybody seated: Rossellini and his lawyer on one side of the couch, Buratti and Griffin on the other. Bennet turned one of the guest chairs around and sat in the open end of the U of the couch. The added height of the chair gave her a dominant position in comparison to the others; that and her body language made it very clear that Rachel was running this meeting.

'Now, Lieutenant Buratti, if you'd be good enough to tell us why you wanted to see Peter.'

'As I mentioned to you on Friday,' Buratti started, 'we're investigating the death of Martin Jury, a videotape editor at Metropolitan Productions and—'

Steinfeld pounced immediately. 'What possible connection could my client have with this death. Just because—'

'Shut up, Irwin. Nobody said there was any connection.' Rachel Bennet made her point immediately. 'Go on, Mr Buratti.'

'We'd like your help with some information.' Buratti paused; this was where it was gonna get tricky. 'In investigating Mr Jury's death, we believe there's a possibility – and it's only a possibility'– he looked directly toward the singer – 'that you might be in some danger, Mr Rossellini.'

'What! What *exactly* do you mean?' Steinfeld and Bennet's reactions were immediate and intense. Peter Rossellini took in the information quietly and stared back at Buratti.

'Just what are you saying, Lieutenant?' Rossellini's quiet voice prevailed.

'Since Friday, we have learned of another death, a probable murder, that could be connected. The point of connection is that both deaths occurred at places where your videos were made.'

The assembled group was quiet for a moment. Rossellini, still looking at Buratti, said, 'Go on.'

Buratti glanced at his notebook. 'Randy Vos was found dead at the Colony Beach Club in Branford a week ago Saturday. From our information, you filmed a video at the beach club earlier this year. Mr Jury's body was found on Stage C at Metropolitan, where your first video was shot.'

'Good God,' Rachel Bennet said quietly. Irwin Steinfeld looked sideways at Rossellini like he was seeing his client with a fresh regard. Like he was wondering if Rossellini was going to die. Then he turned his attention back to Buratti, with only a hint of his usual contentiousness. 'If these – ah, deaths – happened what? – a week ago, over a week ago, why are we just hearing about it now?'

'I called Friday as soon as we made the connection about Martin Jury. We didn't know about the death at the Colony Beach Club until Sunday. Dr Griffin called me from Connecticut to let me know.'

Rachel Bennet focused her attention on Mac. 'And you, Dr Griffin. Your part in this?' Rachel Bennet was desperately trying to regain a sense of control. She thought conducting the meeting would give that to her.

Buratti responded, although the question had been directed to Mac. 'Dr Griffin is a consultant to the department. She is a specialist in the topic of star stalkers' – Ms Bennet vocalized a slight moan at the word 'stalkers' – 'and I asked her to come with me today to give you some idea of what we're dealing with. And she can ask you for some of the information we'll need better than I can.'

As she drew her notebook out of her briefcase, Mac made eye contact with the three people across from her. Rachel Bennet radiated concern; Irwin Steinfeld looked like someone had hit him over the head with a cast iron skillet; Peter Rossellini's expression had barely changed from when Buratti had started speaking. His eyes were alert, his concentration intense, and his expression remarkably self-contained. Mac had doubts if that much self-containment was a healthy thing, given the circumstances.

'I'd like to be able to give you some definite answers. I can't,' Mac began. 'Let me start with a few questions. Lieutenant Buratti checked and there has been no record of your filing a complaint against any fans or admirers harassing you, Mr Rossellini. Is that correct?'

'Yes, that's correct,' answered Rachel Bennet. Mac saw Rossellini lower his head with a small rueful smile, presumably reacting to Ms Bennet's preemptive answer. 'Do you agree with that, Mr Rossellini?' Mac asked.

'With what?' Rossellini looked up at her, a little surprised at the direct question.

'Are you aware of any fan – or anyone, for that matter – harassing or threatening you?'

'No, no. Not at all.'

'Let me go over the patterns of harassment that we know of, just to make sure. Is there anyone writing to you repeatedly, telephoning frequently, following you, or showing up at every one of your public appearances?'

While Rossellini shook his head, Rachel Bennet jumped in to answer. 'Peter doesn't see all the mail directly. We have someone handling that, and he gets a few pieces each week. And his number has been unlisted for about a year and a half now. I don't think that's gotten out at all. Has it, Peter?'

'No.'

'How about anybody following you on the streets, or at public appearances, Mr Rossellini? Are you aware of anyone attending your performances repeatedly?'

'I've had people come up to me in restaurants and on the street, sure. Usually just for an autograph, maybe a picture. Most of them are real nice.' He paused for a moment. 'I really haven't done that many live performances, Doctor. Since I became a solo act, anyway. I toured last spring, just after the album came out, opening for The Trinity Project,' he said, naming one of pop music's supergroups, 'and we finished midsummer, around the middle of July. When the album really started happening, in the fall, I did a bunch of industry things and some charity appearances, but that's about it.'

Now that she'd gotten to hear him speak more than two words, Mac was struck by the smooth, throaty quality of Rossellini's speaking voice. 'And no one showing up all the time?' she asked again.

'No. Wish I could help.' He said the last with a slight shrug of the shoulders.

'That's all right,' Mac assured him, turning to Rachel Bennet. 'You said that Mr Rossellini doesn't see the mail. We'll need to review the mail that has come in for him.'

'Of course,' replied Ms Bennet.

Steinfeld, who'd set a record by not speaking for close to five minutes, said, 'We get some stuff in over at the office because of the publishing. Marge Masterson handles it. Maybe you should look at that, too.'

'Publishing?' Buratti looked at Steinfeld with a puzzled look on his face.

'Peter writes almost all of his own material.' Rachel Bennet jumped in before Steinfeld knew there was a question in the air. 'All the songs, and the copyrights, the licensing, the royalties, all that, are handled out of Irwin's office.'

'Gotcha,' Buratti said.

Mac looked to Steinfeld. 'Then, yes, we will want to take a look at that material as well.'

Buratti leaned forward. 'I assume you've got some security firm that works for you. We'll need to speak with them.'

Despite her attempts at control, Rachel Bennet still looked shell-shocked. 'That's John Monaghan. Michelle will get all the names and phone numbers together for you before you leave.'

Mac stepped back in to the conversation. 'I'd like to be able to reassure you, Mr Rossellini. But we're dealing here with a variation on a pattern that we've never seen before. We're not trying to alarm you, but you should be aware of the possibilities and be very cautious.'

Buratti followed up as soon as Mac finished. 'And of course, contact us immediately if you think of anyone or anything later on.'

Rachel Bennet's business sense started to flow through her body again, and her body language reflected it. She sat straighter and leaned toward the police officer and psychologist. 'Peter is opening at Radio City next week, starting his summer tour. This will all be taken care of by then, I presume.'

Buratti wanted to laugh. Like he could 'take care' of this on schedule. 'I can't promise anything, Ms Bennet. And I can't promise you any help – like protection or anything. We got our hands full with two murders. Well, one of them here in the city. But I will talk to your security guy and give him suggestions about beefing up your protection. That's about as much as we can do.'

Rachel Bennet stood up and walked around the desk. 'I'll have Michelle get that information together for you.' She picked up the phone and pressed the intercom.

Mac raised her hand to catch Rachel's attention. 'I'd like to get a copy of all the videos as well.' Rachel nodded her agreement.

Within fifteen minutes, Mac and Buratti each had a copy of a list with the names, addresses, and telephone numbers of the people they would need to see. Rachel and Steinfeld, together, had made calls to each of these people instructing their cooperation.

Rossellini bent down to help Mac, who was trying to fit the video cases into her slim briefcase. 'Have you seen any of these before or will this be your first time?'

Mac looked up at him. 'My first time, actually. I really don't watch videos. I'd rather listen to music than watch it.'

Rossellini nodded with an almost contrite expression on his face. 'Yeah. Know what you mean. Still'– he tilted his chin toward the full briefcase – 'you'll have to give me your reviews.'

'Wish I could just concentrate on the artistic merits. We'll see,' Mac said. She stood, nodded to Mario that she was ready to go, and extended her hand to Rossellini. 'It was a pleasure meeting you, Mr Rossellini. I'm sorry it had to be in such circumstances.'

He took her hand and shook it firmly. 'Yeah, right. And thanks, I guess. I mean for your help with this. I really don't know what to make of all of it. But thanks.' Mac looked at him squarely and knew he was sincere.

Rossellini was quite a package all right. Handsome, talented, and now even polite. And possibly, or even probably, the object of someone's obsession.

FIVE

John Monaghan couldn't remember the exact moment he decided to be a cop. As far as Monaghan could tell, it was born into him, like his curly blue-black hair. He had never considered doing anything else.

Monaghan could pinpoint for you, however, the exact moment he decided to *stop* being a cop. He was sitting in the emergency room of Montefiore Hospital, waiting to see if his partner would survive the gunshot wound he'd just sustained on a routine patrol of the neighborhood.

Monaghan had been a cop for ten years at that point; his uncles had been cops, as had his grandfather, so he was acquainted with the life. He had paid attention during his academy training and he'd even attended a few cop funerals himself. But somehow, even with all that information and experience, Monaghan had never developed a sense of personal danger. It was always abstract, always the other guy. Until his partner was shot, until he heard the bullet whistle by his cheek – or had he felt it? he still wasn't sure. Sitting in the squad car, with Hungash slumped toward him bleeding what looked to be quarts of red paint all over the front seat, the reality finally sank in. *Holy Christ! Somebody's trying to kill me!*

Like many former cops, he immediately went into the private security business, but he selected a special niche. He provided security for entertainment types. Location filming, celebrities visiting New York, special appearances at stores, that kind of thing. He'd been in it almost five years now and was doing pretty well. Okay, he wasn't in Donald Trump's league, but then again neither was Donald Trump anymore. Monaghan made a good living, and even if the entertainment types were a little flaky, at least they weren't shooting at you.

His office, in a building on Fifth Avenue in the Thirties, was modest. A small secretarial/reception area and a small inner office for Monaghan. The low hum of the air conditioner that sat in the window closest to the desk kept the traffic noise from below to a minimum. Monaghan leaned forward in his executive-styled chair, gesturing toward Buratti, who was trying to make himself comfortable in the one small guest chair.

' . . . but some concert jobs I just won't take. Like these rap groups. Kee-rist, unless you put a metal detector by the entrance, you can't guarantee anybody's security, and even then who knows. I don't need that shit. The venues are turnin' them down, too. They can't get insurance anymore. Another thing I'll never do again is heavy metal bands. We did tour protection for one group last summer. I won't mention the name, since I promised myself it would never cross my lips again, but it was one a them that has a reputation for satanism in the lyrics. These bright lights decide to tour the South and Midwest, like the buckle of the bible belt. I never seen so many Jesus freaks in my life. Practically every town, there's some committee tryin' to stop the concert, and they got picket signs and people throwin' themselves down in front of the limos. I tell you it was a nightmare. Plus the band members were assholes. By the last week of the tour, I was considerin' lettin' the Jesus freaks at 'em.'

Buratti nodded. That was all the encouragement Monaghan needed to continue.

'Yeah, we coordinate with the locals or the private cops that they got on site, but basically we're there for the celeb. Like for example, Cher did another perfume introduction at Macy's about a year, year and a half ago. Whatta scene! You couldn't believe the crowd. Now, the Macy's security is there to make sure the whole perfume department ain't trashed. But me, I don't care about the glass counters and such, I'm there with my people to make sure Cher's okay. That was some crowd, I tell ya. They musta thought she was goin' to show up in her skivvies. Hell, she practically did.'

Buratti and Monaghan had exchanged cop pleasantries, had quickly established that despite sharing the brotherhood of the badge, they neither knew one another nor even knew anybody who knew one another, and now Monaghan was regaling Buratti with his equivalent of war stories. Like Cher at the perfume counter of Macy's. It was a very different kind of war.

'Tell me about security for Rossellini.' Buratti was trying to edge the conversation along.

'Peter – he's a great guy, isn't he? My brother-in-law works in the studio that he records in, so I know him from when he first started, y'know? Happy that he's making it so big. We haven't done that much for him here in the city, 'cept when he's performing. And then the kind of service we provide for him, you might call it more like a limo service. You know, drive him to the venue, make sure he gets to his dressing room, get him on stage, get him through the crowd after the show.'

'Any problems in the last few months?'

'We're getting ready for the tour now. Like I said, we really haven't been on Rossellini much. March, I think it was. Yeah, he had the Grammys, and then they did a video shoot late that month.' Monaghan leaned back in his chair. 'The Grammys, hey, that was a big night for him. We only handled his personal security, him and a few others. One of the big outfits had the event security, and we coordinated with them. We didn't have any problems that I can think of. I'll check with my people who've worked with him on the other nights. But I'm sure if there was any problem, they woulda told me about it.'

'You got any files on Rossellini, threats against him, that kind of thing?'

'What's going on here, Lieutenant? What ain't you tellin' me?' Monaghan got up and walked around his desk. 'If I'm responsible for the guy's security startin' in about six days, I gotta know the deal.'

'Just checking out some possibilities. Martin Jury, a videotape editor over at Metropolitan Productions, was found dead on a soundstage Friday.'

'Yeah. So?'

'Over the weekend we found out another dead guy showed up at the site of another of Rossellini's videos. At a beach club up in Connecticut.'

'Holy shit! I remember that place. That's the video I was talking about.'

'Did you work security?' Buratti pulled out his notebook. Details from the scene of one of the videos was an unexpected bonus.

'Yeah. The Connecticut one I did myself. Thought it would be a nice day at the beach, y'know. But it turned into one of those really cool days. Froze my ass off.'

'Any problems with the locals? Notice anybody hangin' around?'

'Not that I remember. For sure there was no problems. The place was pretty deserted, and a few people maybe stopped by, but nothing . . .' His voice faded as he tried to recall the unmemorable. 'I have my notes from that trip around here someplace...'

Monaghan perked up a little and Buratti hoped maybe some helpful detail would be forthcoming. 'The thing I remember most about that day was wondering if Peter had turned into this great actor or somethin'. He had on summer-weight pants and a cotton T-shirt, and he had to go wading in the water over and over while they were shooting this one part. Honest to God, I thought he'd probably die of pneumonia. But he looked comfortable, just like it was ninety degrees in July. Impressed the hell outta me, I can tell you that.'

'Look,' Buratti said with a trace of impatience. The last thing he needed right now was an assessment of Rossellini's acting ability. 'We're thinking we might have a problem with a stalker type. Somebody seems to be doing in guys in places Rossellini did his videos. How 'bout any of the other videos? You cover those places?'

'The studio work, no. When they go out on location, yeah. But I gotta tell you, Lieutenant, I don't remember anything. Like I said, I'll check with my people, but they woulda told me if something was up. I think we got *nada* for you.' Monaghan leaned forward over the desk. 'A stalker? You really think so?'

Buratti nodded as he closed his notebook slowly and slipped it back into his pocket. This guy had not been a great help. Nothing against Monaghan; so far, nobody and nothing had been.

He rubbed the center of his forehead, hard, trying to erase the headache that had built up over the last few hours.

SIX

Marge Masterson had started in the music business more than thirty years ago, working for a vicious little bastard with the friendly-sounding name of Clarrie Goodman, whose most closely held belief in life was that everybody, but everybody was out to screw him. Clarrie owned a music production and publishing company. He expected his employees to work their asses off, and he was still offended when he had to pay them twice a month. Clarrie distinguished himself as one of the cheapest SOB's to live in twentieth-century Manhattan.

Marge was almost eighteen when she started working for Clarrie, one of the thousands of immigrant daughters the good sisters churned out of Cathedral High who were well skilled, generally bright, and, best of all, compliant. They were also known for being phenomenal workers, a characteristic that Clarrie took advantage of daily. Work was pretty much all she did. Marge had never married, never really dated much, devoting what little free time she had to taking care of her parents. By the time they had both died, she was in her early forties. She inherited the house in Queens where she'd been raised, and stayed on there by herself. Her big extravagance was having the outside of the house painted the same year as the inside.

Then, two and a half years ago, Clarrie up and died, too, at the age of seventy-eight. Out of pure meanness, he'd worked right up to the end, railing every day against what the music business had become, at how it had passed him by. And he was right. But he had a catalogue of standards whose royalties brought in a handsome living and he'd kept his hand in producing musicals on and off Broadway.

Despite the fact that Marge had worked for him for thirty-one years, and was the last of his longtime employees still with him, and despite the fact that Clarrie left a bountiful estate, no provision was made for her in his will. In fact, she was quickly out of a job when his heirs liquidated the company within weeks after Clarrie's death.

So Marge found herself, close to fifty, having interviewed for a job only once in her life, out pounding the pavement. She had no idea how to market the fact that she'd become over the years a talented administrator, skilled negotiator, and superb office manager, since, as far as she was concerned, she was just doing her job.

Marge had negotiated with Irwin Steinfeld a few times early in his career, and she surprised him by being one of the few people he couldn't sway with bombast or bluff. She didn't know him well, but they had run into one another a few times every year at industry functions. When Marge was walking Madison Avenue one day on her way to yet another employment agency, she literally ran into Irwin as he hurried through a revolving door. When he heard that Marge was available, an idea quickly gelled.

Irwin had been unhappy, to say the least, with what was happening to his clients' music-publishing interests. Starting in the late seventies, continuing through the eighties, takeover mania had hit the music publishing business. One company bought another, or, in the vernacular, acquired the catalogue, only to be acquired by yet another, larger company. As the perceived value of the music catalogues increased, these catalogue acquisitions had to be heavily financed, and then every possible penny had to be squeezed out of the company to make the interest payments. By the end of the decade, it seemed there were only three major music-publishing companies left, each controlling hundreds of thousands of copyrights. The years of changing ownership had left a complicated paper trail, and the people working at the three remaining publishing companies were adrift in a sea of copyright registrations, songwriter agreements, and all manner of licensing deals.

The music of one of Irwin's clients had been caught in one of these huge corporate quagmires. His client,

Roger Camden, the main songwriter of the phenomenally popular group Lighthouse, had signed a publishing agreement in the early eighties with Temple Music, one of the companies that spent the rest of the decade doing the takeover waltz. Camden had received regular advance payments from Temple, in anticipation of royalties the songs would generate. Lighthouse hadn't really hit until the deal had run its course, so a good percentage of all the advances he'd received was still sitting on the books. Temple, or actually the company that had bought the company that had acquired the Temple catalogue, still controlled the songs.

At a fundraiser for one of the charities his wife was involved in, Irwin was approached by an advertising executive he knew through just these kinds of social functions. Too bad they couldn't work out something on Camden's song 'Make Yourself Happy,' the executive said to Irwin. What? Irwin wondered aloud. The advertising guy explained that his agency had contacted the publisher on Camden's song, trying to license it for a huge new advertising campaign that would introduce a whole new line of health-conscious products from General Foods. The license fee in the first year alone would have been upwards of $200,000. Repeated letters and phone calls to the publisher had gone unanswered and they finally had to go with their second choice.

Irwin went ballistic. He was able to control himself through the remainder of the party, although he could feel his ulcer acting up. He saved his imitation of a fire-breathing dragon for his appearance the next day in the offices of the president of the conglomerated publishing company, wherein he threatened to eviscerate said president in the middle of Times Square. By the end of their little meeting, Irwin had wrested control of any and all songs by any and all of his clients.

That particular meeting had occurred the week before Irwin body-slammed Marge on his way out of the building. Cartons were starting to show up in his office and he wasn't sure what he was going to do with them. As soon as he heard that Marge was available, he knew.

Marge had moved into two tiny back offices at the firm of Steinfeld, Getz, Hume, and Nakamura, PC the following Monday. Within a month, she had all the licensing and financial data on the songs superbly organized, and she had tracked down an additional $30,000 in income on Roger Camden's catalogue of songs that the publishing company had failed to collect. Irwin was pleased.

In the two years since, as his other clients' publishing interests became available, Irwin turned everything over to Marge. She was responsible for well over two and a half million dollars a year in publishing income; that two and a half million in royalties brought the firm an administration fee of $264,000 last year, so Steinfeld, Getz, Hume and Nakamura were all pleased. And Marge made

$48,000 a year, more money than she had ever dreamed of earning, so she was pleased.

Marge greeted Dr Griffin in the reception area, and showed her to the tiny room she used at the back of the offices. The room had only enough space for a desk, a small credenza behind the desk, a guest chair, one lateral filing cabinet, and a bookcase. Four issues of *Billboard* were precisely arranged on top of the credenza, next to an up-to-date and compact computer that Marge reluctantly used. The metal card file on her desk duplicated most of the information that was in the computer, and Marge was much more comfortable with the index cards. A small window looked out on the narrow airspace between buildings. The room carried the fragrance that Marge wore, and Mac recognized it as one of her mother's favorites.

When Dr Griffin declined her offer of coffee, Marge took it to mean that they would get right to work. She just wasn't sure what that work was. 'When Irwin and Rachel called this morning, I understood that I was to give you absolute cooperation. I'm just not sure what you're looking for.'

Mac sat down gratefully and eased her briefcase, still crammed with videotapes, to the floor. She and Buratti had reconnoitered in the coffee shop in the manager's building to work out their schedule. She'd made phone calls from the booth to set up this appointment and one with the head of Rossellini's fan club. It was now just after one and she hadn't eaten yet; she foolishly had only coffee in the coffee shop. Now she was hungry and her feet hurt from walking from West Fifty-seventh Street to East Forty-sixth in heels.

'Well, I don't think this will take long,' Mac started, as she took out the sheet that Rachel Bennet had given her earlier, 'and then you can get out to lunch.'

'Oh, don't worry about that,' Marge said quickly. 'I've already had lunch.' Mac's stomach growled in reply.

'Good,' Mac lied. 'We can start right in. I will be meeting tomorrow with Marianne Santangelo, from Peter Rossellini's fan club.' Marge smiled at the mention of Marianne Santangelo's name. 'But Mr Steinfeld mentioned that you also receive mail here from fans, admirers, that type of person.'

'Sure. Some. Mostly if it has to do with publishing. What exactly are you looking for?'

'Anyone who writes to Mr Rossellini repeatedly, anyone who seems unusually . . . zealous . . . in their admiration?' She wasn't sure why, but Mac was phrasing this as gingerly as she could.

'No. Not that I can think of. Unless you mean the real crazies,' Marge said matter-of-factly.

'The what?' Mac asked, startled at the term.

Marge got up and inched around the desk to the file cabinet. 'I keep the letters here in my fruitcake file.'

'The fruitcake file?'

'Sure. Here.' Marge withdrew a file folder, riffled through the sheets briefly, and handed Mac a letter that had been laboriously printed on lined notebook paper. 'This guy says he wrote "How Can I Show You." ' She handed Mac another letter. ' "One Heart," ' another letter, 'and "What Will It Take." And whatever song Peter releases next, I'll probably get a letter here saying he wrote that, too.'

'Do you know if he is even a songwriter, or is this pure delusion?' Mac asked, fascinated by the letters she held.

'I don't know the technical term for it. All I can tell you is that I know this guy has claimed that he wrote a couple of Stephen Foster's songs, some of Irving Berlin's, and the whole Rodgers and Hammerstein catalogue.'

'Do you have his address?'

'Sure. Well, I have the envelopes that they came in. We can see if there's an address.' There was.

Mac looked across the desk at Marge. 'Do you have anything else like this?'

'Sure. Maybe not as many from one person. But here's one' – she handed a sheet of flowery pink stationery to Mac – 'saying "What Will It Take" is obviously a cry from Peter's soul, and he should know that it only takes the Lord to make us happy. Here's another guy who says he wrote "How Can I Show You" and demanding royalties from Peter. And here's one from a woman saying she knows Peter is in the

Mafia and she's going to turn him over to the FBI unless he pays her.'

Mac looked at the embarrassment of riches she had in her hands. 'What happens to these claims that other people wrote these songs?'

'Something like this I just ignore.' Marge sat back in her chair. 'If a real problem comes in, it comes with a lawyer letter on top of it. Like the whole thing with Joey Lemon.'

'Who's Joey Lemon?'

'Oh, I thought you would have known about him. Actually, I just saw the first papers that came in, and then Irwin's been handling it since. Peter and Joey were songwriting partners. They were looking for a new publishing deal, and Irwin was representing them. They split up not quite two years ago – just before Irwin got Peter signed to the label. Joey is suing Peter for breach of contract, but I don't know any more of the details than that. It really doesn't affect the songs I'm handling.'

Mac leaned toward the desk. 'Ms Masterson, are you aware of any other . . . situations . . . like this concerning Peter Rossellini?'

'Sticky stuff, you mean? No, not that I can think of. Although I did wonder for a while if there was going to be a palimony suit.'

'A palimony suit? From whom?' Mac tried to keep the surprise out of her voice.

'Judy. Judith Stone. She and Peter were an item for five years, as I understand. I only met them in

67

the last year they were together. They broke up a few months before Peter and Joey split. She saw him through some rough times, or so the story goes, and they broke up just before the glory. Isn't that the way, though?' Marge finished with a rueful smile.

SEVEN

The offices of Circus Maximus Records were located in the lower quadrant of floors of one of the many huge, anonymous towers dotting Sixth Avenue in the Forties. Buratti waited in the reception area while the perky young woman at the desk buzzed word of his arrival back to Mark Palmer, vice president of video production. Buratti slowly made his way around the whole reception area, studying the photographs of the Circus Maximus artists that filled the walls. He recognized Rossellini and one other – a country singer of considerable charm he'd seen on the 'Tonight' show some months back.

'Mr Buratti? You can go back now. Mr Palmer is expecting you.' Buratti had decided on the spur of the moment not to present his police ID to the receptionist; instinct told him word would get around fast that cops had been to see Mark Palmer, and he wanted to keep a low profile for the moment.

'Which way is it, miss?'

'Oh, I'm sorry, I thought you knew the way back.

Now let me see.' She furrowed her brow. 'It's so much easier to show you the way there, but I can't leave the desk.' She pointed to the door to her left. 'Go through this door, take a right, then another right, about halfway back in the building take a left, and Mark's office will be almost directly ahead of you.'

Buratti followed her instructions as he went through the maze, and her instructions were precise and accurate. As he approached a row of offices that, if his internal navigation was right, overlooked Sixth Avenue, a sandy-haired man in his late thirties opened the door to an office forcefully and stepped out into the corridor. The nameplate next to the door identified the office as that of Mark Palmer.

'Lieutenant Buratti?' The fellow extended his hand. 'Mark Palmer. Glad to meet you.' You could tell this guy was a professional charmer. People rarely said 'Glad to meet you' to a cop. 'Come in and have a seat.' He stepped aside and waved Buratti into the office.

Buratti was right – the office did have a view of Sixth Avenue, looking toward Radio City. The office was spacious, perhaps fifteen by eighteen, but crowded. In addition to Palmer's desk, there was a small round table with four chairs, and a low three-tiered wall unit that held two television monitors, three videotape machines, and countless videotapes and books. The wall nearest the desk was covered with large framed corkboards; papers and photographs were pinned over the entire surface of the boards, with an occasional cartoon peeking through.

'Sit wherever you're comfortable, Lieutenant. It is Lieutenant, isn't it? Sorry I wasn't here when you called on Friday. Dan Pfeiffer and I were out on location.' Palmer was a wiry man, and he spoke rapidly. Buratti suspected that coffee and cigarettes were a regular part of his diet. 'I'll be happy to give you any help I can, Lieutenant, but I hope we'll be able to move this along pretty quickly, okay? I've asked Dan to join us. Hope that's not a problem.'

Buratti was surprised when Palmer actually paused for a reply. He pulled out one of the chairs at the small table and sat. 'I don't think it's a problem. Who is he?'

'Oh, right, you wouldn't know. Pfeiffer is Peter Rossellini's product manager. He was working on the video at Metropolitan. He'll be here any minute.' Buratti was right about the cigarettes. He spied a large ashtray on the desk just as Palmer lit a Marlboro, snapped the lighter shut, and slipped it back into his pocket. He came around the desk, dropped a file full of papers on the table, and walked to the open door. He poked his head outside, and apparently spotted Pfeiffer immediately. 'C'mon, Dan, let's get going.'

Buratti decided to luxuriate in the pleasure of having a cigarette indoors, sitting down, during a work day, and lit up as well.

Dan Pfeiffer rushed up to Palmer, almost out of

breath. 'Sorry, sorry, sorry, Mark. I had a million things fall on me this afternoon. I didn't even get lunch.' He followed Palmer into the office, and plunked the legal pad and magazines he was carrying down on the table. 'Hi, Dan Pfeiffer here.' He extended his hand to Buratti. 'You're really from the police?'

Buratti smiled. 'Yeah, really from the police.'

Palmer moved things along quickly. 'Lieutenant Buratti wanted to talk to us about Martin Jury over at Metropolitan. I told him you were the one working on Peter's video at Metropolitan.'

'Yes. Absolutely. Absolutely. Anything I can do to help.' Pfeiffer had taken the chair opposite Buratti, and his posture indicated that he was all attention. He leaned toward Buratti with a just-between-you-and-me air about him. 'Given that the police are involved, are we to assume that foul play was involved in Marty's death?'

'Not sure, Mr Pfeiffer. That's why we're investigating.'

That stopped Pfeiffer only for a moment. 'I didn't hear about Marty until about noon on Friday when I called from the shoot to check on something with him. It's ghastly. Just ghastly. I mean, you're working with a person one day and the next day they're *dead!* I mean, it's *crazy*. And he was so good-looking, too.' Buratti suspected this was not the first time Pfeiffer had stopped to appreciate Jury's good looks.

'Can you tell me when you last saw Mr Jury?'

'Sure. Thursday night. I left him in the edit bay about six forty-five or so. Yes, it was just about six forty-five because I was trying to get down to Forty-sixth Street by seven. Just made it.'

'Did you notice anything unusual about Mr Jury? Anything out of the ordinary?'

'No. He said he just had to finish up one quick thing and he'd be out of there, too.'

'Did he say anything about coming back to the studio later? Anything about bringing somebody with him?'

'No. Wait. He said something about meeting someone for dinner. Yeah. He said he was starved and couldn't wait to get to the restaurant. They were going Italian.'

'Wise choice.' Buratti smiled at his own humor. 'Did he mention who he was meeting?'

'Nope. But I don't think it was a date or anything. More like he was meeting a friend. Sorry I can't tell you more.'

'That's okay. Can't tell what you don't know. Let me ask you something else. Jury always work on Rossellini's videos?'

'I can answer that one.' Palmer had taken a chair in between Buratti and Pfeiffer, turning their seating arrangement into a triangle. 'Unless there's an unresolved schedule conflict, Marty works on all our videos—'

'Worked,' said Pfeiffer.

73

'Right. Sorry. Marty has – had – a real talent for re-creating the music visually. And he'd listen to you. He'd turn out the video you wanted, not the one he did. A good guy.'

'He sure was,' Pfeiffer added. 'And the nicest fellow.' Pfeiffer paused for another moment of appreciative remembrance. 'You just never know in life, do you?'

'Can you tell me how you go about choosing your locations for these videos?' Buratti asked.

Palmer jumped in immediately. 'Depends. What kind of budget you have, how you're trying to position the artist. You start with the song, and sometimes the ideas come out of this department, sometimes from the artist, sometimes from the management office. With some of the established artists, we use independent video production companies, young filmmakers. Ideas come from all over.'

'Remember where the ideas for Rossellini's videos came from?'

Palmer opened the file before him and ran his finger down a list on the left side of the file. He hesitated only a moment. 'Let's see. The first one was a studio shoot, strictly a budget decision. The one at Ten Bridges was dictated by the song. It's sort of an update on "One for My Baby," you know? Had to be sung in a bar. Ten Bridges has a great-looking bar and it was pretty cheap to do it there. "One Heart" starts at the Seaport to give us that great Errol Flynn pirate look, pushing Peter's romantic image – I think Rachel's office came up with that one, right, Dan? Then the rest of it was shot all around the city.' He paused, flipping the page over. 'And "Look This Way," the one we shot up at the beach, Rachel's office arranged for the club—'

'Wait,' Buratti said, 'you were talking about the one at the Seaport. You used other locations for that video?'

'Yeah. Lots of them. All around the city.'

'Like tell me how many.'

Palmer and Pfeiffer looked at one another and mentally conferred. Pfeiffer started. 'Let's see, there's Times Square, the top of the World Trade Center, the Cloisters . . .'

'Central Park, too. That was a bitch to shoot that day,' Palmer added.

Buratti picked up a scratch pad that had Palmer's name on it, lifting it as if to ask 'May I?' Palmer nodded, and Buratti started jotting down the list of the locations they'd mentioned.

'This next one's gonna be much easier,' Pfeiffer said.

'What next one?' asked Buratti. He almost didn't want to know. And he really wanted another cigarette.

Pfeiffer leapt at the chance to answer his question. 'At Radio City. It will be fabulous. Peter's doing five songs from the new album in the act. We'll be shooting some rehearsal footage and then the performances. We'll have our choice for the next single. Edit it together, it'll be great.'

Yeah, Buratti thought, just great, and he added Radio City Music Hall to his list. He could feel his stomach tensing as he read down the list.

EIGHT

By the time Mac walked through the door of her apartment, it was almost four o'clock and she was tired. It was close to three by the time she'd gotten all the information from Marge. When she left the building, there were still no cabs to be found on Madison, so she stopped in one of the storefronts and had a frozen yogurt, hoping a cab would magically appear when she was done. That didn't happen, so she ended up walking to Second Avenue and taking the bus downtown. She made it to the end of her apartment's entrance hall before she dumped her briefcase and purse and eased out of her shoes.

Mac's apartment suited her perfectly. It was on the first floor of a high rise, and in its original form probably had the white shoe box look to it that so many apartments did in Manhattan. But this place hadn't seen its original form in a while. Two apartments had been combined a few years before, and although the result had meant far more room, the combined apartment also had four rooms of approximately the same size in an odd layout. To keep the dining area near the kitchen, for example, one of the rooms on the back of the apartment that had originally served as a bedroom was now a living room. It worked splendidly, however, because you could then sit on the couch and look out onto the reason Mac had bought this apartment in the first place: a patio with a garden.

The size of the patio paled in comparison to what she had been accustomed to in Connecticut; it was not quite as wide as her whole apartment, maybe thirty feet, and only about twelve feet deep. But in New York, having any outdoor space at all was a luxury. After her first few years in the city, she realized that the one thing she desperately missed from her parents' home was the garden, and when she picked out this apartment, the little backyard was the deciding factor. She'd make her own garden in the midst of the city.

After the first summer, she'd given up trying to grow anything in the New York City dirt that edged the cement patio. She instead had acquired a collection of good-sized containers, some wood, some clay, some beautiful, and others merely functional. She'd planted the first of this summer's flowers only three weeks ago, and the annual herbs as well. The herbs were an indulgence; she really didn't cook very much, but she loved the smell of the fresh herbs. They reminded her of Stella, the housekeeper, and the hours she'd spent sitting in the kitchen talking with her while she cooked.

She was tempted to go and putter with the flowers, but it was only a brief temptation. What she really wanted to do right now was to soak in a tub for a long time and hope that her feet would forgive her for walking all over midtown in heels instead of running shoes. But first she had to check in with Buratti.

She walked into the second bedroom, which she used as an office, and headed for the phone. Both this room and the living room had French doors that looked out onto the patio; at least she would be able to look at the flowers while she took care of her calls. She had two lines coming into the apartment, one strictly personal, one for professional purposes. Blinking lights indicated there were messages on both lines.

The messages on the professional line were from Buratti and Rachel Bennet, both asking her to call as soon as possible. The personal message was from the manager of the wallpaper store down on Twelfth Street that her paper was finally in. Her kitchen and living room were supposed to be painted next week, and she was splurging on an amazingly expensive mural wallpaper for one wall.

Her two weeks off weren't turning out quite the way she'd planned. When Buratti had called her Friday morning, she was just finishing up the last of the paperwork required of her by the dean's office before a two-week break until summer session. This was supposed to be her goof-off week; there were a few movies she wanted to catch up on, an exhibit at the Met that she and her friend Sylvie wanted to see, and she had also planned on indulging herself with some genuinely free time.

Next week would be devoted to getting the painters in and out of the apartment as soon as possible, and putting the apartment back together before starting school and resuming a full schedule again. The weekend following the first week of classes her brother and sister would be coming to see her and she wanted to relax and enjoy their visit. Her sister, Whitney, was coming down from Boston, and her brother, Chad (for Chadwick), was coming up from Washington – the Three Musketeers together again, as her sister put it. 'Mackenzie, Chadwick, Whitney – and didn't you say your father's name was Walker?' Buratti had said when they were talking about their families one day. 'What the hell you people got against first names?'

She sat at the desk, one leg folded underneath her, and returned Buratti's call first. They filled in one another and agreed to meet early the next afternoon, since Buratti had to head to New Haven first thing in the morning to see what he could find out about the Vos case in Branford. That schedule would work out well, since Mac was supposed to meet with the fan club president in Mineola the next morning. Buratti mentioned they'd be getting some help. Once the captain had heard about the Connecticut case, he'd assigned a young detective to work with Buratti.

'Putting additional resources on the case, hey Mario? Does this mean I'm on the payroll?'

Buratti hesitated a moment. 'Not yet, Mac. But think of all the research you'll get out of this. Y'know, breaking new psychological ground. Like you said, this is a real twist. Those psych journals will be calling *you*.'

Mac laughed at Buratti's attempt at smooth-talking. Confirming the time they'd meet the next day, she ended the call and dialed the next.

It seemed like the receptionist at Berman and Bennet Management had been alerted to Mac's call, since she put her through to Rachel Bennet immediately. 'Dr Griffin.' Rachel sounded relieved to hear from her. 'Thank you for calling.'

'What can I do for you, Ms Bennet? Let me first say that we don't have much more information than we did this morning.'

'No, no, I realize that. No, I'm more concerned about Peter.' Bennet's concern came through in her voice.

'Concerned in what way?' Mac asked. Other than the fact that someone might want to kill him, Mac thought with a wince.

'He just isn't taking this seriously, Dr Griffin. I don't know if it's some macho thing, or if he just doesn't know about some of this stuff. I've heard some of these horror stories before, and I know how serious something like this can be. One of my friends in Los Angeles, she's a manager, too. Well, one of these nuts came crashing through the glass patio of one of her clients – Lilah. She used to be lead singer for Is It Real, but she's been a solo act for a year or so. Bobbie, the manager, was there, too. Glass all over. And the guy was cut up badly. But he thought it was worth it because he got to touch Lilah. When Bobbie told me this, all I could think of was, lucky he didn't have a gun, y'know?'

Mac waited a moment to see if Rachel had really stopped. 'And how do you think I can help, Ms Bennet?'

'I was wondering if you'd talk to him, tell him about some of what's happened.'

'I don't know . . .'

'Please, Doctor . . .' Rachel started again, and Mac noticed a change in the quality of her voice. Almost as though her throat was thickening, as if she was trying to avoid tears. 'Please. I've got to get through to him. He means everything to me now.'

Mac was trying to reconcile the image of the polished, in-control businesswoman she'd met earlier with the voice on the phone that was near to cracking, when the first Rachel Bennet reappeared. 'Where do you live?' she said suddenly, the voice crisp again.

'Why?' Mac started. Why in the world would this woman want to know where she lived?

'Are you here in the city? Of course you are. It was a local call I made. Or was that your office? I can't remember.' Rachel raced ahead, virtually having a conversation with herself. 'Do you know Hudson's, off Union Square?'

'Yes.' Of course Mac knew it. It was one of her favorite restaurants, and just a few blocks from the apartment.

'I'm meeting Peter there for dinner tonight. Can you join us there? Seven?'

'Look, Ms Bennet—'

'Please, Doctor, just this one time. If he doesn't get it after talking to you, I'll beat it into him somehow. But please.'

'Okay, I'll give Mr Rossellini a *brief* summary of this type of case.' And it would be brief, Mac thought. She knew she had to get to bed early tonight.

'Thank you, thank you, Doctor. See you at seven. Reservation's in my name.' Rachel Bennet got off the line before Mac could add another word.

By the time she'd soaked long enough to turn pruney, Mac's body and feet had begun to forgive her for the day's activities. It was just about five-thirty, and too early to get dressed for the restaurant. She decided to start watching the videos and see what she could see.

She took the video cassettes from her briefcase. The cases were slightly larger than the ones she was accustomed to from the video rental shops. The black case had a large off-white label on it, with the distinctive B and B logo she had seen on the door of the management office. It was just a standard mailing label, Mac realized. Centered on the label was the title of the song, underneath that was the time expressed in minutes and seconds, and beneath that the phrase 'video black with title only – no bars and tone.' She loaded a cassette into the machine and sat back on the sofa, remote control in hand.

This was the 'What Will It Take' video, according to the tape's opening credits. The video started with a shot of Rossellini seated at a deserted bar, fingering a stemmed wineglass. The bar was a long one, made of a dark wood, and there was a metal footrail that ran the length of it. The mirror behind the bar was distinctive: It was framed with stained glass that was softly lit from behind. Mac recognized this bar area; she'd been in that restaurant, but she couldn't place it at the moment.

Rossellini's voice was on the soundtrack, but his image on the screen seemed to be singing only sometimes. The lyrics spoke of a lost love, a woman who had left him. The scenes of him alone in the bar were in black and white, but when he sang of the happier times, the images were in color.

The full-color shots showed Rossellini and a beautiful young woman Mac didn't recognize sitting in the same bar, surrounded by a lively crowd of people. Another shot showed them sitting in a dining room, gazing at one another over a candlelit table. Another had them strolling down a sidewalk, arm in arm, and suddenly stopping, turning into an embrace, kissing.

The refrain resumed in black-and-white images, the solitary figure at the bar now singing:

> *What will it take to make you love me*
> *What will it take to bring you home*
> *What will it take to bring our dream back*
> *I don't want to face this life alone.*

The camera closed in on Rossellini and this whole section of the video consisted of close-ups at various angles, with the impassioned expression of the singer filling the screen. He was singing now and either this song meant a great deal to him or he was one hell of an actor, Mac thought. And she was struck once more by how much more interesting black-and-white images can be than color.

She watched another: the 'How Can I Show You' video, the one that was shot on the soundstage where she'd been. Again, color images mixed with black and white, some clear, some very grainy looking. There were many close-ups of Rossellini, and some long shots that included the whole band. Some images whirled around in a kind of distortion, then returned to the focused close-ups of Rossellini. The rapid sequence of images, the various camera angles, and the mixture of the images conveyed an impression of much more activity than there was: a man singing in front of a band.

The video came to an end, and even though the editor's description had prepared her for it, she gasped when she saw how the last shot of Rossellini resembled the body she'd seen on Friday.

She went back to the first one and rewound it to watch it again. She particularly studied the images of Rossellini alone. The man she'd met that morning was good-looking. Very good-looking. Downright gorgeous, as a matter of fact. But the man on the screen was perfect. There was a difference. There were perceptible clues that the man she'd met was human. A redness on his cheek where his skin was irritated from shaving, the hairs of his left eyebrow standing upright at an odd angle. There'd been a sheen to his skin when he came in off the warm streets, enough to let you know he sweat.

The man on the screen didn't look like he would sweat; he would just glisten.

Mac appeared before the Hudson's maitre d' promptly at seven-ten, arriving ten minutes late deliberately so that she wouldn't have to lurk around the front of the restaurant waiting for Rachel Bennet and her client. Mac had learned that one of the punishments of being punctual was that you usually ended up waiting for other people, and she wasn't in the mood tonight.

The maitre d' smiled on recognizing Mac, and though he could barely hide his surprise (with perhaps a touch of haughty disapproval) when she asked for Rachel Bennet, he walked her back to the table immediately. Hudson's had an old men's club look to it – lots of imitation leather, imitation Tiffany shades on the lamps and chandeliers, and what looked to be real wood. Mac caught a glimpse of herself in one of the mirrors, and realized she fit in as well. She wore straight cut khaki trousers, an ivory silk shirt, a classic-cut navy blazer, and loafers. Once a preppy, always a preppy.

Rachel and Peter Rossellini were seated in a semicircular booth at the back of the restaurant. Mac noted with some dismay that Rachel Bennet's linen jumpsuit looked every bit as good now as it did when they'd first met nine hours ago. How the hell did this woman manage to wear linen all day and not look wrinkled?

Rachel Bennet looked relieved when she saw Mac approaching the table. From the expression on Peter Rossellini's face, however, Mac could tell her appearance was a surprise to him. Rachel scooted out, and Mac took her seat in the curve of the booth, Rachel to her right and Peter Rossellini to her left.

Peter nodded to Mac cordially, and then looked straight across the table at Rachel. 'Okay, what's going on here?'

'I'll tell you in a moment, Peter,' she said, signaling for a waiter and then looking at her watch. She turned to Mac. 'What would you like to drink, Doctor?'

'A white wine spritzer, please,' Mac said, looking up at the waiter. Once a preppy . . .

As soon as the waiter departed, Rossellini tried again. 'Rachel . . .'

'All right,' Rachel told him in a harsh whisper. 'If you hadn't been so thickheaded this morning, I wouldn't have had to pull a surprise on you. But you refuse to take this situation seriously . . .'

Obviously, the woman who had teared up on the phone this afternoon hadn't shown up for this meeting, Mac thought. The take-charge Rachel Bennet was back.

'No, I'm just not taking it seriously the way *you* want me to take it seriously,' Rossellini replied in a soft voice. 'Look, I'm very sorry about what happened to Marty, but as far as I know, nobody's been after me. So what am I supposed to do?'

'God, Peter, you're so exasperating,' Rachel whispered. Mac had been facing Rossellini, but turned toward Rachel as soon as she started to speak. It was like watching a tennis match. After pointedly glaring at Rossellini, Rachel turned and faced directly toward Mac. 'Go ahead, you tell him.'

'What is it you'd like me to tell him?' Mac asked. Rossellini half-smiled at her.

The waiter appeared with Mac's drink, and Rachel took those few moments to collect herself. She also glanced down at her watch again. Mac decided she'd get through this as quickly as possible, and maybe she could be home by eight or so.

'Doctor,' Rachel started. 'I mentioned to you on the phone today that I'd heard about some of these cases. Peter apparently hasn't. But then I don't think Peter's heard who is president now.' She glared at him across the table, and then back at Mac. 'I'd appreciate you filling him in on just what can happen. And then maybe he can figure out how careful he needs to be.'

Mac took a sip of her spritzer, using the moment to organize her thoughts. With a big breath and an 'Okay . . .' she was just about to begin.

'Before you get started, though,' Rachel interrupted. 'I have to leave. I'm sorry.' She looked over at Peter, whose obvious annoyance led her to repetition. '*I'm sorry*, but something came up with Robbie – he's my son,' she explained with a glance to Mac, 'and I really do have to go home. I'll sign the check before I leave, so have whatever you want on me.' She slid out of the booth, adjusting the belt of her jumpsuit as she stood. 'And Doctor, I really do appreciate this.' She turned and sped through the dining room.

Mac moved around in the booth, toward where Rachel had been sitting, positioning herself opposite Peter Rossellini. 'She's quite a dynamo, isn't she?' Mac said to him.

'Yeah, and it's all natural. That's what's scary.'

Mac smiled. Pleasantries were over. She took another big breath to begin, but then sidetracked herself this time. 'Before we get started, maybe you can answer a question for me.'

'Sure, if I can.'

'When Lieutenant Buratti and I were at the office this morning, I noticed the name Berman and Bennet – the double *B* – all over. I know who Bennet is, obviously' – she looked toward the archway through which Rachel had disappeared – 'but who is Berman? And where is he or she hiding?'

'Max Berman was Rachel's husband.'

'Was?'

'Yeah. He died just a couple of months ago. March I think, maybe February. I only remember it was cold at the funeral.' He indicated his head toward where Rachel had been sitting. 'That's why she's so anxious about anything to do with Robbie. He took it pretty hard.'

'How old is he?'

'Seven, I think. Maybe eight. Nice kid.'

Mac smoothed away some of the moisture that had accumulated on her glass. 'Ms Bennet seems young for a widow. Was it an accident?'

'No, he was sick for quite some time. Max was a chunk older than Rachel. Twenty, maybe twenty-five years older. He was the one who'd gotten her started in the business, or so I hear. Like her mentor, I guess you would say.' He took a long draught of his beer. 'I was only around the last year or so that he was sick, but from what I saw, Rachel was a champ taking care of him.'

Mac nodded that she understood. 'It seems trite

to say, but I'm sorry to hear that she's had such a difficult time.'

They sat in silence for a few moments. Rossellini finally broke it. 'Now maybe you can answer a question for me.'

'Okay.'

'What's all this doctor business? What kind of doctor are you?'

Mac wanted to laugh at his expression. 'I'm a PhD doctor. A psychologist. Specializing in criminal psychology. I teach over at John Jay College of Criminal Justice and I sometimes consult for the police department.' And sometimes I even get paid for it, Mac said to herself.

Rossellini sat up a little straighter, his eyes wide open. 'Whew. That's . . . that's pretty impressive.' Mac knew from the expression on his face that he was absolutely sincere. 'You're talkin' to a guy who hangs around musicians all the time. A few of us finished college, but most barely got through high school. You sorta forget about the real world.'

'Well, let me fill you in on this part of the real world.' It was past seven-thirty now; she wouldn't be home by eight, but eight-thirty was still a possibility. 'Your particular case – this particular case – is a variation on the usual profile. But let me explain the usual to you first.'

Rossellini settled back into his seat and looked at her attentively.

'The activity is called stalking, and actually the majority of stalking cases in the country involve regular, ordinary people. For the purposes of my explanation, though, we'll concentrate on the ones that involve celebrities like yourself.' God, she was sounding like she was lecturing to students. Oh, well.

'As I mentioned this morning, there are a few usual patterns. Repeated phone calls, in some cases hundreds a day. Or mailings. Two or three letters a day. Following a person, showing up at every public appearance they make, even if it's just at the grocery store.' Rossellini was paying attention, but his expression was still neutral.

'Sometimes, actually most of the time, it stays in the realm of extreme nuisance. People have to change their phone numbers frequently, have people screen their mail. And be careful anytime they leave their house. But sometimes it progresses. You' – she decided to make this personal to him – 'the celebrity become a factor in this person's life. You become the answer to all their problems. If they can just get to you, everything will be perfect. It's like a piece of their personality is missing, and you become what will fill the void. You become the object of their obsession.'

She took a sip of her spritzer. 'You, of course, don't know what role you're playing in their life. To them, the celebrity has become the perfect lover, or wife, husband, partner, child – although it's usually lover, and you don't act the role that they have created for you in their delusion. So they get angry. How dare you? This seems to be the reason why stalkers get violent – they're angry that they've been ignored.'

Rossellini was quiet for a moment. 'But I don't get it. Nobody's been hassling me.'

'Not that you know of. Yes, nobody's been following you or phoning repeatedly. But I met with Marge Masterson today, and she has received some letters that could be construed as threatening.' Rossellini's eyes widened in surprise. 'We'll check them out starting tomorrow. And I'm going to see Marianne Santangelo to see if there's anything in the fan mail that's come in.' He nodded in understanding. 'It's critical to check out these people, to see who has been trying to contact you. A crucial element to these people is that you – the celebrity – are aware of their existence.'

He was quiet for a moment. 'What's happened in these cases?'

'Most, as I said, remain in the area of nuisance. Sometimes extreme nuisance, and many celebrities have been forced into getting a court order against these types. The court orders work with varying degrees of success. Several states have stalking laws now, and some of these people end up in jail for a while. That can be enough to deter some of them.'

'And the others?' he asked.

She looked him straight in the eye. 'Some have turned quite violent. Extreme threats against the celebrity involved. People have had to change the patterns of their lives drastically, and spend enormous amounts of money on security. There've been peripheral actions like killing pets. There have been physical attacks, knifings, beatings, one or two shooting incidents. I know of three cases where the celebrity was severely wounded, and at least two cases where they – the celebrities – were killed. John Lennon, of course, for one.'

Rossellini was quiet again, staring up at the ceiling in thought. Mac sipped her drink again; her throat was dry from talking. Finally, Rossellini looked at her. 'Okay. I get what you're sayin'. But you're just now checking out the mail and what have you. Before you started all this, you thought Marty's death had something to do with me. How come?'

'Mr Jury's body was found in a rather unusual and deliberate setting, to begin with. And then one of the editors at Metropolitan described the end of your video to us. The "How Can I Show You" video. His body was left in a pose that resembled you at the end of the video.'

Rossellini paled at that. 'Ah, Jesus, that's creepy.'

'Exactly. Now I haven't seen pictures of the crime scene of the other murder, but the fact that they both occurred at the site of your videos, that alone is a powerful indication that you are the object of the obsession. Mr Jury and the other gentleman probably filled in for you in the mind of the murderer.'

Peter took a deep breath, trying to find the words for his next question.

'Ooooh, it IS you!' A loud female voice screeched at Rossellini as a hand shot in front of his face. 'I'm one of your biggest fans, really I am.' Both Peter and Mac started at the intrusion, but Peter jumped a little higher. The hand was holding one of the restaurant's menus. 'I can't believe you're really here. Can you sign this for me, please? To Shirley, with all my love. Okay?'

Peter looked directly at her. It took him a moment to speak. 'Sure. Got a pen?'

She didn't, and Mac finally had to dig one out of her purse. The young woman continued to gush while Peter signed the menu and then handed it to her. Shirley looked at it closely, then read it aloud. 'Shirley – thanks for the support. Best wishes. Peter Rossellini.' Her voice betrayed her disappointment at the inscription. She looked down at him, said, 'Okay, I guess,' and walked away.

Her squeal earlier had attracted some attention in the restaurant and people were looking their way – some surreptitiously, some craning their necks, trying to see who was in the booth.

'Listen, do you want something to eat? We can go someplace else if you'd rather,' Rossellini said.

Mac could tell he was a little shaken. She didn't want to leave him just yet; they needed to finish this conversation. And she was getting a touch hungry. If truth be told, she was getting very hungry. Frozen yogurt at three o'clock was now a distant memory.

'Actually, I could go for a chef's salad. They have a pretty good one here, unless you're uncomfortable staying.'

'You mean with the people looking? Nah, that's okay. It's happening more and more. She just threw me, that's all, after what you were saying. Let's order.' He signaled for the waiter. 'And let's talk about something else for a little while.'

'Fine. You can answer a question for me. Which comes first – the music or the lyrics?' Mac said innocently. He laughed, and his face relaxed for the first time in an hour.

It was after nine by the time they left the restaurant, and Peter stepped to the curb to hail a cab for her.

'No, thanks,' Mac said. 'I'm only a few blocks from here. I'm going to walk.'

Rossellini looked at her with a questioning expression. 'Really? Where? I live a few blocks from here, too.'

'Over on Fifteenth Street, just past Third. Opposite the little park. How about you?'

'Irving Place. Just south of Gramercy Park. We're practically neighbors.'

'I guess we are.'

'Well, let me walk you home, then.' Rossellini stepped next to her and they fell into an easy pace.

'At least to Irving Place. I don't want to take you out of your way.'

'Don't worry about it.'

It had been a pleasant dinner, Mac realized. The conversation was light and friendly. He'd asked her about teaching (she really enjoyed it, especially dealing with the guys who never expected to see a woman criminal psychologist). She'd asked him about how he got started singing (he started in college, when the lead singer of the band he was with didn't show up one night). They both admitted that they couldn't imagine getting up the guts to do the other's job. It was a surprisingly comfortable evening. Mac couldn't remember talking with a man, especially such an attractive man of such new acquaintance, so effortlessly.

They'd never returned to the topic they'd discussed earlier and Mac decided that might be a good thing. Mac knew he was trying to deal with all the information she'd given him, to deal with the fact that he might be – probably was – in danger.

It was a lovely spring evening, and when they got to Irving Place, he insisted on walking her all the way home. They reached her building within a few minutes and he stopped as she climbed the first of the few steps that led to the door.

'Doctor,' he began, haltingly. 'Thanks . . . really . . . I want to thank you for tonight, for taking the time to, ah, go over all of this with me. I appreciate it.'

'You're more than welcome. I just wish it could have been a more pleasant conversation at the beginning. And thanks for dinner.'

'Don't thank me, that was on Rachel, like she—'

A loud *BANG!* echoed around the small park that was just across the street. Rossellini flinched and ducked slightly at the noise. He turned toward the park and looked in the direction that Mac was looking. It was a car that had backfired.

'Hey,' he joked to Mac. 'You really got me going.'

Standing on the first step, Mac was just about the same height as he. She looked directly at him. 'Adrenaline is pumping, and you're a little jumpy, that's all. Alert is good. You need to be alert. But try not to be jumpy.'

'I'll see if I can manage that,' Rossellini said with a smirk. 'And you'll let me know what you find out tomorrow?'

'I'm sure Lieutenant Buratti will be in touch with you as soon as possible.'

'Okay. I'll talk to you later then. Good night.'

Rossellini turned and walked back toward Third Avenue. Mac watched him for a few moments.

NINE

May 29

It had been a long time since Buratti had been on one of the commuter trains out of the city. Seven, maybe eight years. He knew that they'd confined smoking to the smoking and bar cars a long time ago. What he'd forgotten is that they'd eliminated the smokers and prohibited smoking even in the bar cars a few years back.

It was an hour-and-forty-minute train ride to New Haven, plus the ten minutes he'd been in his seat before the train pulled out. That was close to two hours without a cigarette. He had picked up a cup of coffee in Grand Central before he boarded. So he'd had coffee, but no cigarette. He was a wild man by the time the train pulled into New Haven. Damn, he was going to have to do something about this.

Sandra Duvall, an assistant in the New Haven County Medical Examiner's Office, was the one who would be picking him up. They'd agreed that she'd pick him up at the station. Buratti hadn't been in New Haven in maybe ten or twelve years, and from the time he took the stairs down from the platform, he glanced around admiring the restoration job they'd done on the old train station. The last time he was in New Haven, the train station was a dump. They'd been doing some good stuff at Grand Central in the past few years, but this place was amazing.

As he rode the escalator up to the main lobby, he let out a faint but appreciative whistle when he craned his neck all the way and looked around. He could see from where he got off the escalator the ticket windows that lined the left side of the room and the shops that lined the right side. The place had huge high windows and was full of light. The walls seemed to be of a pinky beige marble, and long, highly polished wooden benches occupied the center of the main waiting area. Even the bums on the benches looked like they'd spiffed up a little.

He spotted Sandra Duvall in front of the information booth. He recognized her immediately from her description. She was maybe his age, mid- to late forties, with jet black hair and big red-framed eyeglasses. 'Just like Sally Jessy Raphael,' she'd said on the phone. Since she outweighed Ms Raphael by about fifty pounds, that was the only point of resemblance.

They headed first to the New Haven County Medical Examiner's Office. This whole Vos thing was a nightmare when it came to jurisdiction, Buratti knew from his telephone conversations yesterday. When the body was discovered, the Branford police had been called. Then the state police were brought in, as they were in any possible homicide that occurred outside the major cities in Connecticut. But the coroner's office was under the authority of New Haven County. Nothing was going to be easy about this one.

It took only a few minutes to get to the coroner's office, and only a few minutes more until Michael Hackett, MD, joined him in the small conference room.

Buratti had seen this type before. The good Dr Hackett, assistant medical examiner for New Haven County, was a certifiable caffeine freak and today he was wired for sound. It was just past ten o'clock in the morning and he already sounded like a 33 rpm record being played at 45, Buratti thought. Funny, he realized, in a couple of years nobody will know what that means.

'To tell you the truth,' Hackett was saying, 'I'm still not sure about this one. I'll tell you what I think. Vos had a few too many brewskis, decided to take a moonlight stroll on the beach. It's hard to keep your footing on the beach, y'know. Especially if you're loaded. Too much torque on the bod, see? So maybe he slips, falls, conks his head, and then tries to swallow the Sound. Within about, say, six, seven minutes, he's dead. Or maybe he gets conked on the head, then falls, and then tries to swallow the Sound. Same ending.'

Buratti got copies of what he needed from the file

and then he and Duvall headed for Branford. The local guy and the state cop assigned to the case had agreed to meet him there. The drive to the Colony Beach Club was about fifteen minutes, but as they approached the club and started passing the half-million-, maybe-up-to-a-million-dollar homes, Buratti knew it was a world away from downtown New Haven.

This part of the coastline was generally rocky, but the Colony sat in the center of a shallow cove that had a long stretch of sandy beach. The main club house, a rambling clapboard structure, was just above the beach. Farther back, a two-lane road followed the shape of the cove. The road was lined with houses; big Victorian gingerbreads sat cheek-by-jowl with modern chrome-and-glass squares. They all had an unobstructed view of the beach and of the Sound. Buratti estimated the distance from the edge of the water where he stood to where the houses were, at a little less than a quarter of a mile.

It was a gorgeous day. Sunny, maybe seventy-six, seventy-seven degrees. Low humidity. A nice breeze coming in off the Sound. Tromping on the sand wasn't doing his Florsheims a whole hell of a lot of good, though. The local guy, Swett, had been waiting for Buratti when he arrived, and the state cop was just now making his way from the parking lot. After the introductions, George Thomas, the state cop, started them walking down the beach to the point where the body had been found.

'Body was discovered between five-thirty and six a.m. on the morning of the nineteenth, Sunday morning. Mr and Mrs Salazar who live down there' – Thomas stopped, turned slightly, and pointed to the houses at the southernmost point of the cove – 'were out for an early-morning stroll on the beach. Once they spotted the body, Mr Salazar ran back to the parking lot to call 911. Swett here was on the scene within eight minutes from the time of the call. He notified our unit and we were here within about fifteen.' Buratti saw that they were coming up on a pile of rocks, ones that ranged from melon size to huge boulders. Actually it was too well organized to be called a pile, but it stopped short of being a wall. Thomas came to a halt about six feet short of this gathering of rocks.

'Vos's body was found here, just below the high-tide mark. The Medical Examiner's Office set the time of death at approximately three a.m. Mr Vos had a blood alcohol content of point zero nine, within the legal limits, and that coincides with what witnesses told us he was drinking earlier that night. Death was the result of a blow on the head which rendered him unconscious, then he drowned when the tide washed over him.'

'How come the body wasn't swept away?' Buratti asked.

'He was just below the high-water mark,' Thomas answered. 'The water wouldn't have near enough power to move his body at this point. Actually, it's sort of like drowning in a teacup, if you wanna know the truth. He drowned in maybe two, three inches of water.'

'And the blow on the head?'

'Probably one of the rocks there.' Thomas indicated with a nod of his head. 'According to the coroner, any one of them could be the object that hit his head.'

'Any indication that any of them had been moved?' Buratti asked with a trace of hope in his voice.

'Couldn't tell. By the time the tide came in all the way and then started to go out, everything – the sand, pebbles, some seaweed – had settled around the rocks as well. Those rocks looked like they hadn't been disturbed in a hundred years. No traces of blood, hair, nothing. The tide washed everything clean.'

'So basically, you got nothin', right?' said Buratti. 'So how come it's still an open case?'

'Coupla things. Vos's mother is one influential lady in this community. If we say it's not murder, then people will say it's because her son was falling down drunk, and she won't have that. But even more than the mother, it's the clothes,' Thomas said.

'The clothes?' Buratti looked at both men in front of him.

'You got the pictures in the file, there, George,' Swett said, pleased to be able to contribute finally. 'Show him.'

Thomas cradled the standard manila file folder

he'd been carrying and fingered through until he found what he was looking for. 'Friends of Vos's who were with him at the club that night until about quarter to two, just before the place closed, told us this isn't what he was wearing when they left him.' He handed two pictures to Buratti. 'And we can't find the clothes he did have on.'

Buratti looked at the pictures. Vos's lifeless body was sprawled on the beach, his head almost resting on the lowest of the rock pile. He wore what appeared to be light-colored trousers rolled to midcalf and a lighter, probably white, shirt unbuttoned and outside the pants. After studying the clothes, Buratti looked at the rest of the picture. Vos had had medium-dark hair, curly, and it looked like it was long. Shoulder-length long.

Buratti wasn't usually a betting man, but he would put money on the chance that when he got to look at the video that had been shot here, Rossellini would be dressed pretty close to the way the corpse in the picture was. Shit.

TEN

Mac was a bit surprised when the taxi dropped her off in front of the World Headquarters of the Peter Rossellini Fan Club. At least that was the way it was billed on the letter-sized flyer that Rachel Bennet had given her. The World Headquarters of the Peter Rossellini Fan Club, which according to the brochure was 201½ Holmes Avenue, Mineola, New York, was apparently located in a garage. The numerals of the address, 201½, were above the center post of the two-car, two-door garage.

It turned out that the garage belonged to Marianne Santangelo, who happened to be a cousin of Peter Rossellini. Mac had knocked on the front door of the house (number 201) after she'd determined that no one was in the garage.

Then it turned out that the fan club wasn't located in a garage; it was in half a garage.

'Yeah,' Marianne was saying as she led Mac into the right side of the garage, flicking on a light with her right hand. Her left arm was occupied with

107

holding her beautiful nine-month-old daughter, Vanessa. 'This is the world headquarters, all right. The new world headquarters, as a matter of fact. Just moved here from my dining room.'

'Yes, I can tell,' Mac replied. She'd smelled the scent of fresh lumber just as Marianne mentioned the newness and she glanced around now to inspect the surroundings. One side of the garage had been cleared out, and some drywall added on two sides created the sense of a room. There was a good-sized rectangular table in the center of the room with chairs on three sides. At one end was a desk that had been improvised by laying a piece of plywood over two small file cabinets. A standard personal computer setup, keyboard, monitor, and cpu sat on the desk; the fourth chair of the set was in place under the desk. Along the exterior wall were shelves built out of cinder blocks and raw lumber. There was really no way to hide the garage door, however.

'Ha,' Mac said, carefully running a finger along a stretch of raw lumber shelves. 'I haven't seen one of these since my college days.' The shelves, she noticed, held boxes of pictures of Peter Rossellini and boxes of a newsletter entitled *The Rossellini Report*.

Marianne shrugged. 'Yeah, but it gets the job done.' She plopped the baby on the table and drew a chair toward her with her foot. 'Boy, that's a great-lookin' suit,' she said as she sat down, a longing tone in her voice.

Mac wore a tobacco-colored suit; its straight skirt and blousy jacket emphasized her waist. The new mother wore baggy white cotton pants and a multicolored bat-wing cotton top, also very loose fitting. 'Thanks,' Mac said. 'It's very comfortable.'

'The doctor said my waist would snap right back after she was born. Ha! They lie.' Marianne gestured for Mac to pull up a chair on the other side. 'So what can I do for you?'

Mac placed her briefcase on the table and pulled the chair out. 'Tell me how long you've been handling Peter's fan mail,' she began.

'Since it started, I think. Maybe there was a few things he got in from people before the album came out, but not much. I mean, he'd done some club dates, and there were him and Joey's songs, but there really wasn't much fan mail from that, I don't think. Last spring when the album came out and the first single goes crazy, y'know, 'n' after a month or so, the fan mail started piling up. And so Peter's manager asked if there was anyone he knew who could take it over. I was expecting Vanessa here' – Marianne turned her attention to her daughter and started kissing her cheek, adopting the different tone of voice that adults use when addressing a baby – 'wasn't I, sweetie, yes I was' – she faced toward Mac again and her voice resumed its normal tone as she picked up midsentence – 'and I had just left my job. But I knew I woulda gone bonkers without nothing to do.

And I could do this here at home, sort of in my spare time, so it was great, y'know?'

'Just how does the club work?' Mac asked, knowing that she wasn't going to have to drag information out of Marianne. She was exhibiting a characteristic of many women at home all day with a child. When she had someone around to listen, she talked.

'The girls – it's mainly girls, some guys, but not many – anyway, the girls write in here—'

'How do they know to contact you here?'

'If they buy the tapes or the CD, the little insert thing – y'know where the picture is, and the listing of the songs, there's a little box there that says if you want information on the Peter Rossellini Fan Club, write here.' The baby had started to screw up her face, looking like she was going to let loose with a major yelp. Marianne reached into the pocket of her pants and withdrew a small rubbery clown. The baby smiled, reached for the clown, and immediately slurped it into her mouth. 'And there's a couple of the music magazines, the fan-zines, not the business ones, that run articles on clubs. We put the information in there, too.'

'Are you talking about the teen magazines that I see on the stands?'

'Nah, Peter's a little old for those magazines, if you know what I mean. Don't tell him I said that. He got a little crazy when he turned thirty-four last summer. The ones I'm talking about are sorta like that, but it's just about pop music stars, and not just for teenagers.'

'Okay, what do you do then, after they've written in?' Mac asked. It was a challenge to keep up with Marianne's conversational flow.

Marianne rubbed Vanessa's stomach in a slow, even rhythm. 'Then I send them out the brochure, what the club does, how much it costs to join, like that. There's a form for them to fill in if they wanna join.'

Mac was surprised at this. 'They actually pay to join a fan club? I didn't realize that.'

'Yeah, it's like a subscription, sort of. These pictures and stuff cost something to make, y'know. When I first get the brochure thing back, I send out our welcome package. We've done five newsletters now, so I send whichever newsletter I have on hand, an eight-by-ten of Peter, and an official membership card. If they want more pictures, or the T-shirts or stuff, there's a form in the newsletter so they can order.'

'There's even more for them to buy?' Mac said with even more surprise.

'We don't rip the kids off, if that's what you mean. Not that I can say that applies to everyone in the business, if you get my drift. Some of those concert vendors have the nerve, I tell you. I was over at the Byrne Arena last summer for The Trinity Project. Peter was opening for them, y'know. God, it was so exciting. Anyway, there's all these tables of things.

Programs fifteen bucks? *Give me a break,*' she said deliberately. 'And the T-shirts. Listen, I sell T-shirts here, and I know what they cost. Those guys have got the ba—' – she hesitated and edited herself – 'have got the nerve, to charge twenty-five, thirty bucks for them. That's ripping the kids off, if you ask me.' Marianne leaned back in her chair with a big breath, having emphatically made her point. But she still kept one hand on the baby.

'Do people write directly to Peter in care of the club?' Mac asked.

'Sure.'

'What happens to those letters?'

'I go through them. I send Peter a sample of the mail every week or so. And if there's something really special, I make sure Peter gets back to them.'

'Special in what way?'

'Well I got a soft spot for kids, y'know? And I got a letter, or Peter got a letter, from one mother who says her boy, he's six, and he's spent most of his life in a hospital . . . Anyway, he really loves Peter's music and "One Heart" in particular. The kid thinks the song is just for him. So I make sure that Peter sees that one. And I put a whole package together for the boy – and I made Peter call him, too,' she finished with some self-satisfaction.

'Any others like that?'

'Last month a couple of nice ones from kids whose mothers are real big fans of Peter's. The kids wanted pictures signed for their mothers – for Mother's Day.

So I got Peter to sign those personally, with their names and all. Usually, it's just a stamp, or me trying to sign for him.'

Mac smiled; Marianne's pleasure in a job well done was a delight to observe. 'How about the ones you send to Peter – how do you pick those out?'

'Right after Christmas we got a bunch of letters from girls saying that their boyfriends finally proposed to them because of listening to Peter's songs. A couple of them are going to use "Whenever I Dream" as the first dance at their wedding. When I get stuff like that in, I send them in to Peter. He likes to hear stories like that.'

'Are there any particular fans that stand out in your mind?'

'Stand out how?' Marianne asked.

'People who write frequently, whose letters may seem unusual in their . . . intensity or their tone?'

'You mean the real loony-tunes?' Marianne said without hesitation.

'Yeah.' Mac smiled. Amazing how the terms that she normally avoided seemed to keep popping up. 'The real loony-tunes. Can you tell me about them?'

'Sure.' Marianne stood up and carefully moved the baby until Vanessa was in front of Mac. 'Keep your eye on her for a minute, and I'll get the files out.'

Mac moved closer to the table to put her hands on the baby. Vanessa was intrigued with her new companion and dropped the clown to reach for Mac's hair. Mac dipped her head to get out of the baby's reach, but Vanessa interpreted her move as a new game and laughed heartily. Mac was taken aback at the baby's exuberance. Not having spent much time in the company of people under the age of two, she was genuinely uncomfortable in the presence of an infant. So much for the supposed womanly instincts.

'Actually I shouldn't call them all fruitcakes. Some of them are just pretty extreme, that's all.' Marianne returned to her side of the table with a manila folder. She sat down again and opened the folder in front of her. 'Keep her over on that side, okay?' she said to Mac. 'She just loves paper. First she crinkles it and then she tries to eat it.'

Mac smiled as Vanessa reached for her hair again. She was successful this time and yanked, hard. 'Ow!' Mac said, and she and the baby stared at one another, wide-eyed.

'Okay, we got the ones who are proposing to Peter. I got a couple who invited him to their senior proms. One who thinks Peter is her long-lost son. The one who calls every week – from Australia. Where do you want to start?'

ELEVEN

They had agreed to meet at Mac's office at John Jay, both because she had to pick up some books there and because it would avoid any questions from Captain Lenox's office.

Mac dragged herself in from Penn Station at quarter to two, just minutes ahead of Buratti, who dragged himself in from Grand Central. He was carrying a Diet Pepsi and a hot dog, and the aroma of the sauerkraut and mustard quickly filled her office.

'Sorry about this, Mac,' he said, lifting his hands to indicate his lunch. 'But I thought I was gonna eat the armrests on the train. I forgot they don't have any food on the trains midday.'

'Normally I would say that is a disgustingly unhealthful lunch for a man your age. Unfortunately it smells delicious. If you're lucky I won't steal a bite.'

'Really, you want some?' Buratti held the hot dog toward her.

'No, thanks. I'll control myself.'

Buratti kicked a chair into place at the corner of Mac's desk and carefully arranged his lunch, trying not to drop the envelope he had tucked under his arm. 'Beckman should be here any minute. So how'd you do today?'

Mac slowly sat in the swivel chair behind her desk. 'I'll tell you something, Mario. You know the budget cuts in mental health over the last ten or fifteen years?' Buratti nodded yes as he took another bite of his hot dog. 'I wonder if future generations will ever forgive us. The number of unstable people out there is frightening.' She reached for her briefcase and drew out a stack of papers. 'I made copies of some of the fan mail Peter Rossellini has received. These are only the most disturbing ones. There are twenty-seven of them,' she finished as she dropped the file on the desk.

Buratti took a long swig of his Diet Pepsi. 'Beckman's gonna have his hands full. He just made detective last month. We'll break him in.'

Stu Beckman stepped in the door a few minutes later, on the dot of two. He was about Mac's age, early thirties, and could pretty much be described by the word *medium*. He was of medium height, about five-ten, medium build; his hair was medium brown. His eyes, however, were a striking gray, and from the color and tone of his skin, Mac could tell he'd spent a little too much time in the sun. The crow's feet at the corners of his eyes gave him both a sympathetic and humorous look.

Buratti quickly made the introductions and brought Beckman up to date on the Jury murder. Beckman was very deferential to Buratti, very respectful, and Mac could tell that Buratti was relishing his role as the wise elder brother.

Buratti finished the background and was gearing up for the rundown on the Connecticut case. He reached for his can of drink only to realize it was empty; oh, but he would exchange riches for just a couple of swigs of another Diet Pepsi and an after-lunch cigarette.

'How about Branford, Mario. What's the story there?' Mac asked before he had a chance to offer his recap.

Buratti pulled pictures from the envelope he'd placed on the desk. 'If I had a hundred bucks to bet, right now I'd bet that the video they filmed up there has Rossellini in light-colored pants, rolled up to midcalf, and a white shirt, the kind that looks a little big through the shoulders, you know? And the shirt is open. Right, Mac?'

'On the money.'

Buratti placed the pictures in front of Beckman and Mac.

''Cause that's exactly the way that Randy Vos looked when he died.'

'What else we got on this one?' Beckman asked.

'Not much,' Buratti replied, but he relayed the information he'd learned in New Haven and Branford.

Mac gave her summary of the fan club when Buratti had finished. 'I'll go over this group of names that need to be checked out and set the priorities. Agreed?'

'That's a good idea, Doc,' Buratti said.

'I can get on those right away,' said Beckman, looking toward Buratti. 'Unless there's something else you want me on first.'

'One thing. I'm going to see Joey Lemon tomorrow morning. The unhappy ex-partner. Mac, how about you and Beckman going to see the girlfriend?'

'You want the two of us together?' Mac asked. It seemed a little overkill to her. 'Okay,' she agreed.

'Yeah, I want to see if there are any buttons to be pushed with these two – Lemon and the girl. Beckman with you makes it official.'

'Tomorrow then,' Mac said to Beckman. 'What time?'

Beckman left the office as soon as they agreed on a time and place to meet. Mac looked at Buratti. 'Seems like a nice guy,' she said.

'Beckman? Yeah. I like the new ones. They're eager,' Buratti replied.

His voice was flat and tired. Something was bugging him. 'What's with you?' she asked.

'I really hope we come up with something out these two tomorrow. A woman pissed off at getting dumped, a disgruntled ex-partner, these are things I can understand. This stuff' – he nodded his head toward the pictures spread on the desk – 'this stuff I

118

don't understand.' Right at this moment he would give a great deal of money to be able to have a cigarette.

'It's not easy to understand. Probably a good thing.'

'What do you really think about this, Mac? How much time do you think we have?'

'Time?'

'Yeah. Y'know, it's like I got this clock tickin' in my head, and I'm wonderin' when the alarm's going to go off again.'

Mac folded her arms on the desk and leaned forward slowly. 'And it would be nice to know when the clock started ticking.'

'Yeah,' Buratti said on a sigh.

'That we may never know. And right now there's no way to tell when to expect another killing. There really haven't been enough ... incidents ... to establish any kind of pattern or time frame.'

'You mean we gotta wait till we have a couple more stiffs until we figure it out? Great.'

'No, not necessarily. It's just that we don't have enough right now to figure out the pattern. Or even if there is a pattern.'

'How do you mean?' Buratti looked at her intently.

'Time is one of the first things to look for in cases like this. Days of the week, days of the month, the new moon, the full moon, whatever. There's no time pattern evident here. Vos died a week ago Sunday on the nineteenth, and Jury early in the morning of

Friday the twenty-fourth. Does that mean we'll have another one six days later on the thirtieth?'

'Like tomorrow?'

'Yeah. Like tomorrow. Who knows?'

Buratti wished he could answer. 'What other kind of patterns can we look for?'

'You name it. People can see signs in the alphabet, in their horoscopes, in distances, in a deck of cards, in how the cereal sits in their bowl. What I'm saying is that a disturbed person – and I think the overwhelming possibility is that's what we're dealing with here – can be triggered by any number of factors. Something he sees or hears or feels, and that something may not even be perceptible by another person. Remember the Son of Sam case? He said his neighbor's dog told him to kill those people.'

Buratti almost snorted at that. 'Actually, I never believed that crap.'

'Sometimes it's easier for us – more comfortable – to believe that people commit murder out of malevolence than from some insane impulse. We have a grasp of envy and jealousy and greed. We understand those things. But somebody taking the life of another human being because' – Mac hesitated, trying to come up with one of the examples she'd read – 'because the victim's eyes reminded the killer of the GI Joe doll he'd had as a child. How do you fight something like that?'

Mac was glad to make it home before the worst

120

crunch of the rush hour. She quickly changed into cotton knit pants and a top; they were the summer equivalent of the sweats that were her winter at-home uniform. She got a glass of flavored seltzer, pulled one of the long cushions out of the small storage shed and onto a chaise, and stretched out to read the afternoon paper. Even at five-thirty the sun still seemed high in the sky; the long daylight hours of this time of year were a pleasure.

She folded up the paper when she'd finished and concentrated on the flowers for a few minutes. She picked off a few wilted leaves, tested the containers for dryness, and ended up filling the watering can three times. The routine was familiar and relaxing. That was the whole point of gardening, she'd decided a long time ago. Her mind wandered first to her plans for painting the apartment, and then free-floated back to the letters she'd read earlier today.

Most of them, the vast majority in fact, were straightforward fan letters. People who were enthusiastic about Peter Rossellini's music, his videos, and who wanted to let him know. They asked for pictures, for autographs; they asked when he'd be coming to their town. Normal stuff.

There were even some pretty clever ones. A few boys had written to Rossellini asking him to write a love song specifically for their girlfriends, which Mac thought was pretty ingenious. Many a sixteen-year-old girl would be impressed by that move.

It was the other ones that were disturbing. The

ones that seemed to be cries from the heart. Girls who were sure he had read their minds, that he was writing just for them. Girls who pleaded for him to marry them. The grief-stricken mother who was convinced Peter Rossellini was her long-lost son. Some of these were included in the file that she and Beckman would be reviewing. Between those and the names she'd gotten from Marge Masterson, Beckman was going to be busy.

Later, after dinner, she decided to listen to Rossellini's album. She'd heard the music while watching the videos, of course, but she hadn't really concentrated on it. It was time to.

Her stereo was hidden inside a large oak armoire in the living room. Mac had furnished the apartment with a lot of wood and old-fashioned upholstered furniture, another attempt to re-create the feeling of her parents' home, she'd realized. The armoire was large enough to hold her old albums, cassette tapes, and the newer compact discs as well. She hadn't gone overboard buying the new CD releases of some of her old favorites, even though some of the albums were pretty beat up by now. She was convinced that as soon as she dropped a bundle on CDs, the music business would come up with some new technology that would make the compact discs obsolete. O ye of little faith.

She had stopped at one of the music stores on Union Square on her way home that afternoon and picked up a copy of Rossellini's tape. Now she slipped it into the deck, put on the headphones, and stretched out in her most comfortable reading chair. She recognized the first song, 'How Can I Show You,' from the video. The next was a bouncy, up-tempo song with a clever, repetitive lyric. Soon to be heard in many an aerobics class, Mac thought.

The album had only a few like that. Most of the songs would be categorized as love songs, and most of those were of the broken-hearted variety. Rossellini sang passionately of love lost, of love just beyond reach, of love ignored. No wonder those unhappy people thought they had found a soul mate in Peter Rossellini, Mac thought. His voice captured all the loneliness and longing, all the angst of love gone awry.

Mac drifted off to sleep wondering what Rossellini's inspiration for those songs had been. Maybe meeting Judith Stone tomorrow would answer the question.

INTERLUDE TWO

Too soon, it seemed too soon. Too soon to be starting again.

She tossed on the bed, turning over, untangling her legs from the damp sheets. It was hot, and the single window fan made no difference in temperature in the room.

She closed her eyes tight, trying to concentrate. She'd been trying, but it wouldn't come; it just wouldn't come. She couldn't relive it second by second, heartbeat by heartbeat anymore. It got all jumbled with the first one and then it got lost.

She'd hated that first one. It had been cold on the beach. And when the moon clouded over, it was dark and cold, not at all like she'd imagined. He'd gotten drunk, the fool, and then started pawing at her. She hated that.

She got up and stood in front of the fan, the air blowing directly on her breasts and stomach.

It was too bad, really. He'd looked so wonderful wading in the water. He didn't look quite so much like Peter lying there in the rocks, though. But at least that surprised look had left his face.

Funny. This last one, the one with Martin, she'd liked it so much more, but it hadn't lasted as long as the first. Did memories wear out? she wondered. If you relive them over and over and over again in your head, do they simply fade away?

It was starting again, she was certain now. Her breath was coming faster and faster. She put her hands on the frame of the window to steady herself.

She had to have it back again. She wanted it back now. That feeling. The sensation of being with Peter. The memory of being with Peter.

She turned, her back to the fan now. She braced her legs and hugged herself, hard.

It was time. She knew that now. She couldn't live without it anymore. Her heart beat faster just thinking about it. About him.

She had to have it. She had to have him.

TWELVE

May 30

Mac woke up Thursday morning thinking of Peter Rossellini, just as she had gone to sleep thinking about him. She awoke twenty minutes before her alarm was set to go off, awaking with – or because of – an inexplicable sense of trepidation.

Instead of trying to shake the feeling, she tried to focus on it. She'd lectured Mario enough about paying attention to his intuitions; she had to respect her own as well. She kept the apartment quiet: no music on the radio, no morning news programs on television. Quiet would help.

Moving into her routine of setting up the coffee before stepping into the shower, she measured out the beans into the coffee grinder, but didn't grind them, measured the water to be boiled, and put the kettle over a medium-low flame.

She stepped into the shower and adjusted the spray to a gentle pulse. She closed her eyes, turned her back to the spray, and lowered her head so the water would hit her at the base of the neck. She gave herself up to the feeling that still surrounded her.

What she was sensing wasn't anything rational or logical or even identifiable, she realized. It was almost a physical sensation, like something or someone getting closer.

It had been six days since Martin Jury died. She'd told Buratti they had no definite time pattern and that was true. But the sense she had now was of time drawing nearer.

She finished her shower, patted herself dry, and toweled her hair. Waiting for the coffee to drip through, she worked on how to let Buratti know that time wasn't on their side.

Brittle. That was the only word she could think of. Judith Stone was the most brittle person Mac had ever seen.

Beckman had a slightly different term for it. 'Wound a little tight, wouldn't you say?' he'd whispered to Mac when they were following Judith Stone down the hall to her office.

Beckman had confirmed early that morning that Stone was in her office, and he and Mac had arrived precisely at ten.

Judith Stone worked as a product manager in the headquarters of one of the larger and one of the better costume jewelry manufacturers. The offices were on Thirty-ninth Street just off Seventh Avenue. Stone met them in the circular reception area, and

Mac's impression of brittleness started forming as soon as Stone stepped through the door.

Judith Stone was fairly tall, about five-eight, and willowy. She seemed even taller than she was because of her impeccable posture. The posture would have enhanced her appearance if she'd been able to glide with it at all, but she walked with a stiffness that detracted from the whole picture. She wore a silky peach-toned shirt-dress that was basically a very simple dress, but on Judith Stone it looked stunning. Mac looked at her carefully and realized why: She'd never seen anyone quite so well accessorized. Earrings, necklace, bracelet were all different combinations of variously sized beads and shells. The knot on the fabric belt was held together with a pin from the same line. On anyone else it might have been overkill, but on Judith Stone it looked perfect.

She greeted them with no expression on her face or in her voice and asked them to follow her down the hall. There was a conference room they could use.

Brightly lit display cases were set into the walls on three sides of the conference room, and samples of the company's fall and winter jewelry were artfully presented. Necklaces were strewn through fake autumn leaves, bracelets dangled from leafless boughs, and bright red-and-green earrings served as the eyes for a miniature snowman. Coming in off the streets where the temperature was reaching for the low eighties and looking at red-eyed snowmen and autumn leaves registered on the eyes and the brain like a discordant note registers on the ear. The whole atmosphere of the room was slightly off, Mac thought.

As they silently took their places around the conference table, Mac studied the other woman's face as closely as she could without staring. Like her manner of dress, the total effect was stunning, but cold. Her white-blond hair was drawn away from her face and tucked into a severe French braid, but Judith Stone had the face to carry the look. Her complexion seemed flawless, her features perfectly spaced, and her bone structure the type that makeup artists tried to re-create with shadows and highlights. With bones like that, Mac thought, she's going to look great into her eighties.

Stone got up and closed the door, then resumed her seat. 'What is this about?' The voice was still flat and colorless.

Beckman started with the explanation he and Buratti had agreed upon. 'We believe there's a security threat to Peter Rossellini. We're interviewing some present and former associates of his to see if we can track down the source of the threat.'

'Peter's all right, isn't he?' she asked. The voice was still flat, but the speed of her question hinted that there was some concern present.

'Yes,' Beckman said. 'He's fine.'

'Am I a suspect or something?' Judith Stone asked.

Beckman decided not to answer directly. 'We understand that you contemplated a palimony suit against Mr Rossellini, Ms Stone. Is that correct?'

'Yes. My father talked me out of it. My father always liked Peter.'

Mac caught Beckman's eye. She wanted to ask the next question. 'You and Mr Rossellini were a couple for five years, is that correct?'

'Four years and a half,' she corrected.

'Can you tell us about it?'

'About what?'

'About your relationship and how it ended.'

'I met Peter at the spring show for one of the fashion houses. A friend of his was doing the music. We went out together that night and from then on we were a couple.' Her face softened for only a moment.

'Did you ever live together?' Beckman asked.

Judith Stone looked at him, turning her head as though it were on a wire. 'We tried it briefly. But his hours would get so crazy, especially when he was working in the clubs. I need to stick to my regular schedule. So we always kept both apartments.'

'Can you tell us how the relationship ended?' Mac said softly. Despite her emotionless façade, Mac sensed that this conversation was very difficult for Judith Stone.

'It started around the time of my birthday. In September. I had just turned thirty and I wanted to get married. Peter and I had talked about it off and on, but he always wanted to wait until . . . I don't know. Until something. Until he and Joey got a new contract, until he produced a new group, until they set up some club dates, until they finished the club dates. Always something.'

'So you broke it off after your birthday?' Beckman prompted her.

'No, not right away. Peter and Joey were negotiating a new publishing contract. And then Irwin Steinfeld stepped into the picture. That's when things started . . . unraveling.'

'How so?'

'Irwin . . . God, I hate that man.' Even that phrase, Mac noted, was said in a noncommittal tone of voice. 'Irwin started getting Peter alone, talking to him about how Joey was holding him back, how Peter should go solo. He promised he could get Sid Tarcher over at Circus Maximus to sign him to a record contract, but only him. Joey would have to go. And then he started on me.'

'Irwin Steinfeld started on you? How?' This was getting curiouser and curiouser, Mac thought. It sounded like Steinfeld was the one who should be watching his ass. Both Joey Lemon and this woman might want to take a shot at it.

'He and Rachel and Sid Tarcher, too, I think. Peter was about to sign the recording contract. He and Joey had already had their blowup. Then he told me we would have to wait a while to get married. They

– Irwin and the others – said it would be bad for the image they were trying to create for him if it got out that he was a newlywed.'

'And?'

'And Peter asked me to wait until the album was out. But I knew what would happen. Then it would be until the single was out, and then until the next single. I'd already waited three years. I said no.' She looked down at her hands. Her right hand was squeezing her left fingers, tightly. 'My father thought I was crazy. He really liked Peter. He pictured Peter as the father of his grandchildren.'

Mac's sense of the aura that this woman projected changed. Judith Stone wasn't so much cold as she was sad.

'So you broke it off right away?' Beckman picked up the questioning.

'Yes. The Sunday before Thanksgiving. A year ago last November. Peter was due to start recording in December. There wasn't much point.'

'And your father talked you out of the palimony suit?'

'Yes. Partly because a lawyer friend of his had said there was no basis, especially since we hadn't really lived together. And my dad said it would just end up hurting both Peter and me.' She paused, looking at her hands again. 'Like I said, he was really fond of Peter. He would have been so happy about the Grammy awards.'

'Would have been?' Mac said.

When she looked up, Mac could see the beginnings of tears shimmering in Judith Stone's eyes. 'I told him about Peter being nominated, but he never got to see him win. My father' – she paused for a long moment – 'passed away in March.'

Looking now at the still-grieving Judith Stone was the first time Mac could imagine anyone calling her Judy.

Beckman and Mac were quiet riding down in the elevator, and all the way out to the street. Once on the sidewalk, Beckman turned to her. 'So whaddya think? She a possibility?'

'Unlikely, but yes,' Mac replied. 'That much hurt, that much pain, that kind of grief can . . . twist a person. It's just hard to believe that she could kill anybody.'

Beckman sighed deeply. 'We'll know more after I can check out where she was on the nights in question.'

'Yeah,' Mac said with a sigh to match Beckman's. The heavy-heartedness that the interview with Judith Stone had generated would take a little time to shake. Actually, it was more than heavy-heartedness, Mac realized. It was more a sense of dread.

THIRTEEN

Joey Lemon worked out of a small office building in the West Forties. There were a few other music types in the building, too; Buratti had read the tenant listing board while waiting for the elevator. There was even a small recording studio on the top floor.

Joey Lemon's office was small. But then so was Joey Lemon. There was just one room, about ten by twelve. A small desk, papers scattered over the surface, was pushed into the near right-hand corner. An upright piano took up most of the wall at the far end of the room. On the left side of the wall a narrow table held two tape decks, an amplifier, and speakers. There was a piano bench and one chair. That was it. Not much in the place, but it was still pretty crowded. Lemon sat on the piano bench, facing the room. Buratti had pulled the chair away from the desk and faced toward Lemon.

Joey Lemon was midthirties, approximately five feet six, and carried about fifteen pounds too much for a man his size. His orange-red hair was worn long, although not as long as Rossellini's, and was thinning noticeably. His face was freckled, and freckles were obvious way past his forehead. His face was average and seemed even-featured until he turned his profile to Buratti. Then it became obvious that his nose was too long by however many centimeters it took to throw off the proportions.

The total effect was of a funny-looking little guy, Buratti realized. What a pain in the butt it must have been for Lemon to be around a good-looking guy like Rossellini all those years.

Lemon certainly was energetic, however, and his energy translated to rapid speech. 'You got questions about Peter Rossellini?' he'd said when Buratti stated the reason for his visit. 'Is the sonofabitch in trouble with the cops? Good.'

'No, Mr Rossellini's not in trouble with the law. I was wondering if you could tell me about your relationship with him.'

'Sure. We were partners and best friends until he stabbed me in the back.'

'What happened then?' Buratti asked quietly. Lemon was already flushing, and Buratti sensed this guy was like a pot ready to boil over. His skin turned a blotchy deep pink when he got upset, an unfortunate characteristic for an orange-toned redhead.

'Then he and that goddamn lawyer of his left me in the dust while they got Circus Maximus to sign Peter as a solo act.'

'And you thought it should have been the two of you?' Buratti tried to get a picture of Rossellini and Lemon singing together. He couldn't.

'That's the way it had always been, since we were in college. Peter and Joe. Lemon and Rossellini.' Lemon was looking at him intensely, and Buratti realized that there was a good chance this guy was going to cry. 'It was supposed to be for life, man. Like Rodgers and Hart. Like Rodgers and Hammerstein.' Lemon looked down at his hands; they were gripping the piano bench so tightly the knuckles were white. 'We could've been like Elton John and Bernie Taupin.'

'I understand you're suing Mr Rossellini,' Buratti said, making a mental note to ask somebody who Bernie Taupin was.

Lemon had calmed himself somewhat. He looked back up to Buratti. 'Before I answer any more questions, why don't you tell me what this is about.'

'There's been a security problem with Mr Rossellini. We're talking to present and former . . . associates . . . of his to see if we can get to the source of the problem. That's all I can say.'

'Somebody threatening him, hunh? I hope they cut his balls off.' He paused, and his eyes changed as a thought occurred to him. 'Have you talked to Judy yet?'

'I notice that the thought of cutting off his balls made you think of Ms Stone right away. Do you think she might be out for Rossellini?'

'Hell, yes. Peter dumped her the same month he dumped me. A year ago last November. I went first. Judy and I got together a few times for a drink and to bitch together. Hell, I had more to bitch about. She was only with him for four years. Peter and I were together for eleven. She did talk about getting even with him. But that was a year and a half ago. I haven't seen her in a while.'

'Let's go back to my question before. Tell me about suing Peter Rossellini.'

'Yeah, I'm suing him for breach of contract.'

'What kind of contract was that?'

'It was an oral contract,' Lemon said defensively. 'We made each other a promise that we would always work together.'

That wasn't the kind of answer Buratti expected, and it caught him offguard. He hoped that his expression didn't reveal too much. Like the fact that he didn't think Lemon was going to get too far in the courts with a suit based on what sounded like a boyhood pact. 'Was this recent, or a while ago?'

'What difference does it make? A promise is a promise.' He stopped and looked around the office. He walked the few steps to the table, picked up a magazine, and handed it to Buratti, pointing to a spot on the page. 'Now look where he is and here I am trying to break into the jingle business.'

Buratti looked where Lemon was pointing. It was a short, two-column article with the headline 'ROSSELLINI ADDS TWO DATES TO SUMMER TOUR.' Buratti glanced at the bottom of the page. The magazine was a recent issue of *Billboard*.

'I mean it's not bad enough that the bastard dumped me. No, he has to go and put all new material on his album. Only one cut that the two of us wrote.' Lemon paced back and forth the three steps that the width of the office allowed. 'Shit, I could've set up my own goddamn production company with the royalties. The way it is, it'll be next year before I even earn out the fucking advances.'

Buratti concentrated on what Lemon was saying, trying to understand it. He didn't.

'You're saying that if Rossellini had used some – more – of the songs you and he wrote together, you would have made a lot of money?'

Lemon paused in his pacing and looked at him like he was a simpleton. 'Yeah, a lot of money.'

'Like how much?'

Lemon looked up at the ceiling as if he was trying to decide on his answer. He looked down, gestured for Buratti to move his chair toward the table, and shoved the piano bench to the table as well. He rooted around his desk for a clean pad of paper, grabbed a pencil, and sat down to give Buratti his first lesson in the dollars and cents of the music business.

FOURTEEN

Mac stood up to stretch and looked around at her desk. At this moment it was littered with more fast food containers and soft drink cans than the office had seen in the entire school year.

By the time she and Beckman had made it through midtown to Fifty-seventh and Eighth, only a few blocks from her office, he had announced he was starving and suggested stopping at McDonald's to pick up lunch. She begged off on burgers and fries, but encouraged Beckman to go ahead while she stepped into the pizza stand a few doors down. The last few blocks to her office seemed longer than usual as the aromas of pizza, fries, and special sauce mingled directly under her nose.

After her first slice of pizza and Beckman's first cheeseburger, she pulled out the photocopies she'd made of the fan letters. Twenty-seven to work through. Plus the people from Marge Masterson's files.

By quarter to two, they had a plan. Everybody on

either list from the tri-state area or Pennsylvania would be checked out. The others, spread across the country (and the girl from Australia) would get a call to make sure they were, in fact, still across the country and in Australia.

Even narrowing it to the four states, they had six people to check out. Mac went through the letters as Beckman made his notes.

'First, here's Lester Phillips,' Mac said to him. 'He's the one who accused Rossellini of stealing his songs. From what the woman in the publishing office told me, he's used this story before on other people. But I think we should check him out. He's up in New Britain.'

'Next?'

'Also from the publishing files. This woman seems to think Rossellini is using his songs to deny the existence of God. And according to her letter' – Mac skimmed down the page until she found the phrase she was looking for – 'he will burn in the hellfire of eternal damnation if he doesn't repent.' She looked back at Beckman. 'Her letter seems like she's eager to prove her point. Dorothy Sutcliffe. She's up in White Plains. Here's the address.' She handed him the piece of paper.

'Got it.'

'Okay, we start on the fan mail.' The first in this file had several sheets paper-clipped together. 'Here is Janine Lenkow. She's out in Queens. She's been writing to Rossellini since last summer, and the frequency of the letters has increased in the last few months. At first the letters were the usual: I like you, I like your music. They've gotten more and more personal lately. She thinks the songs are written for her; she thinks he's singing right to her. In the last few letters she's getting impatient. Annoyed that he isn't replying personally, that she's just getting stock photographs and a newsletter. The one received two weeks ago says if he doesn't answer her in person, Rossellini will be sorry.'

'Does it say how he'll be sorry?' Beckman asked.

'Nope. Just sorry.' Mac took a deep breath. There was something oppressive and very sad in sifting through these pieces of paper again. Sifting through these pieces of lives.

'Here's Ronald D. Morris. Of East Rutherford, New Jersey. This one's tricky. He associates with Rossellini deeply. He talks about the videos in his letters like he did them. Talks about how good he looks, how the "babes" are really coming on to him. But then he expresses a real contempt for Rossellini as well. I'd be real careful around this one.'

'Gotcha.'

'Okay. The next one is Cassandra Martin from Philadelphia—'

'Jeez,' Beckman interrupted. 'I got White Plains, East Rutherford, New Britain, Queens, and now Philadelphia? I'm gonna rack up the frequent fanny miles on this one.'

Mac shook her head and smiled. She was about to

resume her rundown on Cassandra Martin when Buratti knocked on the door. He used body English to open the door and walked in holding the last of a hot dog and a can of cream soda.

Buratti looked at the food wrappers on the desk. 'You guys ate already. Good,' he said as he popped a bite of hot dog into his mouth. Beckman was sitting on the guest side of the desk, opposite Mac, and that meant the only guest chair was occupied. Buratti disappeared into the hall for a moment and reappeared pushing a wheeled secretarial chair. He moved it next to Beckman and sat down.

'I just finished with Joey Lemon,' he started. From the tone of his voice, Mac knew there was more.

'And . . . ?' she said.

'Is he involved with all this stuff?' Buratti's question was rhetorical. 'Nah. He's really pissed at Rossellini, and there's a part of him that would like to cut the guy's heart out. But he'd like to do it in Macy's window, y'know?' He didn't pause for Beckman or Griffin to answer. 'No, what was really interesting is he gives me the whole rundown on the money side. Do you know how much money Rossellini made in the last year?'

'No,' said Beckman.

'Lots, I would guess,' said Mac.

'No, no. This is beyond lots. Lots is what the commissioner makes. And did you know somebody like Rossellini gets paid every time one of their records is played on the radio?'

'All the people singin' on the radio? Are you sure about that?' Beckman sounded skeptical.

'No, not the singers. The songwriters. Rossellini gets paid because he writes his own songs.'

'How in the world does that work?' Mac asked.

'Wait.' Buratti looked around for a clean piece of paper, just like Lemon had a few hours before. Mac handed him a pad and he picked up a pencil. He also pulled out some folded-up sheets of paper from his inside jacket pocket and looked at the top one. 'Let me go through this the way Lemon went through it with me.

'Okay,' he started, then he stopped to take off his jacket and drape it over the back of the chair. 'Mac, when we were up in Rachel Bennet's office the other day, she told me that Rossellini's album had sold four and a half million copies. That's just in the United States. But let's just talk about last year, and we'll use round numbers like Joey did. Let's say three million copies.' He wrote down *3,000,000* at the top of his sheet.

'Now let's say a million and a half are cassettes and a million and a half are compact discs.' He wrote *1,500,000* on the left and the right sides of the paper. 'Lemon says the companies aren't even releasing albums anymore. Shows you how long it's been since I was in a record store.

'Okay. An artist – and anybody who records anything is called an artist in this business, no matter what they sound like – signs a contract with a record company. For a new artist like Rossellini, the royalty rate is about twelve percent. That's twelve percent of, ah, what did he call this – the suggested list price on the tape or CD.' Buratti looked up from the sheet in front of him. 'Now, you and I know that nobody pays this, especially in New York, but that's how they do the calculations.'

He looked back down at his figures. 'Okay. We got the suggested list price. But before they do the percentage, they do some deductions. One is a packaging deduction, so they lop off twenty-five percent. So a cassette has a list price of ten bucks, say. Nine ninety-nine. Less twenty-five percent is seven forty-nine something. Times twelve percent is eighty-nine point nine cents. So on the million and a half cassettes, Rossellini's royalty is something like a million three hundred forty some thousand dollars.'

Buratti looked at both of them and waited for the figures to sink in. 'Pretty good, hunh? But wait – now we do the CDs. There's a higher price on them. Thirteen, fourteen, fifteen bucks. Rossellini's was listed at thirteen ninety-nine first, then they jacked it up. But let's start with that and less twenty-five percent' – he checked Lemon's papers again – 'is ten forty-nine, times the royalty, is one dollar and twenty-five point nine cents. Times a million and a half is one million eight hundred thousand plus. So Rossellini's royalties for last year – as a singer – come to a little over three million dollars.'

'Jeez, am I in the wrong line of work,' said Beckman.

Buratti was really into this. Mac could tell. His eyes were shining. 'Now Lemon tells me that the record companies hold what they call accounting reserves. So they only pay seventy-five percent of the royalties. The other twenty-five percent is supposed to come along next time. So our Mr Rossellini would only get two million three hundred thousand on the three million one.'

'Poor baby,' Mac said.

'But wait. It gets better,' Buratti said. 'Rossellini also writes his songs. Most of them on the album he wrote by himself, that's what's got Joey Lemon's shorts in such a knot. Only one of the songs that he wrote with Rossellini is on the album.'

'Un-hunh,' Beckman said, encouraging Buratti to go on.

'So for every song that's on an album, you start with what's called a statutory rate.' He looked at Beckman. 'That's with a *t*. Lemon tells me this is from the copyright law. So this changed a while ago, but from what Lemon says, the song rate we're dealing with is five point seven cents for every song.' Buratti paused for effect. 'For every copy of the record sold.' He looked at Beckman and Mac, expecting a big reaction. There wasn't one. They were both waiting for more.

'You gotta see the way these numbers add up.' He sat forward again, and cribbed from Joey Lemon's notes once more. 'Say Rossellini has eight songs on this album, which he does. That's eight times five point seven cents . . . is another forty-five point six cents an album. Times the three million albums is another million three or so. Lemon says the record company doesn't pay the whole freight on this either, so let's round it to a million. So with the other royalties, Rossellini is now up to four million for last year. And he's just getting started.' He plopped the pencil onto the pad.

The three of them were silent for a moment. Mac's response to this information was different than the police officers' who sat in front of her, she knew that. Ever since college, she had made it a point to keep the extent of her family's privilege a private matter, and she was glad of that at this particular moment. Although she made every effort to live within her salary, although buying the apartment had been a stretch, she always knew she had other resources to tap into. The men across the desk from her, one a veteran detective, one who was still congratulating himself on his recent promotion to the detective ranks, had to deal with the fact that what they made in a year, give or take a few extended decimal points, was one to one and a half percent of what Rossellini pulled in last year. That could take the wind out of your sails for a couple minutes.

Beckman finally turned to Buratti. 'And what were you sayin' about the radio?'

'Oh, yeah, I almost forgot.' Buratti sat up

straighter. 'This is a songwriter thing, too. ASCAP and BMI – y'know the ASCAP building up across from Lincoln Center?' He tried to point in the right direction and gave up trying to figure which way was north from the desk. 'They pay the writers what they call performance royalties. It's tied in to how much a song is played on the radio, but Lemon tells me nobody can figure out the formulas they use to pay these guys. Lemon figures what with having three, four hits off this album, songs that were on the radio as much as they were, he – Rossellini – will get another couple hundred thousand.'

Beckman slumped down in his chair and stared up at the ceiling. 'This is getting depressing.'

'Oh, and I forgot this, too,' Buratti started in again. Both Mac and Beckman groaned. He looked at the bottom of the notes Lemon had given him. 'There's foreign royalties. Rossellini's stuff has been goin' great in Europe apparently, and other places. And he's got another album coming out, so he'll have the royalties from that and the royalties on the other million and a half that the first one has sold. So far. Lemon tells me with the second album, with the royalties still coming in from the first one, and with the tour, he'll more than double what he made last year. Probably close to ten million.'

Mac screwed up her face and looked at Buratti intently. 'Why is this such a surprise to you? You've heard about the contracts that Madonna and Prince

– or whatever he's calling himself these days – have signed over the past few years.'

Buratti nodded his agreement. 'Sure I heard about those. But I figured they were phenoms, y'know? This Rossellini – he's got a good voice and all, and hey, he's a *paisan*. I knew we were talking good money, but I had no idea that we'd start talking four, five million a guy's first year.'

Mac picked up the pen she'd been using and started tapping. 'What do you think all of this has to do with the case?'

'I dunno,' Buratti admitted. 'But when I was first comin' up, Lieutenant Willard told me never to overlook the obvious. It just seems like there's this much money around, it's gotta have something to do with it, y'know?' He wiped his hands down his face and yawned. Too long without a cigarette again.

Beckman cleared his throat. 'I'm just tryin' to think here. Could it be somebody who's nuts over Rossellini making so much money? Could they be trying to smear Rossellini, so as to, like, torpedo his career?'

'Smear like in scandal, you mean?' Mac asked.

'Yeah.'

'Don't think so. This is show business, after all. And from what I've read, scandal in show business seems to be like fertilizer around rosebushes. Makes careers bloom.'

Beckman sat back. 'You're right. Forget I asked the question.'

'Okay, how about the other way,' Buratti said. 'Somebody's not trying to deck him; somebody's really trying to give Rossellini's career an extra added boost.'

Mac looked at him, shocked. 'Mario, are you suggesting that someone would actually *kill* people for the . . . to try to boost somebody's record sales? Oh, that's cold.'

Buratti drew back, a little defensive. 'Okay, I'm stretching. But from what Lemon tells me about this business, it's a possibility.'

Twenty minutes later, Mac had finished reviewing the priority list with Beckman and Buratti, and the two men stood near the doorway waiting for Mac to join them. With any luck, this would be her last day in the office until a week from Monday, and she was checking to make sure she had everything.

'You two will give me a call after you've talked to the Rossellini Intensive Care Fan Club, right?' Mac said, stepping around the desk. 'I'll be trying to catch up on my week off.' She grinned at Buratti pointedly.

'You're staying in the city, though, right?' Buratti asked as she locked the office door.

'Yes. I'll be at the apartment. The painters are coming in next week and I haven't done a thing to get ready.'

Beckman said good-bye as soon as they got to the front steps of the building and trotted off toward Fifty-seventh Street. Buratti paused on the stairs, one step below Mac. 'I'll talk to you as soon as we got anything. And thanks for your help on this, kid. I appreciate it. You know that.'

'Thank me when it's over.' Mac turned and trotted down the last few steps.

'Hey, before I forget,' Buratti said. 'Do you know who Bernie Taupin is?'

'Yeah. I know the name.' Her brow wrinkled in concentration. 'Elton John! That's it. He writes songs with Elton John. He does the lyrics, I think.'

'Very good, Mac. You get the gold star for that one.'

She stepped onto the sidewalk and looked back at Buratti. 'Say hello to Gloria and the kids for me.'

'Will do. In fact I'm gonna talk to Michael and see if he's still interested in that guitar he wanted last year. Seein' those numbers that Rossellini is pulling in, I think I should encourage the kid's musical abilities.'

FIFTEEN

May 31

Mac awoke to the sound of her radio on Friday morning. While she wasn't surrounded by the trepidation she'd felt the day before, her first thoughts were of Peter Rossellini. Well, not exactly. Her first thoughts were about the person who was after Rossellini. What were they thinking right now? Were they in the city? Would Buratti and the others reach whomever it was in time?

By the time she'd finished her shower, she'd shaken the thoughts of Rossellini's stalker. She was still in her robe, enjoying a third cup of coffee and a leisurely read of *The New York Times*, when the phone rang at five minutes to nine.

'Hope you've enjoyed your vacation, Doc.' Buratti's voice was still stuck in morning gear.

'All twenty-five minutes of it, you mean?'

'Yeah. Got another favor.'

'Already?'

'Same case, different favor. Or maybe same favor, different day.'

'What is it?' She reached for her coffee and sipped it.

'I just got off the phone with Rachel Bennet. The woman is climbing the walls, and she wants somebody's hide to tack up there for the view. Like mine. Anyway, she wants to know what's happening and she wants to know *now*. So does Rossellini apparently.'

'That's understandable.'

'I've been trying to keep her posted all week, but now she wants to talk to somebody up close and personal. So I'm going up there around lunchtime. Rossellini will be at Bennet's office twelve-thirty, twelve forty-five. Actually, they'd like us both there.'

'Mario, I've got a lunch date.'

'What time?' he said quickly, willing to make this work. 'Can you make it before or after?'

Mac put down her coffee cup. She knew it was useless to get around Mario when he was in a mood like this. So much for a leisurely lunch and checking out the sales at Saks.

'Oh, all right. Let me call Sylvie and see what I can arrange. Where are you and I'll call you back.'

He said he was going to be at his desk and gave her the number. She jotted it on a corner of the paper as she repeated it to him.

'It might be around ten before I can get back to you. I'm not sure when I can reach her.'

'I'll be here. And thanks, Mac. I owe you one.'

Mac gave a snort. 'No, Buratti. You owe me *five*.'

Mac approached the receptionist's desk at Berman and Bennet Management at one-fifteen. She'd met Sylvie for lunch at eleven-thirty at a tiny new French restaurant on Fifty-fifth between Fifth and Sixth, and it had felt good to walk the few blocks to the management office. Even though she'd resisted Sylvie's invitation to split a dessert, she had managed to put away most of the bread basket.

Michelle Wenzel, the assistant who was such a charmer on her previous visit, was apparently out to lunch, because it was Linda Campbell, the genuinely pleasant receptionist, who showed Mac into the office next to Rachel's where Buratti was perched on a small armchair. He looked relieved to see her.

'Hey, Doc, right on time. Hope you didn't bolt down your lunch to rush over here. I been coolin' my heels for about twenty minutes now. The two a them have been goin' at it for the last ten.' His eyebrows indicated that he was talking about the people in the office next door.

Mac listened for a few moments. You could hear raised voices, but not distinct words. She looked at Buratti and mouthed her question. 'The manager and . . . ?'

She hadn't even gotten that past her lips when she heard a loud 'Peter!' coming from next door.

Immediately following was a lower-toned 'No, Rachel, I'm not going to do it!'

Mac caught Buratti's eye. 'The manager and Rossellini, I take it?' He nodded yes.

Within a few moments they heard an intercom buzzer. The office was quiet enough that they could hear the receptionist murmuring into her phone a second or two later. Another few seconds passed. Then Rachel Bennet opened the door to her office and stepped into the room where they were waiting. She looked flushed.

'Please. Come in.'

Just as Mac and Buratti got up to follow Rachel, her assistant Michelle walked in from the reception area. She was dressed, Rachel noted, with the same nunlike severity as before, this time in a navy blue skirt, top, and shoes. 'You're back,' Rachel said. 'Good. I'll be in here for a few more minutes and then we have to go over the schedule for the weekend.'

'Okay,' said Michelle in a noncommittal tone of voice. She then poked her head in the door to Rachel's office, successfully pinning Mac, who had started into the office after Rachel, to the other side of the doorway. 'Hellooo, Peter,' she said in a silky tone. 'Sorry I wasn't here when you arrived.' Mac was startled to hear a pleasant voice coming out of this abrupt young woman. The different personae certain women slipped into around certain men never ceased to amaze her.

Peter Rossellini was in between the large U-shaped couch and the desk, standing with his back to the door. He had on jeans and a baseball jacket and looked great. He'd been staring out the window intently. When he turned to say hello to Michelle, Rachel was already speaking. 'Peter, you remember Doctor Griffin and Lieutenant Buratti.'

Rossellini's eyes lit up when he spotted Mac, which was about a second and a half before Rachel said her name. He was surprised to see her, Mac could tell. But his eyes also let her know that he was glad to see her. And relieved.

Michelle also noticed his reaction and pointedly stared at Mac as she was closing the door behind Buratti. 'No calls,' Rachel reminded her just before the door closed entirely.

Buratti and Mac both took seats on the couch, on opposite sides of the coffee table. Mac realized that the gray knit pants and jacket she wore blended her in to the office decor. Peter moved to the couch and eased into the seat next to Mac. Rachel took the chair at her desk. No guesses this time as to whether or not this was a meeting and who was running it. It was and she was.

She started right in. 'I've tried to keep Peter filled in as you've called me, Lieutenant, but he's got some questions of his own. I do, too.'

'Sure,' Buratti said. This was starting out much better than he'd thought.

Rossellini looked across the table to Buratti. 'I

understand you visited Joey Lemon yesterday. He called and said that I'd probably be hearing from his lawyer.'

'That little schmuck . . .' Rachel started to sit forward in her chair. 'He's still trying to make it in this business, right? Does he think that's going to help him? That lawyer of his is one step away from those "Have you been injured?" leeches that advertise on television. Only his ad would say, "Have you been screwed?"'

Rossellini waited for Rachel's tempest to run its course. But then he looked back at Buratti. 'And there was a message on my answering machine last night from Judy. Judith Stone. Why did you have to bother her?'

Buratti flashed a quick look at Mac. 'Actually, Lieutenant Buratti didn't go to see Ms Stone,' Mac said to Rossellini. 'Detective Beckman and I interviewed her.'

'You?' Rossellini responded quickly. 'Why?'

Buratti decided to answer, even though Rossellini was looking right at Mac. 'Mr Rossellini . . . look. We've got a situation where it seems somebody is out for you. In the course of some of our conversations, we heard about you and Joey Lemon, we heard about you and Ms Stone breaking up. We wouldn't be doing our job if we *didn't* talk to them.'

'It just seems crazy to even think that Judy could hurt anybody,' Rossellini countered. 'Joey . . . hell, I don't know about Joey.' Mac listened to him, realizing that by late yesterday afternoon, she and Buratti had come to the opposite conclusion about the two people in question.

Rachel decided to take back the reins. 'It's now Friday, Lieutenant Buratti. Do we have any more concrete information than we had when you were here Tuesday?'

'Doctor Griffin has been very helpful in identifying some people that we need to look into. Detective Beckman and I started on the followup this morning. But it will take a couple of days.'

'A couple of days?' Rachel snapped. 'How many are there?'

Buratti deferred to Mac on this one. 'In the total number of people to be checked out, almost thirty.' Rachel emitted a small moan. 'Most of those won't take long to eliminate,' Mac said hurriedly. 'There's at least six in the metropolitan area that will need to be interviewed.'

'Six. In the metropolitan area,' Rachel repeated, shaking her head.

'Where did all these people come from?' Rossellini asked, addressing Buratti.

'Doctor Griffin went through the fan mail from the last year.'

'My fan mail?' Rossellini still seemed surprised. 'Out with Marianne? You got thirty people out of my fan mail that have to be interviewed, that look like they could do something like this?'

'Yes, from Marianne's files and from the publishing office, too.'

'Thirty . . . that's unbelievable.' Rossellini seemed shaken.

Rachel sat a little straighter and leaned over her folded hands. 'Lieutenant, perhaps you can answer a question for me. Peter and I were . . . discussing it earlier. I think it's foolish – no, beyond foolish, I think it's dangerous for him to go ahead with the opening next week if we haven't found out who's behind this. Given that it's Friday, and we open on Monday night, we don't have much time to cancel. And even then it will be a nightmare. We might be able to make some of the Sunday papers, and I can still get it on radio.'

'So what's the question?' Buratti said.

'What's your advice?' Rachel opened her hands toward Buratti. 'Should we go ahead with the opening or not?'

Buratti didn't have a chance to form his answer when Rossellini started in. 'I don't give a shit what he thinks, no offense intended,' he said toward Buratti. Buratti nodded that none was taken. 'I say no. I'm not gonna cancel. I won't let somebody like this have that kind of power over me. Over the show. That would be like their getting away with it.' He paused for a breath and addressed Rachel. 'And it's not like they're going to shoot me or anything.' He quickly turned back to Mac. 'Is it?'

'I can't give you an absolute assurance, you know that,' Mac began. 'We aren't dealing with something or someone who is absolutely predictable. But I do think it's unlikely that the person involved in the other incidents would try to shoot you, that's true.'

'You agree with me, then?'

'I can't tell you that you will be in danger if you go ahead with the concert, Mr Rossellini. But I also can't tell you that you will be safe.'

'Now there's a shrink's answer if I ever heard one,' Rachel said snidely. 'It sounds like a cop version of "Why don't you tell me what *you* think?" Not a lot of help.'

Rachel was just turning on Buratti when her phone buzzed. 'Michelle,' she said, addressing the phone. 'I said no calls.' She picked up the phone anyway, and the pissed-off expression left her face almost immediately. 'Of course,' she said, and handed the phone toward Buratti. 'It's for you.'

'Buratti,' he barked into the phone. 'Yeah. Yeah. Go ahead.' He nodded a few times, listening intently. 'I'm over on Fifty-sev— hell, you know where I am. I'll be over there as quick as I can. Meet you there.' He handed the phone back to Rachel. 'That was John Monaghan.'

'*Our* John Monaghan?' Rachel asked, surprised.

'Yeah,' said Buratti, looking at Rachel, and then over to Mac and Rossellini. 'He just got a call from the security desk at your rehearsal hall. They just found an intruder hiding in a maintenance closet, sort of like a stowaway. The intruder was looking for you, Mr Rossellini.'

SIXTEEN

The three of them – Buratti, Mac, and Rossellini – made it out of the office in record time. Rachel had yelled out 'Call me!' as they hurriedly left her office. Michelle was almost blocking the door once again, her face the picture of concern. She'd figured out something urgent was transpiring as soon as the voice on the phone had demanded to speak to Lieutenant Buratti. When Mac glanced back at the two of them, their taut, concerned expressions made them look like figures in a Greek chorus.

Once on the street level, a quick conference had concluded that the fastest way to the rehearsal hall was on foot. It was on Fifty-fourth Street, on the other side of Broadway. Two long avenue blocks and three short street blocks.

Mac never thought of herself as short, but she was having trouble keeping up the fast walking pace of the taller men. Approaching the corner of Fifty-sixth and Broadway, Rossellini realized Mac was lagging behind. He looked back at her, waited, and then took her elbow to help propel her along. It struck Mac as an old-fashioned gesture, one her father might use, and she smiled.

The building where the rehearsal hall was located wasn't large, only four stories. But it looked like more because each of the stories was so high. It had been renovated a few years ago, after being saved from the wrecker's ball by the downturn in Manhattan real estate. A developer had planned to purchase the site, raze the building, and put up yet another apartment high-rise. The entertainment community had howled loudly, complaining that not only were theaters in danger of disappearing, now even rehearsal space was at a premium. No rehearsal, no show. The developer unfortunately hadn't been convinced by that argument; what did convince him were unprecedented vacancy rates in buildings similar to the one he was planning.

Buratti led the way through the double doors into the lobby of the rehearsal building. He flashed his badge at the guard on duty, who directed them down the hall to the manager's office. Buratti paused outside the door, and looked at the two others. 'Mac, you come inside with me. Rossellini, you better wait here for a minute.'

Buratti had been against Rossellini coming with them, but Rossellini had insisted. Bad enough bringing the guy along. Who knew what the hell would happen if the intruder came face to face with the guy.

Buratti opened the door to an empty office. It was a secretarial office, and the connecting door to the next office was open. That one wasn't empty. Buratti walked into the manager's office followed by Mac. John Monaghan had his back to the door, facing the desk that was centered on the far wall. The man Buratti presumed to be the building manager was seated behind the desk. In a wooden chair to the left of the desk was a young woman, probably late teens, and another guard, uniformed like the one in the lobby had been, stood near her.

Mac only nodded while Buratti made the introductions; she was concentrating on the intruder. The girl had peachy toned skin that looked very pale at the moment, and mousy brown hair with the crown pulled back into a ponytail. She wore tight button-fly jeans, a tie-dyed T-shirt, and a denim jacket. She looked fairly petite, probably five three or so. Mac couldn't guess the height too accurately from the way the girl was scrunched into the chair. She looked absolutely terrified; her eyes were red-rimmed and her upper cheeks were gray. She'd obviously been crying, and it was safe to say she wasn't using waterproof mascara.

'So what've we got here?' Buratti asked.

Monaghan was the one to answer. 'I don't think this is who you're looking for. I think what we got here is your basic over-enthusiastic fan.' He glared at the girl. 'One who popped up where she didn't belong.'

'Where'd you find her?' Buratti asked.

'Lincoln here was on the front desk,' the building manager said, indicating the guard. The manager's desk nameplate identified him only as Mr Salkowski. 'My secretary dumped a plant off her desk when she was watering it. She yelled down the hall for him to get the vacuum and other stuff out of the maintenance closet. He did and that's when we think she snuck through the front lobby.'

'I wasn't even gone a minute, sir,' the guard said to Buratti, almost like an apology. Buratti nodded at him; he knew this guy had said the same thing a few times already to the other men in the office.

'Then what happened?' Buratti said to the manager.

'Fortunately or unfortunately, Ms Johnston picked that same maintenance closet to hide in. When Lincoln went to put the vacuum back, there she was.' The girl snuffled again, as if reliving the moment of discovery.

Monaghan picked up the story. 'I'd left word with Salkowski here to let me know if anything untoward happened while Peter was rehearsing here. When he found out who she was after, he called me. I called you. And here we are.'

Untoward? Buratti thought, staring at Monaghan. If anything *untoward* happened? Monaghan must be using one of those vocabulary books, trying to improve his image.

Mac had kept her eye on the girl during the whole discussion. The kid was genuinely scared. 'What's your name?' she asked her.

'Tina,' came the muffled response.

'Well, Tina, can you tell us what you were doing here?'

'I just wanted to see him, maybe talk to him, that was all.'

'To Peter Rossellini?' Mac had leaned over and was looking directly into the girl's eyes.

'Yeah. Him.'

'When'd you start planning this?' Buratti asked from over Mac's shoulder. His voice was gruff.

The girl looked back at Mac to respond. 'Yesterday. Just yesterday. My brother was here – he was auditioning for a summer stock job and they had the auditions here. He told me he saw Peter Rossellini in the elevator and that he was rehearsing here. He knows how much I love him and his music.'

'Your brother knows how much you love Peter Rossellini.' Mac wanted to be clear.

'Yeah. So I asked him exactly where the building was and I got on the train this morning and decided to come here. Like maybe I could see him or talk to him or something.'

'Got on the train from where?' Buratti asked.

'Tarrytown,' Monaghan answered.

'Tina,' Mac asked quietly. 'Have you ever done anything like this before?' She had to ask, even though she was pretty sure of the answer.

'No, never,' Tina replied quickly. 'I've never been in trouble with the cops. Ever.' She looked down forlornly. 'My mother's gonna kill me.'

Mac smiled at the girl's misinterpretation of her question. 'No, Tina, I mean have you ever tried to get in touch with Peter Rossellini before?'

The girl looked at her, puzzled. 'Like how?'

There was a knock at the outer door, a brief pause, and then the door opened. Peter Rossellini peeked his head in the doorway. 'What's going on?' he said.

'It's him! Omigod, it's him.' Tina Johnston looked up at Peter Rossellini as if seeing a holy apparition. 'Omigod, omigod, omigod,' she chanted like a mantra. 'It's really him.' She started to cry again, but hard this time.

'Ah, geez,' Buratti said, turning to Monaghan. The other men, guard included, all looked at Rossellini. He looked at Mac, then at the men in the office, with an expression of helplessness. The other men had almost the same look to them.

There was some kind of male embarrassment floating in the room that Mac didn't quite understand; it was a bit beyond the usual discomfort at the sight of female tears. She stepped out the door to the secretary's desk, where she'd spotted a box of tissues. She took a couple, returned to where the girl was seated, and forced them into her hands.

Mac patted the girl's shoulder as she looked over to Buratti and shook her head 'No.' He knew it, too. This wasn't the one they were looking for.

It was close to two-thirty by the time they got Tina Marie Johnston ushered out the door. Monaghan was personally escorting her to Grand Central Station, and making sure she got on a train back to Westchester.

Buratti, Mac, and Rossellini were still in the secretary's office when Monaghan and the girl departed. Rossellini turned to Mac, looking a tad embarrassed. 'See, that's what I'm used to. Well, not used to. Actually, that's never happened to me before, somebody just busting out crying that way. But it's hard to be scared of somebody like that, that's what I mean.'

'Oh? You haven't had that reaction at your concerts?' Mac said.

'Sure, you can tell people are really getting into the music and all, and some of the women in front are really out there, but they're fifteen, twenty feet away from you. This was out-and-out, in-your-face crying. Whew.'

Buratti drew himself up from the edge of the secretary's desk where he'd been perched. 'I gotta catch up with Beckman.' He said to Mac, 'Funny, for a half-second there today, I thought we were going to be able to call him off.' He headed for the door. 'I'll talk to you later, Mac.'

'I better be going, too,' Mac said to Rossellini as she bent to pick up her purse.

'How'd you like to stay and watch rehearsal?' Rossellini offered quickly. 'We start' – he looked at his watch, and then smiled sheepishly – 'we started twenty-five minutes ago. It might be interesting.'

Mac quickly went through the plans she'd had in mind for the afternoon. The museum, Saks, getting the apartment ready for the painters. It took her a millisecond to decide. 'I'd love to.'

SEVENTEEN

When Rossellini opened the door to the rehearsal space, all eyes turned to the two of them. A dark-haired, dark-eyed man standing in the center of the hall glared burn holes into Peter's chest. 'It couldn't be helped, Jeremy,' Rossellini said firmly. 'Everybody, this is Mackenzie Griffin. She's . . . she's a friend of mine.'

Peter got a chair for Mac and settled her into a corner of the room while the others scrutinized her. There were two men over to one side of the room, where a piano and drums were set up. One sat on the piano bench; the other leaned on the top of the piano. Three women were over on the opposite side of the room, one perched on the low windowsill, staring down at the street. Mac occupied herself by looking around the room.

The space was large, probably thirty by fifty, and incredibly airy. The ceilings were more than fifteen feet high, and one long wall was filled with high arched windows that started only a few feet from the floor. The opposite wall was mirrored starting from a few inches off the floor up to about six feet, and the mirrors seemed to magnify the light that came in through the windows.

Long strips of masking tape striped the floor, and back near where the women were, three small platforms of varying heights were positioned within some tape boundaries. Each of the small platforms had steps up the back, and they were close enough that someone could step from one to another.

Peter conferred with Jeremy and apparently calmed him down. He stepped to the far side of the room from where Mac sat and removed his jacket. Walking back to the center of the room, he rolled up the sleeves of his shirt as if to say, 'Let's get started.'

Jeremy addressed the three women along the back wall. 'Okay. This afternoon we're working, no, we're polishing the heartbreak medley. Remember, this is the centerpiece of the show. *This* is why all those nice ladies out there are going to be throwing all that money our way. So we're going to make it worth it for them.'

Mac didn't get to hear a lot of music in the first hour or so, but she developed a healthy respect for the patience it took to put these shows together. Jeremy walked the three women, who, it turned out, were the backup singers, through the staging of the medley. The three women would be wearing costumes of different colors. For each of the songs in the medley, the three would be in a different arrangement on the platforms, and apparently the lighting would change with each arrangement as well. Jeremy indicated where the lighting changes would be by saying 'Pow!'

Jeremy wanted the singers to move gracefully between the platforms. The word he used was 'float.' Try as he might, he couldn't get one of the women, whose name was Prissy, to do anything more than shuffle from one place to the next. The outfit she was wearing, black leggings, a neon colored T-shirt, and a sweater draped around her hips in an unflattering gathering of materials, didn't improve the appearance of her movement.

'Priscilla, for God's sake,' he finally exploded, 'you're moving like a cow.'

Prissy, a dark-skinned black woman, looked directly at Jeremy, her eyes snapping. 'I ain't paid to move pretty, honey. I paid to sound pretty.'

Mac could see that she wasn't the only one who wanted to laugh. The two other women and the musicians were trying to hide their smirks from Jeremy's view. Even Peter was biting his lip.

Jeremy called for a break and stepped over to confer with Peter. The three singers walked toward the corner of the room where Mac sat. Mac had shifted from the chair to the floor, sitting with her back against the mirror. One of the other women, Julie, was heading out for a cigarette, and the third, Martha, stretched out full length on the floor. Prissy wearily slid to the floor next to Mac, looked at her with a woman-to-woman expression on her face, and leaned toward her slightly. 'That man got a broomstick permanently up his ass.'

Mac laughed softly and Prissy nodded. She was only tellin' the truth after all. She leaned in again. 'My name's Prissy. What'd he say your name is?'

'Mackenzie. Mackenzie Griffin. Or Mac.'

'Mackenzie. What kind a name is that? Irish?'

'I think years ago probably Scottish. But my family is mostly English.'

Priscilla wasn't too interested in her heritage apparently. 'You in the business, Mac?'

'No. I'm a teacher.'

'Oh, that's good. Good, steady work. A cousin of mine is finishing up to be a teacher. She be graduatin' in a couple weeks. Gonna be a big party for that one, that's for sure.'

'That's nice to hear,' Mac said.

'Glad to see Peter bringing a lady friend around.' Mac didn't even have time to protest that she wasn't Rossellini's 'lady friend.' 'Been worried about the boy.'

'You make it sound like you're his mother or his aunt,' Mac teased. 'I'm sure you're younger than he is.' In point of fact, Mac had no idea how old the woman was. Like many black women, Prissy had the bones and the skin tone that let you know only that she was somewhere between twenty and sixty.

'Could be, could be, but I been at this a long time.'

Mac looked at the woman's profile. 'I always

wanted to be able to sing. It must be a wonderful feeling.'

'Anybody can sing, honey,' Prissy said, looking sideways at Mac. 'You just pull up your chest, throw back your head, and open your mouth.'

'Obviously you've never heard me sing, or you wouldn't be saying that.'

'Didn't say it was gonna sound good, honey. I just say everybody can sing. How good it sounds be up to God.'

With a clap of his hands, Jeremy called them back into rehearsal. But this time he gathered them around the piano.

It was evident within the next few minutes that God had spent an extra few minutes on Prissy's vocal cords and those of her sisters in song. Their voices whispered, swelled, and blended in harmonies that made the little hairs on Mac's arms stand up. Even with just a piano accompanying them, they filled the room with sound.

And even though she heard it first in bits and pieces, Mac knew that the medley would be a showstopper. Four of Rossellini's songs were blended with excerpts of four or five other similarly themed songs of the last ten years, songs that had been hits in their day as well. When she finally heard the whole thing put together, Mac realized that the medley ran close to fifteen minutes, and she was amazed at both the emotional and physical endurance that it took.

After the run-through, Rossellini and the three women rehearsed the transitions in the medley – the bridges between one song and another – over and over. With the four singers near the piano, Jeremy got up and pranced around the platforms, demonstrating, complete with 'Pow! 's, just how the movement tied in with the music. Priscilla still looked distinctly unimpressed.

Still standing near the piano, Peter and 'the girls' went over a song that would be used as an encore. Through the rest of the rehearsal, even during the medley, Peter had sung softly, not using his whole voice. But now he sang full voice, and the other singers followed his lead.

Mac not only heard the music, she *felt* it, and she thrilled to it. Lord, what a treat this was, she thought, and what a privilege, too. Some people would kill for a private concert like this. She straightened up suddenly as the thought that had drifted through her mind repeated itself.

Some people would kill for a private concert like this. A chill shook her shoulders and she had to resist the temptation to look around. Odds were that there was at least one person who would kill for just such an encounter with Peter Rossellini. The question was, who would they kill?

A few minutes later, Jeremy dismissed the performers. 'Remember people, eleven o'clock sharp tomorrow morning at Radio City. We've got a full weekend of work ahead of us putting this on the big stage.' A few groans wafted through the air, but their sources were unidentifiable.

The singers and musicians dispersed, leaving Jeremy and Peter in the middle of the room together. Prissy came up to Mac again, introducing her to the other two women as 'Peter's lady friend.' Julie, a very thin dishwater blonde, seemed very shy; she nodded quickly at Mac and bent to gather her things and head out the door. Martha, a light-skinned black woman, was a bit more effusive. 'Glad to meet you, sugar. Too bad you had to sit in on this one.' She rolled her eyes. 'The show won't be boring, I promise. You comin', aren'cha?'

'Yes,' Mac said, enthusiastically. The introductions had helped her to shake off the grim considerations of a few minutes ago.

She hadn't planned on attending the concert before now, but she couldn't resist after the preview she'd heard. 'I'm not sure which one I'll be coming to, but yes, I'll be there.'

The two women left, leaving Mac standing alone. Rossellini and the director finished their conversation and he walked directly over to her.

'So what'd you think?'

'I think . . .' Mac paused. 'I think I'll be too embarrassed to even sing in the shower for a while. You sounded very good, but I've been listening to you for the last few days. Those women were wonderful!'

Jeremy yelled from the doorway, 'Catch the lights, will you Peter?'

'You got it,' Rossellini said, loudly. Looking back to Mac, he said, 'They are good, aren't they? It's really coming along.' He was slowly walking her to the other side of the room where his jacket and bag sat. 'It's hard, you know, when you've had a hit record or a few. The audience knows the records inside out but you have to re-create on stage the sound that you made in a studio.' He loved talking about this, Mac could tell. 'We used a lot of overdubs on a couple of those songs. On one of them I did multiple tracks of my own voice. Can't very well do that in concert.'

'No, I guess not.'

'That's where the girls come in. They're three of the best.' He draped his jacket over his arm, picked up the bag, and guided her toward the door.

'I can't imagine what it takes to put a show together. Just hearing the details you went through this afternoon is amazing to me,' Mac said as they waited for the elevator.

He smiled. 'And this isn't even one of the big shows. We're going out to work some of the smaller venues – some theaters, maybe some bigger places that hold maybe five, eight thousand people. A stadium is no place for a singer like me. So our show is more like a theatrical piece. The big rock shows – the ones for the stadium circuit – it can take months to put those together. And the logistics – it's like a military invasion!'

They stepped out of the elevator into the front lobby. 'Thank you for this afternoon,' Mac said as they approached the door. 'I can't believe I sat there for – what? – over three hours. It was fascinating. Thank you.'

'You sound like you're saying good-bye.'

'Well, it is going on six.'

'How about dinner?' he said quickly. 'On me this time, not Rachel.'

'Oh, I don't know. I thought I'd walk for a while after sitting for so long. And you must be tired.' Mac listened to herself. She could have said an out-and-out 'No,' but she didn't. Maybe she didn't want to discourage Rossellini entirely.

'Nah, I'm fine.' He glanced down at his watch. 'I was scheduled to go over to Metropolitan to look at the montage they've edited, but I can do that tomorrow morning.'

He looked back at Mac. 'You're heading downtown, right?' he asked. Mac nodded yes. 'Then we'll start walking and we'll stop whenever we get hungry. How's that?'

EIGHTEEN

They ended up walking all the way down to Union Square. When they passed a building on Park in the Forties, Peter told her of playing a particularly disastrous lunchtime concert in the building's lobby, back when he and Joey were taking any gig they could find. Relating that incident led to Peter régaling her with stories of all the places he and Joey had played, the nice little clubs, the dives, the school assemblies, the shopping malls. It was a little after seven when they presented themselves before the maitre d' at the very same restaurant where they'd had dinner earlier that week; his eyes practically twinkled out of his face when he saw Mac with Rossellini again. 'I have a nice quiet table in the back for you,' he said, and whisked them to a booth that sat by itself on a narrow section of wall in the rear of the restaurant.

Peter ordered drinks for them, and Mac sipped from the waterglass that the busboy had just filled.

The walk had been exactly what she needed; now she was both hungry and thirsty.

'That was an interesting experience,' she said to Peter, who was already studying the menu.

'What was?'

'Walking down Park Avenue with you.'

'Well, shucks, ma'am . . .' he started in a cowboy drawl.

'No, I don't mean *you* were interesting. It was the people watching you.'

'I wasn't interesting? Well, excuse me. I thought I was holding up my end of the conversation . . .' He seemed very relaxed.

Mac laughed. 'That's not what I meant.'

The waiter appeared with their drinks and asked if they needed a few minutes before they ordered. They did.

Peter started as soon as the waiter left. 'Perhaps you'd like to explain just how I was so uninteresting on the way down here.'

'Now hear me out on this. You're probably getting used to this by now, but that was my first time walking the streets of New York with a celebrity.'

'And . . . ?' He reached for a piece of bread.

'Now don't take *this* the wrong way, but the vast majority of the people didn't notice you . . .'

His hands still poised over the bread basket, Rossellini looked right at her. 'I don't know if my ego is going to last through dinner.'

'Now wait. The next largest group of people recognized you, but pretended not to. I couldn't tell if it was because they didn't want to bother you, or because they were embarrassed for themselves.' She paused for a sip of her seltzer.

'And . . . ?'

'And the rest – the smallest percentage,' she said pointedly, 'the merest fraction – were like those girls at Twenty-eighth Street who almost fainted when they saw you.'

'C'mon, they were nice girls,' Rossellini said, smiling. Then the smile disappeared from his face, and he seemed suddenly subdued.

'Thinking about Tina Marie Johnston?' Mac asked.

'Yeah, that whole scene really threw me.'

They were both quiet for a moment.

'Tell me what you and Rachel were arguing about before we got there today.'

'I will. In a while. Tell me first how you noticed all this stuff in the different people when we were walking down here.'

'How did I notice? I just did. My favorites are the ones who recognize you but can't figure out who you are. That happened to me once.'

'Who was it?'

'I still don't know his name. This goes back a few years, when I was in college. I'd come into the city, and I was up around Bloomingdale's, you know that section where the streets were torn up forever? Anyway, I'd just come up from the subway and I was carefully crossing the street – it had been raining, and I was trying to step around the puddles. I looked up and saw this guy who was so familiar to me. I knew that I knew him; I just didn't know where from. So I blurted out, "Oh, hi, how *are* you?" like we were old neighbors or something. He said hi, and just kept walking. I was halfway down the next block before I realized he was the big heart-throb on the soap opera that my roommate always watched. I had a kind of flashback of embarrassment.'

'That's what they all say.'

'What?'

'That the roommate was the one who watched the soap opera. Or my sister or my mother . . .'

'It does sound like that, doesn't it? But it's the truth.'

'I believe you.' He looked down into his drink, then up at her.

'Did you ever get a chance to watch the videos? What did you think?'

'I don't know enough about videos in general to critique them. And I was watching them for other purposes as it was. But I really like the music.'

Rossellini's face lit up. 'Thanks. I'm glad to hear it. That's what it's all about.'

The waiter appeared again, and they ordered their food and fresh drinks.

'Tell me about making videos,' Mac said when the waiter had left again. 'They look like little movies.'

'They are, I guess. I've never been around a movie.' He sipped his drink. 'It can be interesting, but it can also get on your nerves.'

'Really? Why?'

'Oh, I've never waited around so much in my life as I have doing the videos. And I have mixed feelings about the video thing sometimes.'

'Mixed how?'

'It's hard to explain. You can't ignore them – the videos – that's for sure. It's a huge part of the business. But there are a lot of people around who put the video first and the music comes second. I don't ever want that to happen.' The last was said with unmistakable intensity.

'Do you think it's changed the music?'

'I don't know. I think it probably has an effect on what music gets out there.'

'How do you mean?'

Rossellini leaned back, extending his left arm along the back of the booth, but keeping his right hand on the base of his glass.

'I think . . .' Rossellini continued, 'I think if you have somebody . . . if you have two people, say. Two groups, whatever. And on a scale of one to ten, one of them is nine in the music department and maybe a five in looks, and the other is maybe a six or seven in music, but a nine or a ten in looks, I think the second one has a better chance of getting a record deal these days.'

'You mean people are getting ahead not because

of their music but because of the way they look.'

Rossellini nodded and took a taste of his drink.

'That is depressing,' Mac said.

'Isn't it, though? Makes you wonder what would happen if somebody like Bob Dylan showed up on their doorstep today. Good chance they might pass.'

The waiter arrived with their food. They each sampled their dinners and congratulated themselves on ordering so well.

Peter was busily preparing his baked potato. Salt, pepper, butter, sour cream, the whole works. 'You said before you never watch videos. It sounded like you avoid them. Am I right?'

'Pretty close. It's not a big thing, really. By the time videos came along, I was in graduate school. I think MTV had started up a year or so before, but I didn't see it until it came into the city.'

'That's right. They didn't have it here for a while.'

'I remember the first time I saw it. I was in grad school, like I said, living in a big apartment downtown with a couple of roommates. They were so excited when Manhattan Cable finally added MTV.' Mac paused for a sip of seltzer again. Peter was halfway through his baked potato already. 'Do you remember that wild record of Bonnie Tyler's, "Total Eclipse of the Heart?" '

'Sure.'

'I loved that record. It had everything in it. That

gravelly voice of hers, this incredibly dramatic song. There was even a train in the background, I think. It seemed like a three-act play.'

Peter nodded his agreement and kept eating.

'I came in from classes one afternoon, and my roommates were both glued to the set watching MTV. And "Total Eclipse of the Heart" came on. I ran back into the living room, and there were these weird little English schoolboys wandering around with Little Orphan Annie eyes. I was so disappointed.'

'Why disappointed?'

'I realized that the images I had in my head whenever I listened to the song were much more . . . more appropriate, or more powerful, or more personal – I don't know what the word is. With the video, it was like I was watching one person's idea of that song, that record, and the universality of it was lost.

'Am I making any sense?' she asked after a second or two. Rossellini was listening to her intently.

'I think so. Keep going, though.'

Mac took a bite of her dinner before she proceeded. 'I remember our housekeeper telling me about the difference between listening to shows on radio and then seeing those same shows on television. I guess it's exactly parallel. Somehow listening to radio expands the imagination. Television makes everything so specific.' She stopped abruptly. 'I'm rambling, I know. But I really liked the pictures in my head better. I don't really even know that they were pictures. Maybe just flashes. But watching that video sort of ruined it for me. Listening to that record was never quite as good again. So I decided music videos weren't for me,' Mac finished with a shrug of the shoulders.

Peter Rossellini was still studying her face. 'I never heard anybody put it quite that way. But you make a lot of sense.' He looked back down at his nearly empty plate. 'Sorta scary, actually.'

'How is it scary?'

'If I listen to you long enough, I could talk myself out of a career,' he said with a smile.

Mac looked up, surprised. 'Naah,' she replied. 'Right, Mr Rossellini, your turn for some questions, okay?'

He looked directly at her. 'You called me Mr Rossellini again. I always think you're talking about my grandfather. Do you think you could call me Peter?'

'Your grandfather? Not your father?' Mac asked.

'I've used my mother's name since I started professionally. Mr Rossellini is my mother's father.'

'Why did you change your name?'

'Nobody could spell it. Llywelyn,' he spelled it for her. 'Pronounced lu-ellen. Rossellini is a lot easier. And one booking agent told Joey when we were starting out that Lemon and Llywelyn sounded like some brand of English marmalade.'

Mac laughed at the image. 'I don't think I'll tell Lieutenant Buratti about your real name,' she said. 'Since he loves referring to you as his *paisan*. Somehow Peter Llywelyn doesn't sound like a *paisan*. Now how about those questions?'

'Sure.'

'Tell me about your relationship with Judith Stone and how it ended.'

The question blindsided Rossellini and he looked stunned for a moment. They'd been having a nice personal conversation, or at least it felt like a personal conversation. But this question, out of nowhere, seemed *too* personal. Or maybe it wasn't personal at all for her. Maybe it was professional. 'Why?' he finally croaked out.

'She told me about it when I met with her. If you tell me what happened, it will help me evaluate the emotional content of her s—' Mac was about to say 'her side of the story,' but that sounded too harsh. 'Her version of the events.' Better.

Rossellini leaned back in the booth, staring up at the ceiling. 'That was a hard time, that whole fall. Joey and I were getting nowhere. I told you – all the gigs we were playing, anything we could get and still we were nowhere. Joey had this idea that we were the next Simon and Garfunkel, or the next Bernie Taupin and Elton John.' Mac hid her smile at the reference. 'We weren't.'

He took a long draught of his drink before continuing. 'We'd had a couple of our songs recorded, but our contract was up and the publisher wasn't picking up the option. Nothing was happening. Then Rachel saw us. She came backstage, and she and her partner started talking to me, and they introduced me to Irwin. He said he'd help us out on a new publishing deal. They asked me to think about going out as a solo act. Keep writing with Joey, but go solo as a performer. Hell, I didn't know what to do. When I look back on it now, it's like everything was ending and beginning all at the same time.'

'How so?' Mac prompted.

'Well, in the middle of all of this, Judy starts after me again about getting married. Judy's father – he was a great guy – he offers me a job. He had some real estate management or development company out in Jersey. And he says there's always room for me there. Judy went crazy. This was everything she wanted. A regular life, near her Dad. Get married, have kids. Except I knew it would mean giving up music. Giving up my dreams.' He sat quietly for a few seconds.

'And that wasn't okay with me. It was okay with Judy, and I think that was what hurt the most. Just before Thanksgiving, we had a real blowout. She told me I was an overgrown teenager who was still carrying around his high school dreams and that I should grow up. Instead I walked out. I hadn't heard from her again until last night.'

The waiter came to clear their plates and

they had a few moments of silence until he left. 'It must have been difficult for everybody,' Mac said softly. She had no doubt he was telling the truth. His account of the story was remarkably similar to Judith Stone's; only the emotions were different.

'What was hardest for me was that I had to face the fact that a lot of what she was saying was true. I was thirty-three years old. I hadn't gone to my fifteen-year high school reunion that fall because I didn't want to face all those people and tell them I was doing the same thing I had been doing when I last saw them. Most of them were married; they had real jobs, maybe a house, maybe a kid. What was I? I was a guy with no career to speak of, living in a studio apartment in a not-so-great neighborhood, without even a car. And even my partner of the last eleven years was gone.'

'What happened there?'

'Joey went ballistic when I approached him about still writing together but not performing anymore. I thought he was going to kill me.' Rossellini listened to what he'd just said and quickly looked up at Mac. 'Figure of speech.' She nodded that she understood. 'Anyway, we got a late start on the album 'cause I wrote all the songs myself. All I remember that winter is writing and rehearsing and writing some more. I did some session work for other people, and a few arrangements here and there. But it was this strange, bleak time. We recorded the album in

February, and by spring everything started to turn around.'

'And you had the vindication of having stayed true to your dream, and seeing it come true,' Mac added.

'Yeah,' he nodded. 'Right. How about your dreams? How does a beautiful woman end up as a criminal psychologist?'

She laughed and dipped her head as though taking a bow. 'I thank you for the compliment, but the short version makes me sound like a Miss America contestant. You know,' she changed her voice to a dead-on imitation of any finalist in any beauty pageant, ' "I'd like to work toward peace in the world."' Rossellini laughed appreciatively. 'But the real story is a long one, and we should really get going.'

Once outside the restaurant, Rossellini insisted on walking her home again. When she headed up the steps to her building, his hand on her arm stopped her before she reached the top. 'I'm assuming you're not married or anything,' he said.

She raised her eyebrows. 'What falls under the category of "or anything"?'

Rossellini smiled. 'Like being involved with someone. Boy, this is one conversation I never thought I'd be having with a shrink.'

Mac moved down one step, so she was eye to eye with him. 'I'm very flattered by the question. Why don't you ask it again after all this is over? At the moment, it's possible that you're just comforted by the idea of my being around. A bit of a security blanket, something like that.'

Peter Rossellini looked directly into her eyes. 'I don't think so, but you're right.' He reached up and smoothed a strand of her straight blond hair behind her ear. 'After this is over.'

INTERLUDE THREE

She burst into the room, slamming the door so hard that the hinges momentarily sagged from the wood.

She kicked off her shoes. Where the hell was he? She'd waited for hours, it seemed. Hours. But he never showed. Where the hell had he been?

She threw her skirt across the room, then the blouse. Where was he? *Where was he*? She was entitled to know. She needed to know. He was hers, goddammit! Hers! Didn't he see that? Didn't they all see that?

She braced her arms on the bureau, trying to stop the shaking. She stretched up, her back arched and her head dropping back. She was tired, so tired.

This one wasn't any good at all. She hadn't planned this one, hadn't thought it through, and it wasn't like the others.

She'd known from the first moment that it wasn't going to be any good. His hands were hot when they touched her and she hated that. It was over fast.

Why, why, why did this one have to happen? It

was an accident, that's all. She'd waited forever for Peter, and then decided suddenly to go to the bar. And later, when it was just the two of them, he started trying to pretend, the fool, just like he knew what was inside her head, like he knew what she wanted.

He didn't, of course. They never did. She had to erase him fast.

God, she was tired. She stumbled toward the bed, then lay back, her arm bent to cover her eyes.

There had been nothing in this one, not even a moment that she could salvage. She hadn't concentrated on it, hadn't planned it, and it simply didn't work. But she knew now it was never going to work again. Not without Peter.

Peter. She mouthed his name over and over, rocking side to side. You can't leave without me.

Maybe. Maybe when Peter found out what she'd done, he would see how much she loved him. He'd take her with him. Yes, that was it, he'd take her with him.

But maybe not. Maybe he'd say she was wrong. Or crazy. She hated that the most, the thought that Peter would say she was crazy. Then she'd have to kill him. Like the others.

She drifted toward a restless sleep, repeating his name over and over like a prayer.

NINETEEN

June 1

At seven thirty-five a.m., Mac was standing in the middle of her kitchen, surrounded by a pile of cartons, trying to figure out where to begin. She was dressed in her grubbies, that much she had figured out. And she'd even had two cups of coffee to help get her thinking, but that didn't seem to be working yet.

The painter was coming Monday, and she had to get ready. Not that she was entirely sure what she had to do. But he had said something about her emptying all the cupboards and moving all the 'valuables.'

This whole redecoration thing was turning out to be much more of a to-do than she'd ever expected. She'd decided at the spring break that this interim between the spring and summer sessions was the perfect time to have the apartment done. But only the living room, the dining area, the hallways, the kitchen, and her bedroom. She couldn't deal with moving all the books and the mounds of paper in her office. Besides, her office would serve as her oasis of sanity while all else was chaos around her. Or so was the plan.

When she'd gone shopping for wallpaper six weeks ago, the guy acted like she was some last-minute shopper. What a temperament on him! Then she found out that scheduling the painter recommended by a friend on the third floor was like getting an appointment with New York's top neurosurgeon. That was why she'd ended up with the painting scheduled the second week of her supposed vacation instead of the first week. Lucky for Buratti.

Despite the *tsouris* it had caused, as Sylvie would say, Mac was pleased that the redecoration was underway. It would give the apartment her personal stamp; it would make it her home.

She'd been in the apartment for almost three years now, and it had been painted standard New York apartment white just before she moved in. She hadn't given much thought to decorating at the time. She was just in a hurry to get settled, thanks to dear old Ivan. She'd broken up with Ivan, bought the apartment, and moved in, all within the space of six weeks.

She and Ivan had been an item for five years. Well, not quite. She'd known him for five years; they were together about four. He was a guest lecturer at New York University when she was in graduate school, and her faculty adviser made sure they were introduced. Nothing had come of that meeting, but the following year she was at Riverside visiting her parents when Ivan was a guest there, and something did come of that meeting. She was flattered that a man so mature (Ivan was about ten years older than she), successful (Ivan was under contract for his second book at the time) and good-looking (Ivan thought he looked like a young James Coburn) was attracted to her. Ivan was indeed attracted to her, and also very impressed with her parents. Too bad it took her so long to figure out that he was a little more impressed with her parents' money than their academic accomplishments.

When she looked back on it, it should have been obvious to her. Ivan was always inordinately concerned with what table they got at restaurants, with making sure that they were seen at the 'right' parties inside and out of university circles, with getting his name in print as much as possible – to boost his lecture fees, he said.

It had all come out pretty suddenly. They were planning on getting married late that summer. In the midst of making wedding arrangements, Mac received a phone call one day from the trust officer at the bank in Connecticut. It seems Ivan had been making some preliminary calls inquiring about the terms of her trusts. Mac had to face the fact that while Ivan may have been very fond of her, he was definitely in love with her family's money. When she confronted him about the phone call, he'd tried to reason with her.

She'd ended it with Ivan that day, and a month and a half later was moving into her new freshly painted co-op. Her friend Sylvie had been a champ during that whole time, but she'd been against buying the apartment so quickly. 'Why don't you buy a fabulous dress or get your hair cut like everybody else does?' she'd cautioned Mac. 'Buying an apartment is a little extreme, don't you think?'

Sylvie's advice aside, Mac had been very happy with the move from the Upper East Side. And she'd been very happy to put Ivan in her past. She still saw him on television occasionally – he'd made a career out of getting into the Rolodex of every news and talk show booker, so that if there was a subject that had a remotely psychological slant, Ivan was among the first called. The first time he'd shown up on 'Nightline,' Sylvie had called at eleven thirty-one p.m. 'Hey, kid, this you should hear from a friend. I thought I was seeing things, but Ted Koppel – Koppel himself – just introduced Ivan the Terrible.'

Sylvie had been a champ of a friend for years. They'd first met twelve years ago at Connecticut College when they were both signed up as psychology majors. Sylvie had changed her major three times by graduation, at which point she took her sociology degree and announced that a life in the 'thee-ah-tah' was her true destiny. So while Mac was in graduate school at NYU, Sylvie was pursuing her craft at various academies and acting classes. The last few years, she'd actually made some money at it; she still had to support herself doing other jobs, ranging from temporary receptionist to market research interviewer, but she was sticking it out. 'I'm growing into my face,' she'd said to Mac the previous winter. 'The character parts are going to be pouring in any day now.'

By quarter to ten Mac had filled six cartons and realized she was going to need plenty more. She decided she'd better primp before going to the grocery store and begging for more boxes, and she was on her way to the mirror when the phone rang. It was Buratti.

'Hey, Doc, how ya doin'?'

'Fine. What's up?' He wanted something.

'You know the bar Ten Bridges?'

'Yeah, I've been there. Over on West Ninth? It has a beautiful long wooden bar as I remember.' Wait, she thought to herself. I've seen that bar – that specific bar recently, and not in person. Funny, she hadn't realized it until Buratti said the name. 'It's where they shot Rossellini's video, isn't it?'

'Bingo. They found the owner dead this morning.'

Forty-five minutes later, Mac walked past the yellow crime scene tape and into the bar area of Ten Bridges. It felt good to walk into the air-conditioned cool of the restaurant. The heat was building early; it was well over eighty degrees just after ten a.m. Even though she'd put on cotton slacks, a light blouse, and a matching cotton jacket, the ride over – in a non-air-conditioned cab, thankyouverymuch, made her feel like she needed another shower.

There were three people from the crime scene unit still working around the bar – both in front and behind it. Buratti was talking to one of the uniforms on duty. He spotted her immediately and waved her over. He finished with the uniform and turned to her.

'Pretty quick getting over here,' he said. 'Thanks.'

'What happened?'

'Mickey Nahas was found dead in the bar, actually at the bar, this morning about five.'

'Found by whom?' Mac asked.

'One of our patrol cars, would you believe. They knew the place was usually dark by four-fifteen or so. People clean up, check the till, and all that after the four o'clock closing. They're gone by four-fifteen, four-thirty latest. The patrol spotted the lights at five, and saw the gate was open. They went in and found him sitting at the bar, slumped over. The body was moved just a little while ago, but they should have pictures for me real quick.'

'Was the body still here when you arrived?'

'Yeah. Why?'

'Nahas was wearing a maroon shirt, wasn't he? And the jacket was gray, if I remember correctly. And his hair was about shoulder length?'

'Not quite so long on the hair, but you got it. That's the way Rossellini was dressed in the video, hey?' Buratti said.

She nodded yes. 'Yep. I watched all of them again the other night.'

Buratti shook his head in disgust. 'Here's what we got on this one. Nahas was sittin' at the bar, his hand still stretched out like he was holding a glass. What happened to the glass you're going to ask me, right?'

Mac nodded.

'Best guess is that whoever did him in removed it,' Buratti continued. 'There's a whole rack of dirty glasses behind the bar. No telling which one was his. The sink was still full of dishwater. You know how they dip the glasses, and then put them in the rack for the dishwater? They're still checking, but unless we get some kind of miracle light pointing it out from the sky, we can't find any trace of which glass was his.'

'Cause of death?'

'Not sure yet, but ninety-nine to one it was something in his drink – like somebody slipped him a mickey. No pun intended. But like I said, we can't find the glass to prove that. The people we've talked to so far tell us Nahas was a heavy drinker but not a drug user, so we'll see if anything shows up in his blood.'

'Who was the last one to leave the bar? The last employee?' Mac asked.

'The assistant chef. He's sitting over there with the new manager.' Mac looked over to a table along the wall that separated the bar area from the dining room. A young Amerasian man, the cook, Mac guessed from his white pants and shirt, sat looking anxiously at the crime scene personnel still combing the area. Opposite him sat a dark-featured man in his early thirties, dressed in chinos, a T-shirt, and a windbreaker; he was staring into his cup of coffee as though it held the secrets of the universe. Every few seconds, he muttered 'Jesus' to himself. 'Both a them just got here twenty, thirty minutes ago,' Buratti said in a low voice. 'Took a while to locate 'em.'

'Were you able to find out anything from him?'

'When he came out of the kitchen about two-thirty, he says there were still four customers in the bar. A couple at a table and two people at the bar. A man and a woman. Not together. Nahas waved as the cook passed the bar, said he would be leaving as soon as the last customer was gone.'

'Any idea who the customers were?'

'Hoping that one of the waiters will be able to tell us who the couple was; the manager's goin' through the bills with credit card receipts, and he'll come up with some names for us. Nahas himself was tending the bar, so we don't know if we'll be able to get anything on the two there. We're gonna have to track down the customers, see if anybody talked to either of them, or recognized them.'

Very standard procedure, Mac thought. But there was something Buratti wasn't saying. 'Why did you ask me to come over here?'

Buratti looked at her straight on. 'I wanted to see

if you could get a feel for anything here, see if there was something we're missing.'

'I'm a psychologist, Mario. Not a psychic. What's the real question?'

Buratti was suddenly uncomfortable in the bar. 'Let's go someplace else and get a cup of coffee. I'll give you the whole rundown.' He stepped over to the bar to check with the head of the crime scene unit, then waved Mac toward him as he headed for the table where the cook and manager sat.

'They'll only be another hour or so,' Buratti said to the manager. The man nodded glumly.

'I can check with you by one o'clock or so and get those names?'

'Sure,' said the manager. 'Kevin was on the desk last night, and he'll be here in . . .' He checked his watch, it was just past eleven. 'About a half an hour. We'll go through the receipts as soon as he gets here.'

'I can reach you here all day?' Buratti asked.

'I think so,' said the manager. 'But I'm not sure.' Buratti looked at him quizzically.

'You know, Lieutenant, I stopped waiting tables six weeks ago, when Mickey asked if I would take over the day manager job. I finally decided I should get a nice stable gig, no more trying for the golden ring. But this,' with his chin he indicated the bar area where Nahas had died, 'this makes acting look better and better. I've been thinking of giving my old agent a call. If she'll see me, I'll be out of here for a couple of hours. But they'll know where I am.'

Buratti nodded good-bye to the men and led Mac to the front door.

They found a little coffee shop on Tenth just off of Sixth Avenue. Greek, of course. Standard-issue booths. Buratti picked one near the windows, since the only other late-morning customers were at the other end of the place.

The uniformed waitress brusquely served them coffee and decaf. Buratti sipped his coffee but didn't say anything. Mac realized she'd better start.

'So what's the real question, Mario?'

He poured a Sweet'n Low into his cup and stirred a few times before looking at her. 'Could we have seen this one coming, Mac?'

'What!' she said, a little louder than she intended. 'You're feeling some kind of responsibility for this? Don't do that to yourself,' she said emphatically.

Buratti barely nodded. Then his eyes drifted over her shoulder and he stared at the picture of the Acropolis that had faded in the sunlight.

'Everybody's got twenty-twenty hindsight,' Mac continued. 'You know that. The only way you could've done anything is to post a guard here. And at the South Street Seaport, Times Square, the Cloisters, and God knows where else. And have them watch for what? Any guy with long hair? A little hard to pinpoint in the middle of Manhattan.'

He made eye contact with her again. 'You're right.' That's what he said, but Mac knew he wasn't convinced.

'What's going on with you, Mario? You're not usually like this.'

He sat back in the booth. 'Okay, let's just talk about these two. Jury and now Nahas. Leave the Connecticut guy out of it for a minute. We got nothing. Nothing to go on. Nothing from the scene – it's as slick as a whistle—'

'You don't know that yet about the restaurant,' Mac interrupted.

'Believe me, Doc, when we figured out about the glass, that his hand was found like it was still holding a glass, and then saw all those dipped and rinsed glasses – there's gonna be nothing from that scene. I know it. Unless somebody can tell us about the people who were left in the bar.'

'Nothing more from Metropolitan?'

'Nope.'

The waitress appeared bearing coffee pots in both hands and refilled their cups. Mario proceeded to sweeten his cup again.

'What is it that you're afraid of?' Mac asked.

Buratti laughed. 'You know, that's one of the few times you really sounded like a shrink, kid. "What am I afraid of?"'

'Well?' She sat back, patiently.

'Okay,' he finally said. 'All those places you said before, Times Square, the Seaport, all the other places around town that they shot these videos. What I'm afraid of is that there's going to be more.'

'More victims, you mean.'

'Yeah, we got three bodies at this point, two here anyway. And we aren't even at square one. We're at square zero.' He rubbed his hands over his face.

'You seem tired. Are you okay?'

One half of his face smiled at her. 'Last night was my daughter's graduation dance. Three o'clock I was up. That's when she came home to change to go out to the sunrise breakfast on the beach. I just can't do those hours anymore.'

'That's God's way of telling you you're not the teenager; she is. Well, did she have a good time?'

'I don't know. She was still at breakfast when I left this morning.' He yawned deeply.

'Don't start that. You'll have me going.' Mac looked down at her coffee, wishing it weren't decaf. 'Mario, there's something else we have to go over.'

He picked up on her businesslike tone and looked up quickly. 'Shoot,' he said.

'You brought me into this up at Metropolitan because of the stalker profile I'd worked on.'

He nodded his agreement.

'And I still think there's an element of that here.'

'Yeah . . . ?'

Mac's tone was becoming formal, like she was making a presentation. 'With Nahas's death, I think we are dealing with a bona fide serial killer, and that's a whole different ballpark.'

'Ball game,' Mario corrected. 'A different ball game.'

'Whatever. But it's way beyond my expertise. I

know the department has a team of specialists who profile serial killers, and I know you can get support from the FBI as well. I think it's time you go to Lenox and let him get you the help that you need.'

Buratti didn't say anything, but nodded slowly. The wheels were already turning in his head. 'I worked with one of the special teams once a few years ago,' he finally said. 'A kidnapping. I swear somebody on the team had a direct line to the *New York Post*.'

'That's a risk. You can never tell if that kind of publicity is going to be a help or not.' She finished the last of her decaf. 'I'll be happy to meet with the team psychologists and tell them what I know.' She paused and looked at Buratti. 'Of course, it's not much.'

They were both quiet. They had learned so little in the past week. 'What do you know about the serial killer profile?' Buratti finally asked.

'The basics. We touch on it in one of the units in criminal psych.' She closed her eyes until she remembered the main points of the profile. 'Predominantly white male. The ones who aren't are so few as to be statistically insignificant. They're usually very intelligent. Very good at manipulating people, at charming them. In a high percentage of cases, there's some kind of psychosexual pathology.' Mac stopped for a moment, and concentrated on the window, as if trying to recall something. 'There's usually an identifiable pattern to the killings – a signature if you will. Like the fact that all of these are at the scenes of Rossellini's videos. A signature.'

'What else?' Buratti prodded.

'It's the scariest thing about them, I think. For the most part, they appear overwhelmingly normal.'

'Normal, hunh? Hard to tell what that is these days.' His saucer clattered as he set down his cup, hard.

'I confess I really haven't explored the literature. There's a level of grotesquerie in those cases that I can't handle. I just don't get it.' She looked at Buratti to see if he understood what she was saying. He was halfway with her. 'With other cases, say with the stalker profile we did, I understand how it happens. I understand how a crush could become an obsession. I understand the leap when a fan becomes a fanatic. It's a question of intensity. Something normal that is magnified until it's abnormal. But the serial cases . . .' Her voice faded. 'I give a lot of credit to the ones that can work on them. They must have great strength of soul.'

Buratti stared at her for long moments in silence, then he heaved a sigh. 'You're right, Mac. I've got to go to Lenox on this one and get some help.' He sat back so he could reach into his pocket for some change. 'Let me go call Beckman and tell him to meet us at Lenox's office.' He slid out of the booth and headed for the pay phone near the front door.

Mac watched him place the call. Seconds after the call connected, his posture suddenly straightened. He nodded, replaced the receiver, and walked back

to her with a bounce to his step that hadn't been
there before. He was full of energy.

'What is it?' Mac said.

'We gotta get uptown.' He picked up the bill.
'Rossellini just called the precinct looking for me.
He thinks he got a note from the killer.'

TWENTY

The ride uptown was accomplished in record time,
even without a siren. Mac and Buratti pulled up in
front of the main entrance to Radio City just as
Beckman crossed the street. Once inside, the box
office attendant convinced them that he, in fact,
couldn't open the doors to the theater, and that it
would be quicker to go around to the stage entrance
on Fifty-first Street. They did.

A security guard stopped them just inside the
doorway. One of Monaghan's guys. Once Buratti
identified himself, the guard visibly relaxed and told
them where they'd find Rossellini.

The entrance area gave way to a succession of
hallways. The corridors and the walls had a very
familiar look to them, Mac realized. Even in this part
of the building, you could tell you were in Rockefeller
Center.

Following the guard's directions, they made a
third turn where an arrow pointed to the stage, and
then were faced with a large curtain. The end of the

curtain was several yards to the right, and Mac and Beckman followed Buratti as he groped his way to the end of the material.

They were in an area off the right side of the stage. It was, in effect, a large room that had been created by drawing curtains about the space. All that heavy fabric created a curiously quiet atmosphere, only faintly lit by white work lights from above. Mac recognized Jeremy's voice floating in from the stage area, but even his high-pitched directions were softened by the absorption of the material around them. The space had a distinct aroma to it as well; although it wasn't unpleasant, anyone could tell that it had been a long, long time since any fresh air had penetrated this part of the building.

In the center of this offstage area was a large table, at least two feet by six feet. Atop the table was an assortment of cups and soda cans and one full ashtray. Tucked underneath was a variety of sports bags, shopping bags, and briefcases. One folding chair sat at the center of the table, on the side away from the stage. Peter Rossellini stood, leaning on the back of the chair, looking up toward the rafters. He didn't hear them until all three had come around the curtain, and he looked down, startled.

'Sorry,' Buratti said. 'Thought you woulda heard us coming.'

"S'okay,' Rossellini said. He looked at Mac and smiled. 'Hi,' he said softly to her.

Even in the dim lighting Mac could see that Rossellini's expression was tense.

Buratti started right in. 'Okay, what's this you got? And how did you get it?'

Rossellini reached toward the portfolio case that was directly in front of him. It was the kind that zips on three sides with handles that pull up. Maybe leather, maybe imitation. The case was unzipped and Rossellini flopped it open. On top was an oversize piece of paper, probably nine or ten by fourteen, lined with music staves. Written across it diagonally, in heavy blue lettering, was the message: I KNOW WHERE YOU LIVE.

'When did you find it?' Buratti asked.

'I went to get my notes this morning on some changes for one of the arrangements. I was going through the sheets and found it. It wasn't that long ago. Just before I called you. You weren't there, but the guy I talked to said just to leave it alone, so that's what I did.'

'That was me,' Beckman said. Buratti belatedly introduced the two men.

Beckman stepped next to Rossellini and looked at the case intently without touching it. 'When was the last time you used the case?'

'I use it every day,' Rossellini replied. 'It has everything in it. My address book, my notes, my schedule. I used it yesterday.'

'When was the last time you went through that whole stack of papers?'

Rossellini hesitated. 'I don't know. I've been so busy this week, I've just been cramming stuff in there. A couple of days, anyway, maybe longer. What are you trying to get at?'

'Trying to pinpoint when the note got slipped in. Maybe you were carrying this around for a few days,' Buratti said.

From the expression on his face, that idea obviously didn't thrill Rossellini.

'Is this the kinda paper you use?' Beckman asked. He was leaning over the case, looking at the pile from the side.

'Yeah, I've got a few sheets of it in the back. Or I had a few sheets.'

Beckman looked at the partition that divided the briefcase into two sections. There were mini-pockets for pens, a calculator, and a larger see-through pocket. There was a blue marker in the see-through pocket. 'That your marker in there?' he finally asked.

'Yeah.'

'Does the color of those letters look like it came from that marker?'

Rossellini bent down and looked closely at the printing in the dim light. 'It could have. I don't know. I haven't used it that much.'

Buratti picked up where Beckman was going. 'We'd like to take the whole case if we can. That way we can check the pocket and the marker and the paper. That okay with you?'

'Sure,' Rossellini said. 'Can you leave my other stuff, though? My notes and everything?'

Buratti and Beckman were figuring out how to remove the notes without compromising any of the surfaces the lab would be examining, when Rachel Bennet's voice floated over the top of the curtains.

'Good God! I feel like a rat in a maze. The guard should have escorted us back here!' She walked a few feet beyond the end of the curtain before she realized it and stopped suddenly. Michelle, who was following her intently, walked right into her back.

'Peter! There you are!' She stepped toward the group, squinting and smiling. Then she recognized Buratti and the smile disappeared. 'The police? What are they doing here? Has something happened?'

'It's okay, Rachel,' Rossellini said, moving toward her so as to stop her progress toward the table. 'I just found something I thought might help the police.'

Rachel dodged him and walked up next to Beckman. 'Who are you and what . . .' She looked down at the heavily lettered note. 'Oh my God, is this what you found?' she asked Peter.

'Now don't get all bent out of shape, Rachel.'

Mac watched as Michelle, who'd been left standing by herself, slowly edged her way toward the opposite side of the table and studied the note. The expression on her face was like she had seen a very large cockroach.

'Peter,' Rachel said, her voice almost shaky, 'this

is a threat, an honest-to-God threat. Where did you find this?' He told her. She almost swooned.

'Somebody actually got into your briefcase? Somebody got that close and you still aren't taking this seriously?' She looked at Mac and Buratti in turn. 'Please, Doctor, Lieutenant, tell him he has to cancel these shows.'

'Rachel, look,' said Rossellini patiently. 'If it comes to that, we can cancel Monday night. We'll say I have a sore throat or something. But I don't want to announce a cancellation now. I don't want whoever is doing this to know they have me on the run.'

'If this is some stupid—' Rachel started, but Mac interrupted.

'He might be right, Ms Bennet,' Mac said. All eyes turned to her. 'There's no way to be sure if that kind of publicity would encourage or deter the perpetrator. In any case, Mr Rossellini seems to have very strong instincts not to cancel, so I would go along with those.' Rossellini smiled his thanks to her.

'But please don't stay at your apartment, Peter. At least do that for me,' Rachel pleaded, and there was no doubt that her concern was genuine.

'That I'll go along with,' Buratti said. 'Might be a good idea,' he said directly to Rossellini.

'Okay,' Rossellini said. He looked at Michelle. 'Think you can set me up at one of the hotels nearby?' Rachel's level of distress lowered visibly.

'Sure,' Michelle replied.

Peter put his hand on her shoulder and squeezed.

'Thanks, Shell.' Michelle looked up at him with a puppy-like expression.

'Listen, you folks can figure that out amongst yourselves. Right now we got to figure a way to get this over to the lab,' Buratti said. He and Beckman returned their attention to the briefcase.

'Is the video crew here yet?' Rachel asked.

'No, they're due around two or so, I think,' Rossellini said.

'That's right,' Michelle piped up. 'I talked to Dan yesterday and he said they'd be here from two to five.'

'Okay, Michelle, take some notes.' Rachel's voice changed into an efficient tone. 'If we're going to go ahead with this, we're canceling all the backstage passes and issuing new ones.' Michelle barely had time to snatch her steno pad out of her large shoulder bag. 'And the party invitations, too. We'll redo that list. Be sure to tell Dan and the other CMR people. If I haven't approved a name and it's not on your list, they don't get in. We'll have to coordinate this with John Monaghan.'

Michelle scribbled quickly.

'And that radio station,' Rachel continued. 'Those contest winners. They'll need new passes too, or do you think we can put them off?' She looked at Michelle, who shrugged an 'I dunno' back at her.

'Christ, there are so many details to think of. Michelle, come with me. We'll have to sit down and make a whole new list.' Rachel trooped off in the general direction of the entrance. The whole area was suddenly much quieter.

Only for a moment. Jeremy's voice was audible suddenly and coming closer. Soon the curtain that led to the main stage parted and musicians and singers started drifting through. Mac recognized Prissy and smiled a greeting. 'Fifteen minutes everybody,' Jeremy said, loudly. 'Fifteen minutes *sharp!*'

Peter put his hand on her arm and started toward the stage. 'Let me show you something,' he said.

Mac looked back to the table where Beckman and Buratti had been standing. Only Beckman was there now. With a raise of her eyebrows, she asked where Buratti was. With hand gestures, Beckman replied that Buratti had gone off to make a call and to smoke a cigarette. Mac nodded and let herself be led away.

Peter held the curtains aside for her and she stepped onto the great stage at Radio City Music Hall. She gasped. 'It's something, isn't it?' he said quietly.

She looked out at the thousands of seats, at rows and aisles that curved up with the floor and seemed to meet the ceiling. Lines and arches and curves all cooperated to create a beautiful space that surrounded and enveloped and transported an observer to another plane. 'It's like a cathedral!' Mac said, with a hint of nervous laughter.

'It is, isn't it?' He walked a few steps farther onto the stage. 'C'mon.'

She finally looked across the stage and gasped again. 'Oh my God, it's huge.'

'You bet. Biggest stage in New York. Maybe in the country, I don't know.' Peter took her hand and led her to the center of the stage. It took quite a few steps. He positioned her stage center and put his hands on her shoulders. 'Now stand here and just imagine every one of those seats filled.'

'I can't. I mean I couldn't even walk out in front of all those people.' She turned toward him. 'The fact that you can actually walk out here and sing in front of them amazes me. What must that be like?'

'It's wonderful, and it's scary. I sang here at the Grammys a couple of months ago.' He smiled and shook his head at the remembrance.

'You know, when we were putting this tour together, it was like seeing the dreams that I've had for years suddenly all coming true at the same time.' He let go of her and stepped around her, stopping just short of the lip of the stage. 'And it has been a lot of years. I was seventeen when I decided I was going to be a singer, even if I didn't tell my parents for a couple of years, so it's over half my life.' He stopped, shoved his hands into the front pockets of his jeans, and hunched his shoulders. 'And after playing damn near every bar and joint, every VFW hall up to Boston and down to Washington, I finally get to sing in a place like this.' His voice trailed off into the huge auditorium, and it was hard for Mac to hear. But then he suddenly turned back to her.

'And getting to go across the country! All these places I've never been. Texas, New Orleans, Denver, Seattle, St Louis. I actually get to go across the country and sing my music for people, and they're going to pay to come and listen to me. It's amazing.' She heard his throat tighten, and saw him swallow, hard.

After a few moments, he started again, this time with a vehemence to his voice. 'That's why I won't cancel. I've dreamed about this for so many years, and I've worked, and worked hard. Too long to let some . . . asshole take it away from me!' He looked at her as if she would challenge what he'd said. She didn't.

There was a flapping motion around the curtains at the side of the stage and Buratti peeked his head through. 'Mac, can I see you a minute?' he called to her.

'I'll be right there,' she said. Turning to Rossellini, she spoke in a lower voice. 'And Peter, if I don't see you again before the show, good luck. Or break a leg, or whatever one is supposed to say.'

'One is supposed to say good luck,' he teased. 'Thanks, Mac.'

He walked with her to the stage entrance, and she hurried to the table where Buratti and Beckman waited. 'Mac, Beckman was telling me he's got a couple a things you should know. Go ahead, Stu.'

'First, Judith Stone has no confirmation of her whereabouts on the nights that Jury and Vos were killed. The people whose names she gave me, the people I talked to were with her early – like for dinner. They didn't see her after nine-thirty, ten those nights. She says she just went home alone.'

'Did you talk to her yet, see where she was last night?' Buratti asked Beckman.

Rossellini had followed Mac offstage, and he walked toward the group when he heard Judy's name mentioned. He was going to object to their continued questioning of her when the last phrase stopped him. 'Why last night? What happened last night?'

'Sorry, Rossellini, things sort of got away from us when we started talking about this here.' Buratti lifted the plastic bag that now held his briefcase. 'You know the restaurant downtown, Ten Bridges?'

'Yeah,' Rossellini said slowly. 'Why?'

'The owner, Mickey Nahas, was found dead this morning.'

Mac could see, even in the poor lighting, that Rossellini paled. 'Oh, God, not another one,' he said, almost in a moan. 'This is insane.' He turned and walked away from them.

'Just a minute,' Mac said to the two detectives and followed Rossellini. 'Are you okay?' she asked when she caught up to him.

'No,' he snapped. 'This is nuts. We are talking stupid little videos here. How can three guys be *dead?* It's not worth it; it's just not worth it.'

'None of this is your fault,' Mac said to him quietly. 'Don't take any of this on yourself.'

'How can I not take it on?' He looked at her sharply. 'This guy was dressed like me, too, wasn't he?'

She nodded yes.

'Jesus, this is creepy,' he said loudly.

From over the tops of the curtains they could hear the sounds of the musicians and singers wandering back toward the stage. Rehearsal was about to resume.

'Mac, we gotta get going here,' Buratti called.

She nodded to him. 'Are you going to be okay?' she asked Peter.

'Yeah, it's just going to take a little while,' he said.

'Is there anything I can do for you right now?'

'No, thanks,' he said on a sigh. 'Really, thanks for asking.'

'I'll talk to you later,' she said hurriedly, and returned to where Buratti and Beckman were impatiently waiting.

'What else?'

'Beckman here says that one of the loose screws you dug up out in Kansas isn't in Kansas anymore. She became one of the happy citizens of Manhattan a few months ago.'

'Which one was it?' Mac asked, surprised.

'Agnes Leonard. She was the one who was writing that his songs were like secret messages to her. That his music was the only thing getting her through the days.'

'Yeah,' Mac said slowly. Sad to say, she

remembered only vaguely. It had been just a few days since she'd gone through this material with Beckman, but they had already blurred together in her mind.

'Anyway, I been calling since, what, Thursday? There was a referral on the number I got out of information. Didn't get through to anybody until late yesterday. The lady at the referral number was her aunt. I got an address down on West Thirty-fifth.'

Mac looked at Buratti. This could be something. 'You want me to go with you to talk to her?'

'I was thinking you and Beckman better go, since you two started on this. I'll drop this over to the lab and see if we got anything. What time is it now?' He looked down at his watch. 'Geez, it's almost twelve-thirty. No wonder I'm hungry. Why don't you two head downtown and check in with me, say, three o'clock?'

'There's something else,' Beckman said.

'What?' Buratti said sharply. He thought they were all caught up.

'The guy from New Britain. The one who thinks Rossellini's been stealing his songs?'

'Yeah?'

'I haven't gotten a hold of him yet to talk to him. But the New Britain police tell me they've had him in three times on assault and once on suspicion of murder. But they couldn't pin anything on him. From what the New Britain guys said, he is one big problem.'

Buratti looked at the floor, then up at Beckman. 'How about alibis? Do we know where he was the nights in question?'

Beckman shrugged. 'Don't know. Haven't had a chance to check it out yet. But I'm working on it.'

'Well, first things first. You two get downtown and talk to our Miss Kansas. I'll get over to the lab.' He headed for the curtain, trying to find where to exit. 'Was there a hot dog cart out on the corner when we came in? I'm starving.' Beckman followed him.

Mac quickly picked up her purse that had been sitting under the table and walked over to Peter Rossellini. 'Better?' she said.

He nodded. 'A little. Thanks.'

At that moment, Jeremy burst through the curtains that led to the stage. 'Peter, can you join us onstage now? If I don't get something accomplished soon, I shall scream. *Scream* I tell you.' He jumped up on the table. 'Priscilla is even more cowlike than usual today. But I know she's doing it just to get to me. Ha! Like she could.'

Mac smiled up at Peter, who rolled his eyes at Jeremy's theatrics. Mac waved good-bye and hurried to catch up to the two men in the corridor.

TWENTY-ONE

The three parted ways on the corner of Fifty-first and Sixth, where Buratti had located the hot dog pushcart. Mac and Beckman left him happily munching away on a sauerkraut-and-sausage special.

Beckman had to get back to the precinct before they headed downtown. As usual, it was easier and faster to walk the seven or eight blocks than it was to find any other mode of transportation. They walked up Sixth to Fifty-third and then across, then up Eighth to Fifty-fourth. That route avoided most, but not all, of the patches of midtown streets that were torn up.

Beckman took advantage of the time to fill her in on the interviews he'd done since she'd last seen him. 'You really have a knack for picking these types out of the pile, Doctor,' he congratulated her. 'By the time I got home last night, I said to my wife, "There's no end to the variety of whackos walking around, I tell you." '

'I know you didn't get to see our friend in New Britain,' Mac said. 'Who did you talk to?' They stopped for a red light. Mac noticed that Beckman actually stayed on the curb, which is unusual for a New York pedestrian. But after ten seconds, he edged into the street, Mac following him.

'Got started in Queens. Janine Lenkow. Midtwenties, I would guess, but hard to tell. Real overweight. Works part-time at Queen Lady at that Mall they got out there . . . What's the name?'

'I have no idea,' Mac said. Queens was a mystery to her. A large mystery. 'All I know about Queens is that they give the same street a bunch of different names to confuse outsiders.'

'Different names?' Beckman looked at her quizzically.

'Oh, they have Forty-seventh Street, then Forty-seventh Avenue. That I can understand. But then they go into Forty-seventh Drive, Forty-seventh Place, Forty-seventh Alley, I don't know all the other ones. It's confusing as hell. I got seriously lost out there one time.'

'I bet,' Beckman said. 'So Janine works part-time. Her real vocation, according to her mother, is being a professional fan. She apparently belongs to twenty, twenty-five fan clubs. Spends a good bit of time writing letters, spends a good bit of what money she has on buying fan stuff through these clubs. She's a real case, but I don't think she's our problem.'

'What were the threats about then?' Mac said as they stopped at the next curb.

'That she was going to leave his fan club and join the Quinn fan club. Know who Quinn is?' Beckman said in a teasing tone.

'Nope. Who?'

'It's a new group. Couple of guys, couple of girls. Personally I think they sound like they're rippin' off Fleetwood Mac. But that's me.' He was edging into the street again and started walking when the traffic cleared.

Mac caught up with him when the light changed. 'Okay, Janine is out of the picture. Who did you talk to next?'

'Miss Dorothy Sutcliffe in White Plains. This lady scared the shit out of me.'

'Why?'

'Her house is like something out of the Addams Family or somethin'. Dark, 'cause she keeps the shades drawn and it's like you're gonna see spiders right before your eyes. And she's got candles all over the place. The whole house smells dead. Gave me the creeps.' Beckman's shoulders shivered in remembrance.

'But you don't think she's a problem, either.'

He looked down at her. 'I think she's a problem, but not for Rossellini. She's about seventy years old.'

'I think that pretty much eliminates her,' Mac said. Before Beckman continued, she had to ask, 'How can a seventy-year-old be so scary?'

'She's one of these super-religious types, you know. Everything is Satan and evil and sin and destruction. While I was talking to her, she had one of those evangelists on television, whipping people up into a frenzy, I tell you.' Beckman slowed his step to look at Mac directly, his eyes widening. 'And when I ask her about writing to Rossellini, she goes wild. Heathen music, she says. Pagan. Music for fornicating. Fornicating! She actually used that word! It was wild, honest.'

Mac studied him carefully. 'Sounds like you're glad you got out of there in one piece.' He nodded his agreement. 'Did you get to see anybody else, or did Miss Sutcliffe do you in?'

'No, I made it over to East Rutherford. Good ol' Ronald D. Morris. What a loser. But I got some more checking to do on him.'

'Tell me what you've got so far.'

'Ronald D. is twenty-two. Hasn't had a real job since he got out of high school. Which means never, I guess. His mother said he picks up odd jobs here and there. Mainly he stays around the house and gets stoned. He busted his ass trying to clear away the weed when his mother told him I wanted to talk to him. But his room reeks with the stuff.'

'So we've got a twenty-two-year-old without a steady job, who's an old-fashioned pothead. How quaint. What else?' Mac asked. She could see the precinct up ahead and she'd be glad to get in there and get a drink of water. It was getting close to ninety out, she was sure. And the humidity was somewhere around a hundred and fifty percent.

'Ronald D. talks a big game. It's like he's made up this whole life in his head, and that's what he tells you about. But there's his mother standing over his shoulder shaking her head, telling you no.'

This one piqued Mac's interest. 'What's this other life he's made up?'

'He thinks of himself as some rock and roll consultant, I don't know. He watches MTV a lot – like all day, according to his mother. And he talks about the groups and the singers like they were his friends. Or like he works with them. It's all really weird.'

'Can you give me an example?' Mac asked.

'Sure. He had MTV on when I was talking to him. He's answering my questions when all of a sudden he turns toward the TV and starts yelling. About how they shouldn't have done the video that was playing. They should have done a video on another cut from the album, like he told them. Make any sense?'

They walked along quietly for a moment, then Mac continued. 'And he seems serious about this; it wasn't like he was putting you on?'

'Yeah.' Beckman nodded. 'He seemed serious. Whacko, but serious.'

'What happened when you asked him about Rossellini?'

'He called him a few names that I won't repeat.

Then said he was a slick sonofabitch. And that he was tired of Rossellini stealing his women.' Beckman shrugged his shoulders in a 'that's what he said.' 'Not that this kid's had a date since maybe his junior prom, if he was lucky.'

'Really?' Mac pressed.

'Really. I tell you the kid is living in some parallel universe. It was like a skit from "Saturday Night Live."'

They were at the precinct, and Beckman opened the door for her. 'What about alibis?' Mac inquired.

'He said he was home and his mother backed him up. I don't know if that's the end of it, though.'

'So this was yesterday?' Mac asked.

Beckman nodded.

'So you haven't had a chance to ask him or his mother about where he was last night?'

Beckman shook his head 'No.'

Mac was silent for a moment. 'This one could use some further attention. It would be real interesting to find out where he was last night.'

'Yeah, I'm gonna follow up with him,' Beckman said, and then looked directly at her. 'Y'know, today was my day off. You can see how far I got. And from what Buratti says, especially with another one last night, we're working seven days until something breaks. I'm planning on getting to Philadelphia by tomorrow, or maybe even late today. Maybe I can catch up with Morris again on the way back.'

They'd stopped in the lobby. Mac got a quick drink

from the water fountain. Before leaving Buratti, the two of them had agreed that Agnes Leonard would be her last interview. He was going to have to get some official help from the department.

That new team would take some time getting up to speed, of course. And Mac figured that she couldn't be officially off the case since she was never officially on, so a little guidance for Beckman was not entirely out of order. 'I'd go ahead and check out the Philadelphia woman, but I'd concentrate on Morris. If he's got a drug problem, and apparently a delusional world as well, he may be our guy. Plus the information we have to this point makes a male perpetrator more likely. Yeah, I'd keep a close eye on him.'

A half hour later, they arrived at the West Side Christian Residence for Women on West Thirty-fifth Street. Mac had been wishing the ride was longer, since this time they'd lucked into an air-conditioned cab.

The West Side Christian Residence for Women had started life as a hotel, built in the late twenties. It was bought in the late sixties by one of the women's charities in New York and renovated into a residence for women. It was not intended as a long-term residence, since the rooms were still small hotel rooms. Rather, it was meant, as the description in the brochure at the front desk stated, as a 'safe haven for young women, offering reasonably priced monthly accommodations, a friendly atmosphere, and the security of knowing someone will be watching out for them.'

'I never heard of this place, did you?' Beckman asked Mac in a whisper. They were waiting at the front desk for the woman to get off the phone.

'Not this place specifically, no,' Mac whispered back. There was something about their surroundings that made whispering appropriate. 'But I'd heard about places *like* this. I just didn't think there were any left.'

Walking through the front door had been like walking through a time portal. The wood of the front desk and the archways was curved and striped in classic deco fashion, and the lobby was dimly lit with torchères. There were two sets of French doors, with the same deco feel to the woodwork, and frosted decorative glass. One set of doors was behind the front desk, apparently leading to an office, and the other set was opposite the desk, on the other side of the lobby.

The white-haired, stern-faced woman behind the desk finished her phone call and approached them.

'We'd like to see Agnes Leonard, please. Can you tell us what room she's in?' Beckman started.

'And why would you be wanting to know what room she's in?' the woman replied with a faint trace of a brogue.

Beckman was nonplussed. 'So we can talk to her, ma'am.' Then he realized he hadn't identified himself. He pulled out his badge. 'Sorry, ma'am. I forgot to tell you this is official police business.'

'Well, police business or no, any talking you do will be done down here in the parlor, young man. Men aren't allowed past the first floor.' She started for the phone on the counter behind her, but turned back toward him. 'Was Agnes expecting you?'

'No. No, ma'am,' Beckman said.

'We'll see if she's at home, won't we?' Her tone suggested that the next time he came to see a young woman at the West Side Christian Residence for Women, he would be well advised to call ahead.

Beckman looked at Mac in disbelief. Mac was wide-eyed, but a part of her wanted badly to laugh, and she was biting the inside of her lip to make sure that didn't happen.

Within a minute, the woman was off the phone. 'Agnes will be down shortly. Since she wasn't expecting you,' another pointed look at Beckman, 'she'll have to get dressed to receive visitors. You may wait for her in the parlor.' With a nod of her head, she indicated the double doors across the lobby.

Beckman and Mac backed away from the counter a few steps and then quickly turned and made a beeline for the parlor door. 'What the hell kind of place is this?' Beckman said, keeping his voice low. 'It seems like a convent or something.'

Mac nodded, but she was too taken with the interior of the parlor to do more than agree with him. The time-portal effect continued when you walked into the parlor; time had just moved up a little from the twenties. In the parlor it was 1950.

The parlor was a good-sized room. Big, heavy furniture – armchairs, sofas, and loveseats – was arranged into four or five 'conversation areas' complete with little side and coffee tables. The armchairs had doilies on the backs – actual doilies – and all the furniture had covers on the armrests. All the pieces were upholstered with substantial fabrics in varying shades of green and maroon, and the two colors were picked up again in the long flowered draperies that framed the windows that faced Thirty-fifth Street.

Mac knew the time set exactly because the room was an instant reminder of childhood visits to her great-aunt's house in West Hartford. According to family lore, that house had undergone one great and last redecoration in 1950. Aunt Phoebe apparently hadn't planned on living until 1979.

When Agnes Leonard walked into the room, the time machine cranked ahead a few more years. To the midseventies, and the 'dress for success' look, when women started to dress like small men. Agnes Leonard wore a woven polyester suit in a very dark navy blue, a white blouse with rounded points to the collar, a small string of graduated imitation pearls, and shoes that could only be called sensible.

The image matched perfectly with her letter, Mac thought. She'd gone over the letter when they stopped at the precinct, and she remembered why it had stood out from the rest. What had distinguished the intense, worshipful prose was that it had been conveyed in such a polished manner. The letter was written in impeccably even and beautiful script on high-quality paper. Similar letters, filled with adolescent emoting, had not alarmed her when they were written in ballpoint on sheets torn from school notebooks. Agnes Leonard's letter had set off little bells in her head.

Agnes herself was on the pretty side of plain. She had mousy brown hair worn in a well-cut dutch, bright blue eyes, and even features except for a too-wide mouth. She wore no discernible makeup except a pale pink lipstick, which unfortunately made the mouth look even a little bigger. She was of average height, maybe five-five, and carried an extra ten to fifteen pounds, which gave her a rather typical American build.

She had opened and closed the door to the parlor so quietly, it was a second or two before they noticed she had joined them. Beckman stood up and introduced himself and Mac. They had chosen one of the 'conversation areas' along the left wall of the parlor, the side away from the windows.

'Is this about my job application?' Agnes asked nervously. Her voice was light but not high-pitched. It was pleasant.

Beckman looked down at Mac quickly, then at Agnes Leonard. 'What job application was that?'

'I applied for a job through an agency, and they asked if I was bondable. I didn't know what that was and they said it had something to do with the police. But I didn't think you'd be coming here.' The last part was said with a tone of disapproval.

'No, Ms Leonard, this isn't about your getting bonded,' Beckman finally said.

'Well, can you tell me what this is about then, Detective?' Agnes said.

'Sure, sure,' Beckman said. 'We just want to ask you a few questions. Why don't you have a seat.' He pointed her toward an armchair that was next to the small two-seater loveseat where Mac sat. He took the opposite armchair. Agnes Leonard sat primly, legs angled to one side but uncrossed.

'Ms Leonard,' Mac started, 'we understand you are a fan of Peter Rossellini's. Is that right?'

'Yes, I love his music. I truly do.'

'Have you tried to see Rossellini since you arrived in New York?' Beckman asked.

'I'll be seeing his show Monday night, if that's what you mean.'

Mac again. 'Have you tried to learn where Mr Rossellini lives, or to go to the studios where he records, anything like that?'

'Goodness, no.'

'Ms Leonard,' Beckman said. 'When did you move to New York?'

She looked down at her hands. 'It was the end of March.'

'Why did you decide to come to New York?' he continued.

'I'm not sure. It seems that so much of what's exciting and important in the world happens here.' She looked down at her hands again. 'But it's all so overwhelming.'

Mac signaled to Beckman that she had a question. 'What was it that made you decide to come to New York at the end of March?'

Agnes Leonard looked directly at Mac, and there was pain in her eyes. 'My brother died. I'd been taking care of him for about a year and a half and he died. And I decided that I wanted someplace to begin again.'

Mac decided to back off the direct questioning and hoped that Beckman would pick up her lead. 'We're sorry to hear about your brother. Please accept our condolences.'

A quick nod. 'Thank you.'

'How has the first few months been for you? Finding your way around the city okay?'

'I'm amazed at how expensive things are. Like my room here. You could rent a whole big house with a yard for less than what I'm paying here. And it does take me a little while to get around, but I think that's because I won't go on the subway. I take the bus.'

'That's probably a good idea,' Beckman said agreeably.

Back to the questions. 'Ms Leonard,' Mac started in again, 'when you wrote to Mr Rossellini, you said that his songs sounded like they were meant for you alone. Can you tell us about that?'

'How do you know what I wrote to him?' she asked in a small, still voice.

'We've had to look into quite a bit of Mr Rossellini's fan mail. Can you tell us what you meant in your letters?'

Agnes Leonard looked down at her lap, and then lifted her head to talk to Mac. Her eyes were focused on something above and behind Mac's left shoulder, though. 'I should have said that there was one song that sounded like it was meant for me. Just one song. Maybe two. Some days when it got really hard I played "Keep On" over and over. And "What Will It Take." I like that one a lot, too.'

'When what got hard, Ms Leonard?' Mac asked softly.

Agnes's eyes snapped back to Mac's as soon as she'd started the question. Then she tipped her head back and stared up toward the ceiling. 'My brother was bedridden.' She paused. 'And he was in a lot of pain.' Another pause. 'And sometimes it seemed that no matter what I did, it wasn't enough. That was hard.'

It was obvious that she was trying desperately not to tear up, and both Mac and Beckman gave her a minute. But just a minute.

'Ms Leonard, do the names Metropolitan Productions or Ten Bridges mean anything to you?' Beckman started in again.

'The first one, yes. It's a video facility up on Fifty-seventh Street.' Both Beckman and Mac sat up a little straighter; 'video facility' was not a phrase that rolled off the tongue of your typical new arrival from small-town Kansas. 'The second one, no.'

'So you're familiar with Metropolitan?' Beckman continued.

'I haven't been there, no, but I've talked to a lot of people who work there.'

'Why would you be talking to people at Metropolitan?' Mac stepped back in.

'It's one of the companies that handles videos for us.' She corrected herself. 'I mean for Circus Maximus Records. I've been working as a temp there. For Mark Palmer. He's a vice-president.'

Mac could only hope that her face and Beckman's were maintaining neutral expressions. 'Gee, that sounds like a good job to land, Ms Leonard. How did you do it?'

'One of the women here recommended a temporary agency to me. I registered with them. And within a few days they called me.' She stopped and noticed what she took to be an expression of disbelief on Mac's face. 'I have very good skills. My mother and my teachers insisted on that. And when the agency called, they had two assignments, but the name of this company was familiar to me. The other one wasn't. So I went. And I think Mr Palmer has been pleased with me.' The last she added a bit defensively, still trying to make a point of her worthiness.

'I'm sure he is,' Mac said, turning slightly toward Beckman.

Beckman picked up the ball. 'Ms Leonard, could you tell us where you were last night and the nights of May nineteenth and the twenty-fourth?'

'Of course. I was here.'

'You answered that very quickly. Which is understandable for last night, but how about the others. You know for sure you were here?'

'Yes, every night but the fifteenth of April and the fifth of May, I've been here.'

'Tell us about those nights.' Mac was curious.

'Well, the fifteenth of April, I had just gotten my first paycheck from the agency, and another girl and I went out to the movies and to dinner.'

'And the fifth?'

'That was my birthday, and one of the girls upstairs found out and took me out for a drink. But I don't drink,' she finished with an apologetic smile.

'No more movies and dinner with your girlfriends?' Mac said.

Agnes Leonard sat a little straighter in her chair. 'Do you know by the time we got back here in a cab, it cost me forty dollars that night? Just for a movie and a dinner. I make good money at the agency, but still and all . . .' She looked at them intently. 'Forty dollars, that's crazy.'

A few minutes later Ms Agnes Leonard walked them back to the front desk, where she excused herself and headed for the elevators. The white-haired woman was still on guard duty and seemed surprised when Beckman approached the desk again. He asked if the residents were free to come and go at all times.

'Goodness, no,' she replied. She sounded exactly like Agnes Leonard. Or Agnes Leonard had sounded exactly like her.

'Okay, then, can you tell me how your system works?' Beckman said patiently.

'Very well. From five o'clock in the morning until one o'clock in the morning the ladies are free to come and go. But between the hours of one and five the front door is locked.' She stopped, pleased with her explanation.

Mac stepped in. 'But what if one of the ladies is doing something that will keep her out until, say, two o'clock?'

The woman turned slightly toward Mac. 'She can make arrangements with one of the other girls to sit at the desk and open the door when she comes in. But we discourage that.' The last was said with an expression that reinforced such discouragement.

'Is there any way for you to know that everybody is in, and that nobody is going to be stranded on the front stoop?' Mac continued.

The woman glared at her. 'There's the at-home sheet.'

'What's that?' Beckman got back into the conversation.

The woman sighed and pulled herself up straight.

'When our young ladies come home in the afternoon, or in the evening, we ask them to sign our at-home sheet. It tells us who is here and who isn't.'

'Do you keep these sheets going back a while?'

'Yes.' She stood still as a statue.

'Well, would you have the sheets for April and May?'

'Yes.' She nodded slightly, but didn't move.

Beckman could tell that she wasn't going to give an inch. 'Well, ma'am, do you think I could see them?'

The ma'am seemed to do the trick. 'Certainly,' she said. But from her it sounded like 'Sartenly.'

She reached under the counter and drew out an oversized ring binder, the kind that usually holds financial ledgers, and set it on the counter. Beckman turned it around and looked up the dates he was interested in. As he located each item he was looking for, he put his finger near it and let Mac take a look. He flipped through several dates and found that Agnes had signed in at various times between five-thirty and seven p.m. The two exceptions were the nights she'd mentioned. On April fifteenth, Agnes Leonard signed in at ten-thirty after her forty-dollar dinner. May fifth, at eight-fifteen. Not much of a birthday drink.

He went back to check the dates of special interest to them. May nineteenth, when Randy Vos had died at the beach club, she was signed out for only a brief period in the afternoon. May twenty-fourth, the night that Martin Jury died, she signed in at six-forty p.m. and apparently hadn't left. And last night, the night that Mickey Nahas drank his last drink, she had been safely ensconced at the West Side Christian Residence for Women at six-fifteen p.m.

TWENTY-TWO

June 2

The temperature was a skin-perfect seventy-two degrees at nine o'clock Sunday morning, and the humidity hadn't started to climb yet. Mac had carefully piled *The New York Times* sections next to her chair in order of preference. First came the main news section; a quick scan of the headlines could tell you if there was any earth-shattering news; it was amazing how infrequently there was. Next the Week in Review section, especially for the roundup of editorial cartoons. Then the book review and the magazine, then the Arts and Leisure section. It was a pleasant Sunday-morning ritual that would only have been enhanced if the *Times* would deign to run some comics.

She picked up her cup and sipped the lukewarm coffee. No breakfast this morning, just coffee. She was still coasting on last night's dinner, and she had to meet Sylvie and another woman for brunch at eleven-thirty. Lukewarm coffee was just fine.

On her way into the building late yesterday

afternoon, she'd been waylaid first by the doorman, who announced that some woman had stopped by, asking for her. No name, no note. Probably Sylvie, wondering what she'd be wearing tomorrow. The waylaying continued with her backyard neighbor Oliver, who announced that since it was so goddamn hot already, they – he and Sam – were having an early-summer barbecue and she must, absolutely must, come. 'But Oliver, I have so much to do,' she'd tried to excuse herself.

He stood in the doorway of his apartment, leaning against the frame. 'If you don't come, I'm simply going to blow wafts of barbecue smoke your way and it'll drive you crazy. So get your buns over here at six.' He stepped back quickly and closed the door before she had a chance to say no again.

She was glad she'd gone, too, even though she could have used the time to tame the chaos that now reigned in the apartment. The food was delicious – both Oliver and Sam were wonderful cooks – and Oliver had managed to corral a number of the other neighbors in the building. Everyone had raved over the unusual vinegar-based barbecue sauce that Oliver had prepared. He had a wonderfully involved story of how the recipe originated in his family down in Alabama after the Civil War, but given Oliver's capacity for embroidering the truth, one had to take the story with a barrelful of salt. But, Lord, that sauce was good. Just thinking about it could make a person drool. Mac thought about it, started to salivate, and reached for her coffee.

She'd managed to make the coffee, get the paper at the door, and make it out to the garden without looking at all the cartons that awaited her. The packing and stowing to be done had now grown to gargantuan proportions in her mind, and for a while she couldn't remember why she'd insisted on doing it herself. Then she remembered not only the warning about 'valuables,' but the painters who'd worked on her old apartment and the fine mist of white speckles that she'd had to remove from almost everything that she personally had not packed away.

Somewhere in between the book review and the magazine, she reasoned that if she returned from brunch by two, started right in, and didn't get distracted – a big *if* when packing – she'd easily be done by tomorrow afternoon. That settled, she returned to the magazine until just past ten.

If she was going to meet Sylvie and company at eleven-thirty, she had to leave by eleven-ten at the latest, and she wanted to give herself at least an hour to shower and dress. She wasn't in the mood to rush this morning. Just after ten, she was busy locking the doors that led from her office to the garden when the phone rang. She figured it was Sylvie, who would ask her what she was going to wear; there was a part of Sylvie that had never gotten beyond sophomore year of high school. Or it might be her sister, Whitney, who had a habit of calling

Sunday mornings to complain about her lack of social life in Boston. But when she got near the phone on her desk, it was the other line ringing. She answered it.

'Hello. I hope I didn't wake you.' The deep, throaty voice was Peter Rossellini's.

'No, not at all.' A pause. She didn't know quite how to take this call. Was it personal or professional? 'How are you?'

'I'm not sure.' His voice sounded different to her. Maybe it was just his early-morning voice. Then again, she'd never talked to him on the phone before. 'Maybe if you could just tell me what's going on, it would help.'

This was awkward. 'Have you talked to Lieutenant Buratti?' she asked.

'Yeah, he called a little while ago. Said he has to send somebody over this morning to get my fingerprints. Something about the tests they were running; they have to eliminate my fingerprints, I guess.'

'Of course. Was he able to tell you anything else?'

'Not really. He just said, "The investigation is proceeding."' Rossellini did a perfect imitation of Mario Buratti, whose voice Mac would not have thought was easily imitated. She laughed lightly. 'That's why I'm calling you,' he finished.

'I don't know how much I can tell you. I've talked to some people over the last few days, and Detective Beckman has talked to even more. He has two more to interview today, and he'll be calling me after that.'

'These are the people with the crazy letters you're talking to?' Rossellini's voice was getting impatient.

'Yes,' she replied.

'Well, has anything come up?'

'I can't say yes and I can't say no, Peter. We're still checking into some things.' She heard a sigh of frustration on the other end of the phone. A change of subject would help. 'How are things going at rehearsals?'

'I don't know. My concentration hasn't been great. Rachel's been bat-shit since yesterday. She and John Monaghan have added so much security they're practically singing backup with Prissy and the girls.'

'And how is Prissy doing on the platforms?' This was easier. They were in comfortable territory now.

'She and Jeremy came really close to a pistols-at-dawn shoot-out. But things are calming down a little. I think it'll work out. Hey, are you coming to the show?'

'I'd love to see it, yes, but I'm not sure when.'

'You just give Rachel or Michelle a call and let them know which one you want to come to. Assuming that there are any, of course.' The last phrase sounded discouraged.

Mac knew what he was talking about. 'How will you decide if you have to cancel the shows?'

'I'm not sure. Just go with the gut, I guess. Listen, I better let you go.' He stopped for a moment. 'You know, I think I just called to hear your voice.'

A quick laugh burst out of Mac before she could contain it. 'Ha! No, no, no, you don't understand. You're the one with the voice, Mr Llywelyn.'

Peter's laugh was soft but relaxed. 'I have a feeling I'm going to regret telling you about that . . .'

'Good luck, Peter. Bye.'

At one thirty-five, Sylvie closed the door on the cab, and she and Mac both dutifully waved as the cab pulled away. 'That was the longest two hours I've spent in years,' Sylvie said, her face still frozen in a lips-only smile. 'And look at me, my cheeks are gonna stay like this forever.'

She and Mac fell into a slow pace as they walked down Third Avenue. 'Kristine looks pretty good, doesn't she?' Mac finally said.

'Pretty good?' Sylvie replied. 'She looks goddamn fabulous.' They walked along quietly. 'You know what makes me crazy?' Sylvie finally broke the silence.

'What?' Mac said. Like Sylvie needed prompting.

'I don't want to be married right now. I particularly don't want to be married to the youngest partner in the history of Price Waterhouse in Chicago. But looking at those pictures of Kris's kids . . . And the house! Did you get a load of those pictures of her house? That backyard looks like a goddamn park!'

'Yes, it looks like a nice place,' Mac said calmly.

Sylvie knew Mac was being calm just to annoy

her. 'Does it ever make you wonder about what we're doing?'

'How do you mean?'

'Well, look at us. The three of us graduated together. And there's Kristine with her three perfect children, the gorgeous house, the cottage in Wisconsin, the country club, the cars.'

She stopped before Mac expected her to. 'And?' Sylvie apparently did need prompting.

'Here I am, thirty-two years old, living in a studio that I can barely afford, filling in playing Miss Receptionist or the Telemarketer from Hell, all for what? For my art?! What am I doing, hoping I can get ten lines on a soap opera twice a month so I can make my rent?'

'You're doing better than that, Sylvie. You're exaggerating.'

'And look at you . . . You, who I suspect has more money than God, are living in four rooms that are sort of a jumble – which, make no mistake, I would give my right arm to have – but which you got because you wanted some postage-stamp size garden, am I right?'

Mac nodded. It was scary how easily she could follow Sylvie.

'And our social life is nonexistent. You – you scare away most normal men anyway . . .'

'Thanks so much, Syl,' Mac muttered.

'Well, except for that bum Ivan, it's true. And me. Any man that is attracted to me I immediately suspect must have problems with his mother or something. What a pair.'

'Did you lose out on some audition last week?' Mac asked. Sylvie's really aggressive pessimism usually came out in such circumstances. She only grunted in reply.

Mac looked at the traffic coming up Third Avenue and spotted a cab. She hailed it, indicating that the cabbie should turn onto the side street. 'It's always so uplifting to get together with you like this, Sylvie. Really pumps me up for the week. Talk to you later.' She slid into the cab.

Sylvie was unswayed. 'You know I'm right, Mackenzie. And don't forget Friday!' she yelled before Mac closed the door.

Beckman's bones jolted as he drove over a rough patch on Route 17 heading into East Rutherford. The trip to Philadelphia had been for nothing. He'd found Cassandra Martin all right. He'd walked away knowing she wasn't a threat to Rossellini, just another goddamn flake.

But what a flake. The woman's whole house was nothin' but pictures of pop singers. Male pop singers, that is – starting with Elvis. Lots of Elvis. From the time you walked in the front door, through every room, including the bathroom, the walls were plastered with pictures of these singers – pictures from magazines and newspapers and a few snapshots that she must have taken herself. In her bedroom

even the ceiling was covered. And it wasn't like he'd
had to insist on seeing the rest of the house – she'd
started the grand tour the minute he was in the door.

Now Elvis he could understand. He personally
wasn't around for the young Elvis, but the 'Aloha
from Hawaii' thing was on television when he was
maybe twelve, and that whole outfit with the white
cape and all – hell, Elvis was right up there with the
other caped superheroes. He was a pretty good
singer, too, but his cape, man, that was a whole
attitude thing.

Elvis he could understand. She had some pictures
of the Beatles, too, especially McCartney, and he
understood them, too. But the others – jeez! Tom
Jones and Engelbert Humperdinck, who'd been
around forever. Barry Manilow and Rod Stewart –
hard to tell who was geekier-looking. He never could
understand why women went for them. Then there
was Phil Collins, whose forehead was racing to the
back of his head. Beckman had to agree that the
guy could sing, though, even if he was sort of
average-looking. She had pictures of George Michael
in his various looks; the women really seemed to go
for him whatever he looked like. And this Michael
Bolton guy had the women panting after him, too.
Go figure. Most of the pictures of Rossellini were in
the latest room she was covering – the kitchen. She
loved having her morning coffee with Peter
Rossellini, she told him.

Just a couple of turns after leaving the highway

brought him onto Morris's street. The neighborhood looked like it had been prosperous once. Good-sized brick homes, small yards. But here and there you could see a house in need of a paint job, a yard gone to weed. East Rutherford had been through a few changes in the last fifteen or twenty years. The changes hadn't been for the better on this street.

Mrs Morris answered the door. She was a thin woman, graying, probably in her early fifties, but she looked like she was midsixties. She sighed when she recognized Beckman and opened the door, which squeaked loudly. She'd just gotten the screens in the door yesterday, and she didn't remember it squeaking then. She'd have to take care of that today.

Beckman was back on the road within an hour. He was anxious to get to Buratti to find out if the lab guys had picked up anything at all from the Ten Bridges scene. Old Ronald D. Morris might turn out to be a hot one.

Questioning the kid, he got the same old routine. He was home all night last night, and his mother was his alibi. But when he got talking to the mother, she volunteered that she'd gone to sleep about nine o'clock; that was a little early for her, but it had been a long week and she was tired. After some questions about her sleeping habits, she finally admitted that she couldn't say if Ronald was in the house all night or not – not Friday night, not on the nineteenth, and not the night that Martin Jury died.

* * *

While Beckman was driving into the city, Buratti was prowling around the labyrinth that was the backstage area of Radio City Music Hall. The place was crawling with people today and that fact alone made him uneasy.

Monaghan was doing a pretty good job on security, though. Rachel and her assistant had redone and rechecked the lists, creating one for admittance to today's rehearsal, one for tomorrow's opening performance, and another for the party afterward. The guards had instructions that nobody, but nobody who wasn't on the list was to be admitted, and even then they were to check an ID on everyone whose name was listed.

One of the guys had even stopped Buratti and IDed him; his name wasn't on the list, and Monaghan had to clear him in personally. The guard's apologies had been profuse and loud enough to attract the attention of a feature writer from one of the daily newspapers.

The writer both heard the guard refer to Buratti as 'Lieutenant' and saw the last flash of his badge as Buratti was tucking it away. Sniffing out a story, he'd hustled right up to Buratti and asked why a police detective would be attending Rossellini's rehearsal.

Buratti knew they'd caught one big chunk of luck that the Rossellini connection to the two homicides hadn't leaked out, and he wasn't about to blow it with this guy. Hell, that was just what he *didn't* need at this point – a reporter on the entertainment beat trying to score big with his editor by breaking a story like this.

'I'm a fan,' growled Buratti as he walked by him. 'A big fan. Guy's got some pipes, y'know. But I'm here 'cause my brother-in-law's in the band. He owes me twenty bucks.'

Buratti poked around in the wings while the rehearsal was going on, studying the different vantage points a stalker might have if they went after Rossellini with a gun. He'd have to talk to Monaghan about some kind of metal detector for the backstage entrance.

Rehearsal broke a few minutes later, and Buratti went looking for Monaghan, only to see him and Rossellini heading right his way, with a third man that he recognized as one of the musicians.

'Lieutenant, Peter tells me you sent somebody over for his fingerprints this morning—'

'Yeah?'

'Well, you can call off the lab. The note wasn't from the guy you're lookin' for.' Monaghan looked at the musician impatiently. Buratti glanced at Rossellini, who simply looked tired, and then at the musician, who looked embarrassed.

'It wasn't? How do we know this?'

'Because Mason here sent it.'

'Ah, shit,' Buratti said, thinking of the calls he'd have to make to stop the tests.

'Honest, Lieutenant, I had no idea th—' Mason started.

'You had no idea of what, Mr Mason?' Buratti stepped toe-to-toe with Mason and got right into his face to let him have it. 'No idea that you're interfering with an official police investigation? No idea that I could take you in on an obstruction of justice charge?' That was pretty much bullshit, but Buratti enjoyed seeing the guy turn pale. 'No idea of what?'

'I just heard that they were checking into some of the letters that Peter gets, and I thought it was a goof,' Mason said sheepishly. 'Honest, I didn't know that anything serious had hap—'

'Tony overheard me telling Monaghan about the finger-printing just before we started rehearsing,' Rossellini interrupted. 'And as soon as we broke, he came up and told me that he was the one who planted the note. I got John, and we came right to you.'

Buratti wiped his hand down his face. Damn! He'd really thought they had something. 'Okay. What's done is done. Thanks for coming to me right away. And you, Mr Mason. You stay out of my way.'

'Absolutely, sir.' Mason was already backing away.

'Where are the phones?' Buratti asked. Monaghan pointed him toward the pay phones that were near the Fifty-first Street stage entrance.

Once he talked to the lab, Buratti called Mac to let her know that the note had turned out to be nothing. Not only that, but the lab hadn't turned up anything from the Ten Bridges scene either.

'Nothing at all?' Mac repeated. 'So the lab has nothing from Metropolitan and nothing from the bar? Nothing to determine the cause of death?'

'The ME on the case says she guesses that it's something that depresses the heart action, but she can't find it. Apparently, ninety-five to ninety-eight percent of the drugs or chemicals they look for in these autopsies, they find using one or two drug screens. They've run those and can't find what they're looking for. They found that Jury was taking sinus medication, and that Nahas apparently had the gout and was taking something for that, but they can't find anything that would stop the heart. There are another couple of drug screens, but they're top dollar to run, and the department head has to approve it 'cause of the budget restrictions. And before he'll do that, he has to review the previous tests, and he's not due back until Monday. Is that bureaucratic enough for you, Mac?' Buratti wasn't even attempting to mask the impatience in his voice.

'Well, at least there's something left to check out. It's not entirely a dead end.'

He was trying to work up some appreciation for that fact when Beckman came roaring through the stage door entrance, much to the dismay of the guard. 'I just stopped over at the precinct,' he said to Buratti. 'Have you seen this morning's reports?'

'Just a second, Mac,' he said into the phone, then waved to the guard that Beckman was okay. 'No, I came right here. Why?'

'They found a body down at the Seaport this morning.'

'Mac, did you hear that? Gotta go. Call you later.'

INTERLUDE FOUR

It was strange, picking out the clothes you were going to die in. Strange but comforting in a way.

She was sure now that Peter wouldn't take her with him; she'd thought it through last night. No sense being unrealistic. But she couldn't allow him to go off and leave without her. He was hers, didn't he see that? Didn't everyone see that? She would just have to kill him.

She packed the small bag, shoes on the bottom, top on the top, just like her mother had taught her. She arranged the clothes carefully; she wanted to look good when she got dressed tonight. She would wait until she got to the Music Hall to change.

She'd been sad last night when she first realized that she'd have to kill Peter. But this morning she'd cheered up when she decided she'd kill herself, too. Then they would die together.

Yes, she thought, a peaceful smile lighting her face. Peter and me. Together forever.

TWENTY-THREE

June 3

Mac didn't hear from Buratti again until close to noon on Monday. When he did call, he confirmed what she had suspected when she didn't hear from him later Sunday: The body at the Seaport was unrelated to this case.

Beckman was on his way to New Britain, Buratti told her, to question Lester Phillips, the man who'd accused Rossellini of stealing his songs. Once Phillips was questioned, that was it for the letters that Mac had picked out. It was either go back to the well or start rechecking all the people who'd been questioned so far. Maybe there were some alibis that wouldn't hold up to much inspection.

Just considering the alibis that she knew about, Mac realized that there were some pretty good-sized questions. Just how difficult would it be for Agnes Leonard to dodge the sign-in procedure at the West Side Christian Residence for Women? And if Ronald D. Morris's mother was as exhausted in fact as Beckman's description of her appearance indicated, would she really know if her son was up and out of the house after she'd gone to bed? And then there was Judith Stone: home alone.

Mac tried to shift her concentration back to the task at hand. The painters were due tomorrow at eight a.m. She'd worked yesterday into the night, and had gotten her bedroom taken care of. She'd stayed up too late, but somewhere she'd gotten stuck sorting all her summer clothes. They were painting her closets, too, and that meant that everything, but everything, was going into cardboard boxes.

Beside her office, the only other space that wasn't being painted was the second bathroom that was next to her office, since she decided that having both bathrooms out of commission at the same time was too stupid to consider. Her available wardrobe for the next few days was hanging from the shower rod in the smaller second bathroom, and she had moved all of her cosmetics and toiletries in there this morning. How strange to have a four-room apartment and to feel like you were living in twenty square feet of it.

By midafternoon she'd finished up the kitchen and dining area, leaving only basic dishes and utensils for the next few days. It looked like she was going to be taking advantage of the take-out restaurants in the neighborhood for a while.

By quarter to four she relaxed a little bit. There was only the living room still to do, and there wasn't all that much to pack up in there, but what there was would take a little longer. She had some vases, small picture frames, and other *objets d'art* that she wanted safely tucked away. And once she wrapped up the framed pieces from the wall, she wanted to be sure to patch the holes. No telling anymore if the painters would do it.

After a quick iced coffee break, she got her roll of brown paper and a fresh roll of tape and cleared space on the dining table to wrap the framed posters and paintings. She'd had the radio on all day and it was time for a change. She turned on the television and flipped between 'Oprah Winfrey' and 'Donahue' until she could figure out what today's topics were; she passed on both of them.

Remote control in hand, she scanned through the channels until she came to MTV. She listened for a moment, but the video playing was from one of the harder hard rock bands and she certainly wasn't in the mood for that. She continued through the channels until she came to VH-1. A Billy Joel song was playing, one she particularly liked. Think of it as radio with pictures, she said to herself as she adjusted the volume and returned to her wrapping project at the table.

For the next hour, she watched and listened. Well, she started out listening, but her curiosity was piqued after just a few videos. Three or four current songs played, and then a song from ten years back. The older video already looked dated, even to her untutored eye. The newer ones had a polish to them, a look that the older one didn't have. The cross-editing of black and white with color, which she had found so interesting in the first of Peter's videos that she'd watched, was actually quite common in the videos of more recent vintage. As was the rapid and constant editing of the images. The eye barely had time to adjust to a new image when yet a newer one replaced it. It was almost dizzying.

She was entranced with a video that included some animation. During most of the song, the camera held the singer, a beautiful young blond woman, in a tight close-up; when the background singers chimed in during the chorus, they were represented by tiny animated figures who hopped in a halo around the singer's face. Mac felt herself smiling and waiting for the next chorus to come up.

She glanced at her watch and stood up in a flash. This stuff was addictive. It was now just past five and she'd only gotten one framed piece wrapped in the last hour. She turned her back on the screen and headed back to the table; the first few notes of the next song were familiar, but she steadfastly kept her eyes on the oversized piece she was trying to wrap up. It wasn't until she heard the voice join in that she looked up at the screen. It was Peter singing 'Look This Way.' This was the video they'd shot up at the beach club.

Mac walked away from the table and sat in the chair directly in front of the screen. It was different, somehow, seeing his video this way, in the context of all the others. It seemed more immediate.

She'd watched the video before, studied it actually, but now she sat back and admired the figure on the screen in an entirely different way. Peter's shirt was open well down his chest, and his pants were rolled up to midcalf as he waded in the shallow water near the small breaking waves. He got to the chorus of the song:

Look this way, you'll see the man who loves you
Look this way, you'll see the man who cares
Look this way, I can't do it for you
Darlin', just look this way.

The scenes of him alone on the beach were intercut with others of a group of five or six people, including one stunning young woman who continually ignored Peter. The group was picnicking on the beach; the woman was apparently with one of the other men, but the Rossellini character was carrying the torch for her. The video worked very well since the little scenario reinforced the message of the song: Love might be waiting right next to you if you just look that way.

Mac watched the whole video appreciatively, enjoying the pictures as well as the music, much to her own surprise. As Peter sang the last notes of the song, the tide and credits appeared in the lower left side of the screen. That Mac had seen before. But what she hadn't seen before was an emblem in the lower right side of the screen, an emblem that said 'World Premiere.' What? What did that mean?

She knew what the words meant, of course. But they didn't make sense. How could they still be premiering a video that was a couple of months old? 'Look This Way' had been filmed in March. Surely they'd shown it by April, or the beginning of May at the latest. Okay, maybe it was only a month old. But it had to have been on at least by early May; it had to have been airing before Randy Vos died at the beach club. Unless . . . unless . . .

She looked at her watch. Five-fifteen. Maybe she could catch her. She dialed Rachel Bennet's office. Linda Campbell, the receptionist, recognized Mac's name immediately. This girl was on her toes.

'No, I'm sorry, Dr Griffin, Ms Bennet's over at the Music Hall already. Can I take a message for you?'

Much as she hated to, she had to ask the question. 'Is Michelle there?' She might snarl at me, thought Mac, but she might know the answer to the question.

'No, she's over at the Music Hall, too. Sorry.'

'Do you expect to be hearing from Rachel soon?' Mac asked.

'I think she will be calling in, yes. But I'm not certain just when.'

'Ask her to call me, please.' Mac gave her number. 'And ask her to get to me as soon as possible.'

Mac depressed the button on the phone and dialed a familiar number. Sylvie was always informed on most anything in the entertainment world. Maybe she could tell her.

Sylvie answered after a few rings. Mac put the question to her quickly. Sylvie screeched, 'Mackenzie Griffin, you're working on a case that involves Peter Rossellini and you didn't *tell* me? I may never speak to you again!'

'Sylvie, tell me what the World Premiere thing means.'

'Well, if you're going to be pushy about it, it means that they just started showing the video, and it might mean they have an exclusive on it as well.'

'Just started showing . . . like when?'

'Hard to tell. They might have an exclusive for ten days, two weeks, a month. Now I don't know if they'd keep billing it as a world premiere, but they might. So tell me, what's he like?'

'Talk to you later, Sylvie. Thanks.' She replaced the phone in its cradle.

She walked into her office. The videocassettes that Rachel Bennet had given her were still sitting on her desk. Fortunately they hadn't been wrapped or packed away. She took them all out of their cases and looked at the labels. They all had only one date on them, the same date – May 15. That must have been the day these copies were made. There was no way to tell the sequence of the videos looking at the cassettes.

Rachel Bennet called at twenty to six. 'What is it, Dr Griffin?' she said brusquely. 'I'm terribly busy.'

Mac explained how she'd just seen the broadcast of the video and asked her question.

'Yes, it just started over the weekend. Saturday night, seven o'clock I think. They were doing a special show on acts touring this summer and we authorized the first airing for that show. It went into their regular rotation yesterday.'

'Ms Bennet, this video was finished a few months ago, right?'

'That's right, around the middle of April. Doctor, I really must be going.'

Mac grabbed the phone a little tighter. 'Just one more thing, please. Who would have had access to the video before this weekend?'

'Well, besides our office, the people at the record company, up at Metropolitan where they finished the edit. And the people at VH-1 would have had it since last Monday or Tuesday.' Her voice changed and she hissed an 'I'll be right there' to someone other than Mac. 'Doctor, I hate to be rude, but I must run.' The line clicked dead.

Mac stood for a moment, holding the quiet phone, concentrating. She set down the phone, went for her briefcase, and dug out her notebook. She found another number and dialed it.

Marianne Santangelo answered on the second
ring. Mac could tell that she was holding the baby,
since the baby's cry came through the phone lines
clearly.

'Marianne, I hate to bother you,' Mac said after
identifying herself. 'Did you print a—' She stopped
midquestion. 'Marianne, why aren't you at Radio
City for Peter's opening?'

'Tonight's for all the big shots. A couple of the fan
clubs in the area got blocks of tickets for tomorrow
night and Wednesday, so I'm going to those shows.
Why?'

'Just curious. Listen, did you do an article about
the video they shot up at the Colony Beach Club in
Connecticut?'

'Yeah. Why?'

'Did you print a picture with it?'

'I think so, why?' She tried to hush the baby.

'This is very important, Marianne. What picture
did you print? Was Peter in the outfit – the costume
he wore walking on the beach or not?'

'Geez, I'm not sure. Let me go look. Hold on a
minute.' Mac could hear the baby's cry receding and,
after a few moments, footsteps approaching the
phone. Marianne must have left the baby in the other
room.

'Dr Griffin? I got that issue in front of me. Yeah,
we printed a picture of Peter and the director
along with the manager of the Beach Club. And no,
Peter's not in costume. He's got on what looks like

273

a medium to dark shirt, I can't really tell 'cause these are black and white, y'know? Anyway, he's wearing a denim jacket and jeans, I think. Does that help you?'

'It does, Marianne. Thank you.'

Randy Vos was killed at the beach club a little over two weeks ago. No one outside the business would have seen the video until Saturday. And now she knew that not even the subscribers to the fan club magazine would have known how Peter was dressed in the video. Yet Vos had died wearing clothes that looked like the ones Peter wore in the video.

It was getting close to six. Fat chance Buratti would be at the precinct, but she decided to give it a try. No luck. He was on his way to Radio City.

She washed up quickly. There was little in the way of available clothes. Radio City would have to see her in her painting overalls, that was all. But she managed to find a fresh oversized T-shirt that fit under the overalls, and then threw on a lightweight man's workshirt. Looking like Little Orphan Annie, she was out of her apartment by five after six, hailing a cab.

She settled into the backseat of the taxi and stared unseeingly out the window. All the time they'd spent checking out the crank letters, all a waste. It wasn't some overzealous fan they were after. It was somebody on the inside.

Somebody on the inside. Just the kind of person

for whom the red carpet was being rolled out tonight. Just the kind of person who would have no trouble getting past security.

TWENTY-FOUR

It was a torturous ride uptown. Mac had forgotten just how long the 'rush hour' lasted in New York. The taxi inched crosstown through midtown traffic and then the last few blocks up Sixth Avenue.

It was six thirty-five by the time she got out of the taxi. A few fans were already gathering in front of the main entrance, and a few more stood outside the stage door entrance on Fifty-first Street.

She presented herself to the guard at the stage entrance, and it took some time even to get the man to pay attention to her. Maybe she should have changed out of her painter's overalls. She finally pulled out her ID.

'Look, I'm Dr Mackenzie Griffin. I'm a consultant to the police department on security matters.' No sense telling this guy the whole story. Who'd believe it, anyway? 'I've been working on a case with Mr Monaghan and I need to see him right away.'

The guard hesitated another long minute and said, 'Okay, I'll send somebody for him. You stand right here.' He pointed to a place on the floor directly to the side of the podium he stood behind, and Mac moved into exactly the position he'd indicated.

She waited, and while she waited she watched as the big door onto the sidewalk opened and closed repeatedly. The people who'd gathered on the side had attracted even more people, and there was now a crowd of fifty or more.

The notion of absolute security becomes absurd once you start studying a crowd, Mac thought. If somebody really wants to take you out, they can, if they're willing to give their life for it.

Ten long minutes later, Monaghan finally walked toward the guard's podium. 'What're you calling me down here for?' he said brusquely to the man.

'I called you down, Mr Monaghan,' Mac said. 'Mackenzie Griffin. We met over at the rehearsal hall on Friday?'

Monaghan stared at her for a while before it clicked. He sized up her clothes questioningly, then looked back at her face. 'Yeah, now I remember. Dr Griffin, isn't it?'

'That's right. I called the precinct and they told me that Lieutenant Buratti was due here. I need to speak to him as soon as possible. Do you know if he's arrived?'

'Buratti? Yeah, I seen him just a couple of minutes ago. Come on in, and we'll check.' They went off down the hall.

They started down the first corridor at a good pace.

'We need to find Rachel Bennet and get her list of backstage passes and the people invited to tonight's party as well,' Mac told him.

'Why, what's going on?' Monaghan asked.

'It'll be easier to tell you both together. Where did you say Buratti was?'

He pointed her in the right direction to look for Buratti and he went in the opposite one to look for Rachel and her list. They agreed on where to meet.

Mac worked her way down the hall. This place was confusing enough before, when it was empty. Now it was jammed with people. Peter had told her that they'd added strings and horns to the band, so there were more than twenty musicians in the show now, plus Peter and the three girls. Plus all the stagehands and technicians. It was madness.

A video crew was roaming the hall as well, catching some decidedly candid backstage shots. She saw a couple of people with press passes, and then four people who looked amazingly out of place, in the company of one tall, thin, satin-jacketed hyperkinetic man. As soon as she heard his voice, she recognized him as one of the disc jockeys on a popular radio station. She glanced at the tags on their passes. These were the contest winners Rachel had been talking about; from their expressions, they thought they were in Oz.

Jeremy appeared around the corner. He was

walking directly toward her, accompanied by a nervous-looking young man who clutched a small tape recorder to his chest. If he recognized her, he didn't show it. He never broke stride. ' . . . doesn't get those fucking lighting cues right at the end, I'll personally tear every hair out of his head one by one,' Mac heard him say as he passed her. The nervous young man whispered something into the tape recorder, concentrating hard on whispering and walking at the same time.

Mac stopped at an intersection of corridors and looked down to her left. That hallway was less crowded, but she didn't see Buratti. She spotted Michelle Wenzel at the far end of the corridor, just turning to her right. Mac considered yelling out to her, but in the seconds she took to consider it, Michelle disappeared around the corner. No big loss; there was not much likelihood that the churlish Ms Wenzel would be of assistance, anyway. Suddenly the door closest to where she was standing opened and Prissy stepped into the hallway.

'Hi there, girlfriend. I didn't know you was coming to tonight's show.'

Mac started to mumble a reply, but it was too long a story. 'Yeah,' she finally said, but Prissy wasn't really paying attention.

'You going to see Peter?'

'Oh, is this the way to his dressing room?' Mac asked.

Prissy looked at her with one eyebrow arched.

'Like you didn't know.' She gave Mac a thorough once-over, sizing up the outfit.

'I don't mean to be critical, honey, but ain't this look a little *too* casual?'

'I'll tell you all about it sometime, Prissy. Listen, have you seen . . .'

Just then Monaghan spotted her from down the hall and called her name. Buratti was next to him. She excused herself from Prissy and trotted toward them.

'I found an empty dressing room over here,' Monaghan said. 'It'll be a lot quieter for us.'

Monaghan flipped on the lights. One overhead light came on, as well as a whole line of bulbs over the mirror that extended from one side of the room to the other.

From the look on his face and his body language, Mac could tell that Buratti was enjoying his brush with show business. 'Poor Beckman,' he said as he half-sat on the counter that ran the length of the wall under the mirror. 'He hauls ass all the way up to New Britain today, gets to the station, and the guys tell him Lester Phillips slipped out on them. Seems he headed up to Bangor to see his brother without telling the locals.'

There was a streak in Buratti that was relishing this story. 'So he gets back here a little after five, hot, tired. I send him out on a dinner break a while ago, but I didn't know they have some spread set up right down the hall. Some great catering company,

I tell you. Better than most weddings I been to.' Buratti moved slightly as Monaghan settled in next to him. 'Okay, Mac, whaddya got?'

'I was watching VH-1 this afternoon—'

'Don't rub it in, Mac. Some of us got to work for a living,' Buratti cracked and looked toward Monaghan to see if his joke was appreciated.

'Listen to me, Mario. The "Look This Way" video, the one that was shot up at the Colony Beach Club . . .'

'Yeah, what about it?'

'It just premiered over the weekend.'

'And?' Buratti asked.

'The "Look This Way" video was broadcast for the first time on Saturday. That means that prior to Saturday, only somebody inside the business could have seen the video. According to Rachel Bennet, only somebody at the management office, the video place, or the record company. And since Randy Vos was killed a little over two weeks ago, it means that we've been chasing down blind alleys.'

'Holy shit . . .' Buratti said.

'Whaddya mean about the blind alleys?' Monaghan asked.

Buratti stood up straight. 'What she means is that we've been talkin' to every loose screw this side of the Monongahela River who's ever written to Rossellini, fans, all kind of oddballs. But none of them could've seen the video, and Randy Vos bought it dressed like Rossellini was in the video. Am I right so far, Mac?'

'Right.'

'So here we are, thinkin' we got Rossellini in a pretty secure place for tonight, 'cause only people authorized by the management office are allowed in.' He stopped talking and twisted his lower lip in a grimace of concentration.

Monaghan shook his head. 'Holy Christ, if this don't beat all.' Buratti paced the small room briefly, then stopped and looked directly at Mac. 'How'd we miss this?'

'We heard that the video was done in March. It never occurred to us. All the people we've talked to in the business have been seeing the video for a couple of months, so it's old news to them, too.' Mac paused. 'I even listened to most of his album. I never noticed that "Look This Way" wasn't one of the songs I was hearing.'

Buratti paced again. 'Okay, next step?' he finally said.

'The list, I think,' volunteered Mac.

'Yeah, we need to get a hold of Rachel's list and see who's been cleared for here and for the party,' Buratti started.

'You talked to the people at Metropolitan and the record company, didn't you, Mario?' Mac asked. When he nodded yes, she continued, 'Anybody come to mind that we should be looking out for?'

Buratti thought for a moment. Nobody from Metropolitan occurred to him. That Pfeiffer guy over at Circus Maximus had seemed enthralled with

Martin Jury, but not particularly with Rossellini.

'Let's stop guessing and get the list.' Monaghan stood up and walked toward the door. Once outside the door, he checked the number. 'Okay, let's spread out. This place is like a maze. Rachel could be on the other side of that wall and we'd never know it. Let's all check back here at' – he looked at his watch – 'seven-fifteen. That gives us almost fifteen minutes to find her. We'll meet back here in Room 108 if we find her or not.'

'Okay, we'll spread out and find her and her list. But relax, Monaghan. There's no reason to guess that whoever is doing this is going to do him in tonight. Is there, Mac?'

She looked down at the way she was dressed. How to explain why she shot out of her apartment like someone had lit a fuse under her. But reason? No, it wasn't a reason, it was a feeling. 'It's a perfect opportunity. No reason to think they're *not* going to.'

The chaos in the halls had gotten worse in the last ten minutes. It seemed like each person in the show had invited their entire family backstage. If this was the result of a tightened security list, Mac thought, she didn't want to see what the usual crowd would be like.

She ran into the video crew again. This time they were taping Prissy, Martha, and Julie parading down the corridor in their costumes. The three women were dressed in form-hugging sequined dresses that had chiffon capes flowing back from the shoulders. The sequins and the chiffon had graduated hues, darkest at the bottom and lightest at the shoulders. Each dress was in a different primary color.

Prissy spotted her coming down the hall again. 'Hey, Mackenzie, look at this.' She lifted the chiffon capelet out to the sides. The other women followed suit, all for the benefit of the video crew. 'We our own rainbow coalition,' Prissy said with a laugh.

Mac smiled at the joke, and asked Prissy if she'd seen Rachel. She hadn't and Mac continued around the maze.

She managed to find her way back to Room 108 at seven-fifteen on the dot. Buratti was just walking down the hall. Monaghan was there already. In his hand was a clipboard with the lists. 'Where's Rachel?' Mac asked.

'I thought this would be easier without her, so I told her some story about checking the door,' Monaghan said.

'I owe you one for that,' Buratti replied.

Buratti and Mac stood on either side of him, scanning the list.

Most of the names meant nothing to Mac. But close to the bottom, a name leapt off the page. Agnes Leonard!

'Oh my God, how did she get on there?'

'Who, Mac? Whaddya see?'

'Agnes Leonard. She's the one from Kansas Beckman and I talked to. She said she was working temp for the record company, but I never figured that would give her access to a place like this!'

'Have you seen her in the halls? What does she look like?' Buratti's voice was picking up speed. It usually did when he sensed he was on a roll.

'No, I haven't seen her. And looks? She's about five-five, mousy brown hair, very ordinary looking.' That alone would make her stand out in this crowd. The only people she'd seen tonight that Agnes would fit in with were those radio contest winners. She concentrated hard to remember them. No, she wasn't in that group.

'Would this Agnes Leonard have seen the video?' Monaghan asked. He was a little lost.

'I guess she could have. She told us she was temping at Circus Maximus Records. I'm sure that's one of the first places the video would be seen.' Mac paused. 'Wait, that video crew that's here. They're from the record company?'

'Yeah, I think so,' Monaghan said.

'They should be able to tell us if Miss Kansas is here. That what you're thinkin', Mac?'

The three set off down the hallway and almost ran into the video crew as soon as they turned the corner. Buratti quickly determined that one Steve Vartan was head of the crew. But he had no idea where Agnes was.

'Yeah, we put her name on the list when it looked like my regular assistant was going to miss it.' He looked toward a thin young woman, hardly more than a girl, who was toting several black nylon bags. 'But Marilyn felt better by late this afternoon and showed up right on time. Poor Agnes – she was so excited. Thought she was gonna faint when we asked her if she wanted to help on the crew.'

'Was there any particular reason you asked Agnes Leonard?' Mac inquired.

'She's been working for Mark Palmer for a couple months now. She's great. A great worker. Nothin' she won't do to help you. That's a nice attitude to see. Thought she could help us, that's all.'

'Do you know if she was planning on coming to the show tonight?' Mac asked. 'As part of the audience, I mean. I think she mentioned that she was planning on seeing the show.'

'Gee, I don't know about that,' Vartan replied. 'Sorry.' He headed back to his crew.

They were near an intersection of two corridors, and Monaghan got the other two out of the flow of traffic to the side of the hall. 'I'm going around to the Fifty-first Street door and see if my guy remembers her coming in. Her name being on the list and all, she might have tried to get in that way.'

'Good. Good idea,' Buratti said. 'Do that. It would help to know if she's really here.' Monaghan took off down the hall. Mac suspected he was headed the wrong way to get to the Fifty-first Street entrance, but she was so turned around herself, she couldn't be sure.

'Where the hell is Beckman?' Buratti said to

himself and to Mac. 'I'm going to call the precinct, see if anybody knows where he is, then we're going out front to see if the guys in the lobby spotted anything.' He walked toward the pay phone that was down a few feet on the opposite side of the corridor. Mac leaned against the corner of the wall.

Even given all the information they had now, Agnes Leonard hardly seemed like a credible suspect, Mac thought. It was just too hard to believe that sensible-shoes Agnes was the type to go around killing people.

Mac had to straighten up when a woman whooshed around the corner quickly and bumped into her. She was a stunning woman, tall but with good-sized heels on, a mass of reddish blond curls. Her manner of dress seemed exotic to Mac, but it was probably tame for the circumstances: dark-toned stockings, a very short black skirt, and a generously cut denim jacket with a sequined flower design on the back with what looked like a shiny tank top underneath, and a good-sized bag slung over her shoulder. The strong scent of a perfume trailed after her, and only hit Mac once the woman was already a few steps down the hall.

Funny. The woman seemed vaguely familiar. Maybe it was one of the models Mac had seen in Rossellini's videos. The makeup certainly fit in with that possibility. Heavy but well done. She tried to think back to the specific videos, but couldn't recall a woman who resembled the one she'd just seen.

Mac rubbed her hip lightly. When that woman had come around the corner, it was her purse, and a heavy one at that, that had hit Mac square on the hipbone. Thinking back, it was a large metal zipper pull that had hit her. No, it was more like an ID, because it said 'Mickey.'

The chill of recognition shivered down her spine, and Mac stood bolt upright. That exotic creature who'd just passed her in the halls was Michelle Wenzel! The transformation of the Michelle she had seen at Rachel Bennet's office, the severe, even dowdy Michelle, into the exotic Mickey was more than surprising – it was alarming! Now she knew who the threat to Peter Rossellini was. She knew who the killer was. Michelle. And she'd been headed in the direction of Peter's dressing room!

Waving for Buratti to follow her, she darted down the hall. At the next turn, she stopped and located herself. She was next to the dressing room the three singers were sharing. Just as Mac approached the door, it opened and Prissy stepped into the hall. Mac grabbed her by the shoulders and turned her until they were face to face. 'What's the matter with you, girl? You're going to mess my dress!' Prissy said disgustedly.

'Which dressing room is Peter in?'

'Honey, we goin' on in twenty minutes, it's a little late to be goin' visitin' . . .'

'Which room *exactly*, Prissy?' Mac's tone of voice left no room for doubt.

'Last one on the left down there. The one closest to the stage.'

'See that man, Prissy?' She indicated Buratti with a glance. 'Get to him and tell him that's where I'm going! Okay?'

Prissy nodded solemnly. 'Okay.'

Mac raced down the hall and stopped outside the last door on the left. She put her head against the door to see if she could hear anything; the metal felt cool against her cheek. She heard a voice, faint at first, and then stronger. It was Peter. She heard the next part clearly. He said, 'Michelle, what is this? What are you doing?'

Mac positioned herself with her hand on the door, counted to three, and threw the door open.

'No, no, not you!' Michelle cried when she saw Mac. Peter looked equally startled to see Mac burst into the room, and he saw Michelle start to react.

'No, Michelle, no. It's okay. It's gonna be okay,' he said soothingly.

Mac looked around the room quickly. Peter was standing in front of the long counter that ran across the width of this room just like in the other dressing room. He stood with his back to the mirror, in bare feet, his shirt pulled out of his trousers, and open halfway to the waist. Mac noticed that he was trying to calm Michelle down. Then she saw why: Michelle had a gun in her right hand. Now she thrust the gun toward Mac.

'What's *she* doing here?' Michelle said loudly. She moved the gun more vehemently in Mac's direction.

'I asked her to come, Michelle. I asked her.' Rossellini was doing his best to keep her calmed down. Mac wondered if he realized how very critical that was.

'You asked her?! *You asked her?!*' Michelle was getting more and more excited. Mac could smell the heavy perfume that she'd first noticed out in the hallway. The scent was overtaking the room, released by Michelle's increased heart rate and body heat.

Mac decided to step in. Surely, some of the hostage negotiating techniques she'd taught would be applicable here. 'Michelle, I—'

'Shut up, bitch.' Michelle stared her straight in the eye. 'I'm not talking to you.'

Mac looked at Rossellini quickly, and with her eyes and the slightest shake of her head tried to communicate that they needed to be very, very careful with Michelle.

Michelle let the gun drop slightly, her arm moving down in a gesture of fatigue. 'No more, Peter, I can't take it anymore. I won't take it anymore.' She edged back from the center of the room, toward the far wall, turning her attention to Rossellini. 'I saw you. At the office. Right in front of me. Your eyes all over her. When *I'm* the one who's always doing for you, *I'm* the one who's always taking care of everything.'

'Yes, you are, Michelle. You do, and I've always

appreciated that.' Rossellini's voïce was calm, and his tone sincere. He'd apparently figured out, without Mac's assistance, that he needed to do whatever it took, say whatever he needed to say to placate Michelle.

Mickey/Michelle watched him intently, her eyes starting to tear up. 'It's just not fair, Peter. It's not right. After all we've been through together, after all I've done.'

Rossellini looked at her intently, then dropped his head and looked toward Mac. Mac squeezed her eyes shut and shook her head slightly, trying to communicate that he shouldn't look in her direction.

'What are you looking at her for?' Michelle spit out. 'Was she there when you split with Judy and were hanging around the office day and night? Huh?' The tears that had been building overflowed her eyes, leaving tracks of the dark mascara as they ran down her cheeks. 'Was she there making sure you got your wake-up call so you wouldn't miss your first album sessions?'

'No, Michelle—' Rossellini started to reply.

She wouldn't tolerate the interruption. 'Was she there to buy the cake and champagne for you – and clean up afterward – when you got your Grammy nomination?'

Rossellini shook his head, looking down at the floor.

'Look at me, Peter,' Michelle said vehemently, pointing the gun directly at him. 'Look at me. I made

myself over for you. Just like the girl in the video.'
She spread her arms and arched her body into a
caricature of a fashion-model pose, the gun held high
like it was the latest accessory. She returned to her
normal posture after a few seconds, and the gun was
now pointed toward Peter again. 'But you didn't
notice, did you? Did you!?'

'I've never seen you like this, Michelle. You
look . . . you look great.'

Mac watched intently, feeling like she was on the
sidelines of some high-stakes competition. Saliva was
accumulating in her mouth, and she tried to swallow
as silently as possible.

Michelle slouched, shifting all her weight to one
hip, but the arm that held the gun was still upraised.
'I tried to get along without you, Peter, I really did,'
she said, brushing away the tears from her cheeks
with the palm of her left hand, leaving smudges of
gray streaked across her face. 'I tried to make it work
with the others, but it just couldn't work, so that's
why I had to kill them.' She spoke in a very matter-
of-fact voice, with just a trace of impatience. 'They
weren't you.'

Rossellini tried to control his surprise at the
confession, but Mac could see his eyes widen. 'They
could never be you,' Michelle said, her voice
softening. 'But now you're leaving. For weeks.
Months. I'd never get to see you. Never get to talk to
you . . .'

Mac noticed that Michelle's eyes had gone glassy,

appearing unfocused, and her voice stayed soft, with a peculiar tone to it, as if she weren't really talking to Peter Rossellini but rather repeating a conversation that she'd had with herself many times before.

'And I can't let that happen, Peter,' Michelle kept on. 'I can't. What would I do without you?' The voice was getting stronger again, and she looked straight into Peter's eyes. 'That's why it will be better to end it here. Tonight. Together.'

Rossellini's shock didn't show in his voice at all. 'Now, Michelle,' he said in a placating tone, 'I never knew you were interested in me. Now that I know—'

'DON'T LIE TO ME! DON'T PATRONIZE ME, YOU SONOFABITCH!' Michelle screamed, straightening her arm so that the gun was even closer to him. 'You think I don't know what you're doing? Do you think I'm stupid?'

The room was quiet for several seconds. Mac broke the silence. 'No, no one thinks you're stupid, Michelle. Or should I call you Mickey?'

'Call me whatever you want, bitch,' Michelle said, looking sideways at Mac for an instant. 'It won't make any difference.' She turned more toward Mac. 'You think I don't know about you, too, don't you? I saw how you came in, with your fancy clothes and your perfect hairdo, and that oh-so-cultured voice. But you were just after him. You were just going to take him right away from me, weren't you?'

Placating didn't seem to work. Maybe cool and rational would help. It was worth a try. 'Michelle,' Mac said as she inched toward the back of the room, away from where Rossellini was standing. 'You know better than that. You know I was brought into this case by the police, by Lieutenant Buratti. I'm a consultant, that's all.' She looked toward Rossellini to make sure he saw what she was doing. 'Mr Rossellini and I have a professional relationship. That's all.' Michelle was in between them now, her eyes moving nervously from one to the other. 'That's all,' Mac repeated and she signaled Peter with her eyes.

They both rushed her at once, Mac grabbing the right arm and straightening it, Rossellini taking hold of Michelle's left arm and shoulders, trying to push her to the floor. Mac had both hands on the woman's arm, trying desperately to find the nerve that would release Michelle's grasp on the gun.

There was a knock at the door, and Buratti walked in, seeing the three bodies in a struggle, just as the gun dropped to the floor and discharged, sending a bullet into the wooden baseboard.

'Judas Priest, Mac. What the hell's going on?'

Mac stood up, leaving Rossellini kneeling on the floor. Michelle was cradled in his arms. He held the woman tight to his chest. Through her sobs you could just make out the words. 'I love you, Peter, I've always loved you, always loved you.'

TWENTY-FIVE

It had been a long, sad evening. Mac arrived at the opening-night party close to midnight. She was there only because she'd promised Peter and Rachel she'd come and fill them in on the initial interrogation of Michelle.

She presented herself to the doorman at the well-known club on Fifty-seventh Street. At first, the doorman had assessed her disdainfully, but Mac could hardly blame him. She was still wandering around in painter's overalls and a workshirt. But the doorman snapped to when he heard her name. 'Yes, ma'am, Doctor. Ms Bennet said to get you inside right away.'

She was ushered through the entranceway, directly past the archway that led to a good-sized bar area, and beyond, to the main room. There the circular dance floor was surrounded by a large circle of tables. The music pounded from the room, and Mac could see knots of people through the bar and on into the big room. She was thrilled that she was being steered toward the stairs.

The young hostess that the doorman had handed her off to guided her up the stairs to a private room. 'Ms Bennet asked me to let her know as soon as you arrived. I'm sure she'll be right here. Can I get you anything?'

Mac smiled. She wanted a drink, a meal, a bath, a bed, and about eighteen hours of uninterrupted sleep. But that seemed like a fairly steep order for this young woman. 'Anything cool and not carbonated. Some iced tea maybe?'

'I'll be back in just a minute,' the hostess said as she closed the door behind her.

The room was a private dining room apparently, one that could hold a table for eighteen or twenty. There was one lone table for four in it now, with a few miscellaneous chairs here and there. The room was a beautiful peach color, and the lighting came from pink-toned bulbs fitted in wall sconces. Very flattering. Not that good lighting was going to help her appearance any, Mac thought as she wearily pulled out one chair from the table and sat.

In the quiet she thought back over the events of the evening. Beckman had shown up shortly after Buratti had come into the dressing room, and the two detectives arrested Michelle. At Rossellini's request, they kept as low a profile as possible, although the magazine writer Buratti had run into the day before was buzzing around like a bee in heat. He was put off, at least momentarily, with tales of an overeager fan, and the sound of the gun discharging was attributed to a stagelight exploding.

Rachel had arrived in Peter's dressing room minutes after Buratti and Beckman and had practically swooned when apprised of the situation. When she recovered, she started chattering about the announcement they'd have to make canceling the show.

Rossellini, who had been relieved of the sobbing Michelle only minutes before, refused to cancel. 'Announce a delay; say it's a technical thing,' he'd insisted. 'Just give me a half hour.'

Beckman had moved Michelle out into the hall. Buratti and Mac were still in the dressing room. 'Judas,' Buratti had whispered to her when he heard of Rossellini's decision. 'This guy's got balls made of titanium.'

Buratti had asked her to come along for the interrogation of Michelle. 'We got to find out how it all happened, Doc. But this is a tricky one, I know. We could use your help.'

She'd agreed to go along, but was stopped by Peter's voice before she could follow Buratti into the hall.

Peter was leaning on the counter, supporting himself on extended arms, and he caught her eye in the mirror. 'Mac . . .' he started, and then shook his head. He turned to face her. 'I don't even know what I want to say.'

'You don't have to say anything,' she replied.

'Yes I do, but there's too much spinning

around . . .' His voice faded, and he stepped toward her. 'You'll come back?'

'What?'

'After they question her. You'll come back here? Or to the club? I really need to know what all this is about.'

'Okay,' she agreed and turned to leave, but Rossellini reached toward her, caught her left hand in his, and just squeezed for a moment as he stared into her eyes.

The only sound in the room was the two of them breathing, until Buratti called from the hall. 'Mac, you comin' with us?'

'I'll see you later,' Peter said, gently letting her hand go.

'Later.' She nodded.

She'd run into Rachel in the hall, and repeated the promise to come here and fill them in.

The door opened, and it was the young hostess returning with her tea. While the door was still open, Rachel appeared. She waited at the door for the hostess to leave, then closed it firmly, and walked to the table where Mac was seated.

'Thank you so much for coming, Doctor. Peter will be right in. He's just finishing up some interviews in the next room.'

Now that she was close, Mac could see that Rachel's eyes were red-rimmed. 'Are you okay?' Mac asked.

'Don't mind me,' Rachel said, sniffing. 'I've been

doing this all night. Telling people it's an allergy attack.' She looked down at the tissue in her hands. 'I can't believe it, I just can't believe it. Our own Michelle.'

'Yeah, it is a little hard to believe.'

'I know she confessed, but are we absolutely certain it's true? Could Michelle really have killed those people?'

'Yes, it's true. Detective Beckman went out to Michelle's house while the interrogation was going on. They found Randy Vos's shirt in the bottom of her closet.'

And that wasn't all, according to Beckman. They also found what he described as a 'shrine' to Peter Rossellini. Pictures, mementos, even a note he scribbled to her on a memo pad. A picture of the two of them together, Michelle and Peter, taken in Rachel's office during what looked like somebody's birthday party, was blown up to poster size.

They'd also found her father's room, still set up virtually like a hospital room. According to Beckman, it still smelled like a sickroom.

Rachel was still twisting the tissues in her hand, absorbing this latest information that Mac had told her. The two women sat in silence.

Suddenly the door opened, and Peter Rossellini appeared. Mac took a deep breath when she spotted him. She was inordinately glad to see him.

He walked directly to Mac, reached for her hands, and pulled her gently from the chair. He clasped her to his chest in an embrace that had little to do with romance or even friendship. It was an embrace of comfort and reassurance, like those between the survivors of a disaster. Or at least it started that way. When the two of them felt it becoming something else, they parted quickly, both remembering Rachel's presence at the same moment.

'I'm glad you're here,' Peter said after a few seconds of quiet. 'Even if I still don't know what to say.'

Mac looked up at him, and simply nodded her acknowledgment of his thanks. There wasn't anything to say.

Mac stepped away from him and sat down again. Rossellini walked around to the other side of the table from Rachel and took that chair. 'Can you tell us about tonight?'

'I'll try. It's a long story.' Mac took a deep breath and started. 'Michelle was an only child. Her parents were German immigrants who came here after the war. They were in their forties when Michelle was born, almost fifteen years after they arrived here.'

Mac tried to condense the information she'd heard over a three-hour period into a coherent narrative. It was hard. 'It sounded like she had a strict upbringing. Old World kind of strict.'

'Was she abused?' Rachel asked quietly.

'Not physically, not from what she said, or sexually if that's what you mean. But it sounds like there was a lot of abuse, yes.'

'How do you mean?' Peter said.

'Verbal abuse. It amounts to psychological abuse. She was told they wished they'd never had her, that she was an accident, that she wasn't good enough, smart enough, pretty enough. You hear that often enough in your childhood, and you begin to believe it.' Mac paused in her recitation. 'Never allowed any friends, really. Dating was out of the question.'

'I don't remember Michelle ever talking about her family,' Rachel said. 'Now I understand why.'

Mac took a deep breath. 'She apparently got away once. After she'd finished school, started working, she moved into her own apartment when she was twenty-two or twenty-three. But her mother got sick a few years later, and they got her to move back home. Her mother died a little over two years ago, and then her father got sick. He died in March.'

'I remember that,' Rachel said. 'She was very closed-mouthed about it. Only took maybe two days off.'

'I didn't know her father died,' Peter said.

'I took care of it,' Rachel responded. 'I sent flowers from us.'

Mac let that rest for a moment. 'Apparently after her father died, when she had the freedom to live her life like she wanted to, she couldn't. The core of what was Michelle had been so damaged, she couldn't even live out her own dreams. She had to make up somebody else to do that. So she came up with this alter ego of Mickey.'

'Alter ego? Is this like some kind of split personality?' Rachel's face was full of curiosity.

'There are some similarities, but it's a different type of personality dysfunction,' Mac replied. 'At any rate, by the time Mickey came along, she – Michelle – had already developed an obsession about you' – she looked at Rossellini – 'and Mickey was the one who acted it out.'

'What does that mean?' Peter asked.

'From what Michelle told us, she was the one who talked to these men from your office, she was the one who made the initial arrangements with the Colony Beach Club, with the restaurant—'

'Omigod, that's right,' Rachel interrupted. 'And she's the one who always talked to the people at Metropolitan, too.'

'Right,' continued Mac. 'In a way, Michelle would do all the advance work, smooth the way. Then Mickey would show up.' She paused again. 'She was the most obvious point of connection actually, and the one we absolutely overlooked.'

'But why these men? Was it the videos?' Rossellini asked.

Mac couldn't spare him from the answer. 'Yes. She developed a real fantasy life around you and around the videos. I don't know if she distinguishes between the real you and the one in the videos. But she would try to re-create the scenes and she would get so far, and the fantasy would fall apart. Reality would hit, and then she would kill them.'

'But why, why did she have to kill them?' Rachel was deeply disturbed by Mac's account. Her voice was shaky.

'From the way she talks about it,' Mac replied, 'it's almost like she was erasing a tape, doing another take, correcting a mistake. She's very detached about it. The first one – Randy Vos – upset her. It turns out she did hit him over the head and watch him drown, and that was too violent for her.'

'How did she kill the others?' Rachel asked.

'She slipped some of her father's heart medication into their drinks after they'd had a few. Very toxic to a healthy heart. Even more so when there's alcohol present in the bloodstream. We knew that Nahas had been drinking right before he died. And we knew that Martin Jury had alcohol in his blood. What we didn't know was that she and Jury had split a bottle of wine right there in the studio. She'd brought the wine and the glasses with her, and she took them when she left.' Mac stopped, thinking back to seeing Martin Jury stretched out on the floor of the studio. 'She brought the rose, too.'

'Will she have to stand trial?' Rossellini asked.

'I don't think so. I'm not sure. There are two states involved here. And she's confessed,' Mac paused. 'They got a lawyer in for her tonight. From Legal Aid.'

Rossellini looked over at Rachel. 'Let's find Irwin and have him get the best lawyer for her.'

'Peter, you've got to be—'

'I'm serious, Rachel. Get her a good lawyer. I know what she's done, but she needs help. I want to see her get the care she needs, not just end up in some prison that doesn't have anything.'

'All right,' Rachel acquiesced. 'I'll go for Irwin.' She stood up, but turned back to Mac. 'You know, when you were telling us all this, I kept remembering a friend of mine, a lawyer at one of the record companies until she quit. We were having lunch one day. She said that some woman would be smart to get into the financial department at any of the big record companies and start cooking the books. Her point was that, in this business, women are so invisible, one could get away with embezzlement – or murder, I guess.' She stopped and gave a small, mirthless chuckle. 'And I guess she was right. I'm only embarrassed that Michelle was invisible to me, too.' She turned and walked out the door.

Mac's hands rested on the table in front of her, and Rossellini reached for them. 'How are you doing, really?'

'I'm okay. Just tired. And sad.' She smiled at him. 'That's very good of you to help Michelle out with a lawyer.'

He shrugged his shoulders, still holding on to her hands. 'That whole scene tonight was unbelievable. Absolutely unbelievable. And you. How does a person say, "Thank you for saving my life"?'

'You just did,' Mac said, turning her hands and clasping his. 'Now I've got to get out of here or I'm going to fall asleep on this table.' She stood up.

'We've got some cars downstairs, I think. I'll have one of them take you home,' Peter said, following her lead and standing next to her.

'You have no idea how wonderful that sounds.'

'I'd head downtown with you, but I've got a lot of people to see downstairs.'

'That's right.' Mac turned to him as he started ushering her out of the room. 'Opening night. How did it go?'

'It was okay. Not quite the opening I'd imagined, but everything went okay. I don't think the audience knew anything except that we were late. Which was the way I wanted it. But I don't think I've ever concentrated so hard in my life.' He kept his hand on her arm as they walked down the stairs. 'So when are you coming to see it?' he said as they hit the bottom step.

'Let's see, it's what, Tuesday morning at quarter to one?' Mac said, looking at her watch. 'Oh, God, I'm not going to get any sleep until—'

'Rest up today, come tomorrow. Wednesday. I'll send a car for you,' Peter said quietly.

'That's not necess—'

Prissy strolled into the entranceway and interrupted her midsentence. 'Girlfriend! Is that you? I tell you I like to die with all that goings-on tonight. But I got him for you, just like you said, didn't I?'

'That you did, Prissy. And thanks.' Mac patted the woman's arm and what Prissy was wearing finally registered on Mac's tired brain. The woman looked absolutely luminous in an outfit of gold lamé, and Mac realized that the two of them standing side by side was an image that bordered on the ludicrous.

'Now, honey, the next thing we got to do is something about these clothes. Yes, yes, something about these clothes. You come see me when you come to the show, okay? I got to run now.'

'You bet I will,' Mac said with a smile, and Prissy took off out the door. 'She's amazing,' she said, looking back at Peter.

'No, you're the one who's amazing,' Peter said.

Mac smiled almost shyly at the compliment and started edging toward the door. 'Well, thanks for the ride downtown.'

'No, wait.' Rossellini grabbed her arm to stop her. Mac turned to him, an inquisitive look on her face.

'Do you remember what you said to me a couple of nights ago?' he asked as he smoothed a strand of hair behind her ear.

Mac looked at him quizzically. She had no idea what he was referring to. But she did know that his hand in her hair felt awfully good.

'You said I might be thinking of you as a security blanket.' His hand was on her neck now, the fingers slowly massaging the tension away. 'Well, I thought about it. In fact I was thinking about it on stage tonight.'

Mac's eyebrows arched up in surprise.

'I decided you were wrong. And now all of this' – he looked up and shrugged in an all-encompassing gesture – 'all of this craziness is over.'

Peter smiled as he slipped his arm around her and pulled her toward him. 'But this, Dr Griffin, this is just beginning.'

More Thrilling Fiction from Headline Feature

Steve Martini

COMPELLING EVIDENCE

'[It] will leave you dazzled' Edward Stewart

'A taut, tense tale that I simply could not put down'
Dominick Dunne

Paul Madriani, a brilliant criminal defense lawyer,
had a once promising career with a prestigious law
firm, until an ill-judged affair with the senior partner
Ben Potter's wife led to his resignation. Now he
scrambles for work amid the ghosts of his doomed
affair and the remains of a failing marriage.

Then Potter is found dead, an apparent suicide. But
as details come to light, the case turns from suicide to
murder and the needle of suspicion points towards
the victim's seductive wife, Talia Potter. Indicted and
arrested, Talia turns to Paul, her former lover, to
defend her against the mounting evidence in a case
that for her could result in the gas chamber.

'A wonderfully crafted and clever courtroom thriller. We
unquestionably have a new literary lion in the fictional
crime genre' Vincent Bugliosi

'Authoritative debut novel ... refreshingly candid'
Publishers Weekly

'Beautifully constructed courtroom thriller'
San Francisco Chronicle

FICTION / THRILLER 0 7472 3989 4

Colin Harrison
BODIES ELECTRIC

'Mr Harrison's novel is a cause for celebration . . . a daring, haunting book' *New York Times*

Jack Whitman, thirty-five, is already a top player inside the country's largest media-entertainment empire. Several years earlier, Jack's pregnant wife was killed in a senseless spasm of New York City violence. In his grief, Jack's blind fury has become blind ambition.

Enter Dolores Salcines. One night, returning from work, Jack sees a beautiful, ravaged woman and her child sitting across from him on the subway. Against every rule of urban survival, against his proper judgement, against the dictates of his class, Jack thrusts his business card at her. Soon he rescues Dolores and her daughter from their Times Square hotel – to take them into his home.

But as Jack falls in love with Dolores and begins to learn her secret history, he finds himself caught in the middle of a corporate coup. His scheming CEO is determined to push aside the company's aged but cunning Chairman to make way for a merger with the Corporation's German-Japanese counterpart. That deal will make the new company the new century's world-wide media colossus.

Soon after Jack discovers the Chairman has his own designs on him, he is confronted by Dolores's jealous, street-smart husband, Hector. Jack finds his life spinning wildly out of control – until he must fight not just for his job and for Dolores, but quite possibly for his life.

'Intricately plotted, packed with fibrillar detail BODIES ELECTRIC is a blockbuster with *gravitas*, a Nineties thriller with a Victorian sense of moral purpose' *Evening Standard*

'Like Scott Turow's *Presumed Innocent*, this is a serious piece of work that examines the rotten heart of the yuppie dream with an uncompromising intensity' *The Sunday Times*

'A taut, nerve-wracking drama . . . a beautifully balanced thriller in which high-tech corporate power struggles are contrasted with the incendiary passion for family' *Publishers Weekly*

FICTION / GENERAL 0 7472 4434 0

A selection of bestsellers from Headline

BODY OF A CRIME	Michael C. Eberhardt	£5.99	☐
TESTIMONY	Craig A. Lewis	£5.99	☐
LIFE PENALTY	Joy Fielding	£5.99	☐
SLAYGROUND	Philip Caveney	£5.99	☐
BURN OUT	Alan Scholefield	£4.99	☐
SPECIAL VICTIMS	Nick Gaitano	£4.99	☐
DESPERATE MEASURES	David Morrell	£5.99	☐
JUDGMENT HOUR	Stephen Smoke	£5.99	☐
DEEP PURSUIT	Geoffrey Norman	£4.99	☐
THE CHIMNEY SWEEPER	John Peyton Cooke	£4.99	☐
TRAP DOOR	Deanie Francis Mills	£5.99	☐
VANISHING ACT	Thomas Perry	£4.99	☐

All Headline books are available at your local bookshop or newsagent, or can be ordered direct from the publisher. Just tick the titles you want and fill in the form below. Prices and availability subject to change without notice.

Headline Book Publishing, Cash Sales Department, Bookpoint, 39 Milton Park, Abingdon, OXON, OX14 4TD, UK. If you have a credit card you may order by telephone – 01235 400400.

Please enclose a cheque or postal order made payable to Bookpoint Ltd to the value of the cover price and allow the following for postage and packing:

UK & BFPO: £1.00 for the first book, 50p for the second book and 30p for each additional book ordered up to a maximum charge of £3.00.

OVERSEAS & EIRE: £2.00 for the first book, £1.00 for the second book and 50p for each additional book.

Name ....

Address ....

....

....

If you would prefer to pay by credit card, please complete:
Please debit my Visa/Access/Diner's Card/American Express (delete as applicable) card no:

Signature .... Expiry Date ....